Betrayal

Choosing Family
Book 3

Jennifer Raines

Betrayal
Copyright © 2024 Jennifer Raines
All rights reserved.

ISBN: (ebook) 978-1-964636-15-3
(Print) 978-1-964636-16-0

Inkspell Publishing
207 Moonglow Circle #101
Murrells Inlet, SC 29576

Edited By Yezanira Venecia
Cover art By Emily's World By Design

DEDICATION

Thank you to the members of Romance Writers of New Zealand (RWNZ) for the conversations, competitions and conferences which have taught me so much and nourished my creative soul.

JENNIFER RAINES

CHAPTER ONE

Clutching a champagne flute of mineral water, Anna Turner turned away from the bar to face the marketing conference party crowd. Her penance, as representative of Changing Minds—Creative Solutions, at this exclusive venue overlooking Sydney Harbour, was to observe competitors and promote the superior skills of Changing Minds in brand management and product promotion across traditional and social media platforms.

"Ditch the scowl, Anna," her friend Beatriz Gomez whispered. "We're here to soothe, not rouse the savage beast."

"I *don't* scowl." Anna beetled her brows. "Remember that exercise at last year's conference with the face-reading experts?"

"They *claimed* a company could increase client signups with the right smile."

"They rated mine as winning."

"Emphasis on the smile, girlfriend." Bea looked her up and down. "And they didn't see you in that dress."

"This old thing?" Anna shrugged, and the décolletage on the flaming-red, figure-hugging short cocktail dress slipped a half-centimetre closer to her navel. The dress was a crude but effective tool for identifying the obvious lechers without saying a word.

"Seeing the stunned disbelief on that company exec's face remains one of the highlights of my short life." Bea didn't waste time on polite fictions, one of the reasons they were close friends. "He couldn't believe you'd chosen that dress to tell him he didn't have a chance in hell of scoring with you."

"The sexist so-and-so deserved it. Claiming his company would cancel their brand marketing contract with Changing Minds because I wouldn't sleep with him. Did he miss several centuries of female emancipation?" Anna infused scorn, disgust and I'll-kill-him-if-I-see-him determination into her voice. Childhood drama classes had to have some benefits.

"There's steam coming out of your ears."

"I'm seriously pissed off." Anna lacked the patience to deal with sleaze tonight.

"I'd never have guessed." And a lot of people never guessed sweet-faced Bea did sarcasm.

"It's worse than when that idiot threatened me." Anna waved her drink in the air, and some sloshed over the rim, just missing her feet—her stilettos continued the blood-red theme. "His boss overruled him. Anyway, that was just money."

"Ah! Money!" Bea sighed. "We don't care about money." Bea had to care about money, though, regularly helping her immigrant parents pay their bills.

"This is more important than money." Anna curled her lip.

"Your childcare centre." Bea leaned closer and dropped her voice. "I forgot. You were signing the lease for the premises today. Let me get you out of this crowd." With a few words and a smile, Bea navigated a path through the mass of people away from the packed bar. She made a beeline for the windows overlooking the Sydney Opera House and Harbour Bridge, then tucked the two of them into a corner. "This is quieter. Tell me."

"I was meant to sign the lease before the entire building was subject to a hostile takeover. Some infantile troglodyte in a feud with his equally infantile father."

I worked out too late that competition with some fathers is the first step on the highway to hell.

"Who won?

"The son. And he cancelled all pending leases. From the few business blogs I checked, if one of them sniffs out a distressed estate, the other tries to beat him to the purchase. About as logical as teenage boys in a pissing contest."

"I'm sorry, honey," Bea commiserated. "A new owner usually wants to negotiate their own leases. And if the original owner's in trouble, your lease might have gone pear-shaped in a few months anyway."

"That's what Antonio said."

Anna had been with her boss, Antonio Perez, CEO of Changing Minds, long enough that when she'd approached him about the need for better childcare options for company staff, he'd given her the lead on finding a solution.

"What else did Antonio say?" With four younger sisters, Bea listened to every version of a story before making judgement.

"Sleep on it. We'll regroup in the morning." *A perfectly rational assessment.* Antonio was better at rolling with the punches than Anna was. "Normally I love his positivity, but I've promised, Bea." Although Anna's original promise to help hadn't been to the young mother currently on her team but to three other women two years ago, one of whom was now dead. Tonight's dress was her roar of frustration at her failure.

"It's unlike you to promise before you have everything stitched up and in triplicate."

"A matter of hours before I signed the lease. Due diligence complete. I was as sure as I could be, and Nadia is holding on by the skin of her teeth. Even with Antonio providing financial help, Nadia's childcare is at one end of town, her crisis accommodation the other, and commuting to the office is an isosceles triangle on steroids. The distances are killing her." Anna was hoping for a miracle before she had to tell the newly single mother the bad news.

"You can't save every woman trapped in an abusive relationship." Bea's pragmatism was as hard-won as Anna's determination to make small differences.

"I'm not trying to save every woman. Or even most women. One childcare centre is not a solution to domestic or partner violence, it's an option for a few women under pressure. Apart from Nadia"—whom Anna would lose if she didn't pull a rabbit out of a hat—"we have two other employees looking for work closer to their childcare. We don't want to lose them."

"What else did Antonio say?"

"The new owner might be financially stretched enough to welcome the offer of a long-term lease on one floor."

"He's got a point."

"You're right, and the property's perfect." Anna sighed. "So I'll be charm personified when I try to reopen negotiations, even if the owner has an electronic calculator in place of a heart and a father fetish."

"Who bought it?" Bea prepared for her meetings with meticulous care.

"H. S. Thompson was all the managing agent would give me. Who names their child after a famous dead journalist, for Pete's sake?"

Bea held up a hand. "So, why didn't you send an apology for this shindig?"

"Antonio wanted a presence and reminded me it was my turn to come. 'Cocktail parties loosen tongues and increase personal contacts,'" Anna repeated Antonio's encouragement.

"Networking—naughty and nice?" Bea grinned. "Bet you didn't tell him you were gonna wear your *Killing Eve* dress. He's an understanding boss, but Antonio was present when you took that last dude down, and it probably wasn't what he had in mind tonight."

"I'm wearing it tonight to exorcise my rage, so I can renegotiate from a place of calm." Anna waved her hand from her head to her belly in a gesture of serenity. "But, you're right, I should go."

"On the basis that researching the buyer trumps glad-handing strangers?"

"On the basis I might bite someone's head off when I'm meant to charm. Like the guy looking this way." Anna had been aware of the guy for a while. Now, she put her hand on Bea's arm and adjusted their positions. "Make it casual. Over my shoulder, about two o'clock. The guy with the lean and hungry look." Anna's pulse raced, a lick of interest curling through her body.

"He's just looking at this stage." Bea's husky contralto oozed intrigue.

"Who is he?"

"I don't recognise him, but he wouldn't have got past security without an invite." Bea took a sip of her drink. "Mid-thirties, tall, dark, broody rather than handsome, and on his own. He's perfected the stiff-backed, imperious, don't-mess-with-me look. Out of place in a crowd like this. Do you want me to find out?"

"Yes." Anna sipped her icy mineral water and waited a heartbeat. "No."

"Well, that's clear." Bea flashed her dimples.

"Yes, because I should care if he's competition. And Antonio would expect me to." Anna frowned; her charming, vivacious and interested impulses were flatter than a cane toad daring to cross a Queensland country road. "No, because I've exhausted my store of goodwill for rich, entitled entrepreneurs."

"You've never had any time for rich and entitled." Bea flicked a glance back toward the stranger. "Although it's impossible to tell if someone's rich or an entrepreneur by their Rolex or bespoke suit these days—think Mike Cannon-Brooks. But broody guy's a possibility." She wiggled her shoulders sexily. "Be still, my beating heart."

"You want him?" Anna rolled her eyes.

"I just got a little distracted"—Bea sighed—"but he looks way too complicated for my lifestyle. Anyway, returning to our topic, how do you figure H. S. is entitled?"

"Because it's a raid." Anna bit her lip. "The property wasn't on the market. He's made an unsolicited purchase."

"If you keep flouncing about like that, your dress will slip straight off your boobs and you'll create the kind of feeding frenzy you hate."

"My subconscious was sabotaging me." Anna used her drink as cover for her quick tug on her dress. "I dressed with H. S. and Armageddon in mind."

"In this crowd, the only people likely to approach you will be people who don't know you and have minds turned to mush by lust." By contrast, Bea looked wholesomely sexy in a classic, self-patterned powder-blue jumpsuit.

"You've convinced me." Anna started to edge toward the door. "I'll leave now."

"Warning," Bea stage-whispered. "Mr. Two-o-Clock is coming this way."

"Damn." Despite her indifference to the lavish compliments from the face-reading experts, Anna summoned her sincere, interested, likely-to-instil-confidence-in-the-most-cautious-of-clients professional smile. The expert had never seen it paired with *The Dress*.

"Hello. I don't believe we've met." His pick-up line lacked originality, but the gravelly baritone could launch an entire collection of intimate apparel. He'd inherited a face of sharp angles, slashing cheekbones, and a chiselled jaw—conventionally handsome, although she understood Bea's choice of broody. His dark chocolate gaze held her attention despite her desperate need to escape, his eyes hinting at secrets he never intended to share. "I'm Hunter."

"Is that your name, or your current intention?" Bea's gasp told Anna she'd actually asked the question out loud.

His mouth quirked up. "I'll let you find out."

"If you'll excuse me, I think I need a drink." Bea turned on her heel, balancing her almost full glass of wine carefully.

"I'm Anna Turner." She paused, her heels enabling her to be on eye level with him. "I'm guessing you already knew that."

"I asked another guest."

"Why?" Anna was fresh out of small talk. She wanted to go home and howl at all the malignant gods of the universe who'd conspired to thwart her meticulously researched, carefully negotiated, and enthusiastically anticipated childcare centre plan.

"You interest me." He edged closer, and the only clue he'd moved was the whiff of his sandalwood scent.

"I'm flattered." *Or I might be in some parallel universe*. "But you've caught me at the wrong time. I'm about to leave."

"Why don't I buy you"—he considered her champagne flute, half full of mineral water—"another drink somewhere quieter where we can talk."

"Are you looking to share marketing tips?" Antonio would expect her to check, and Hunter wasn't responsible for her black mood.

"Will a yes or a no improve my chances of you staying?" When he made the effort to smile, he moved up a notch from broody-handsome to gorgeous. His slim-fitting jacket conveyed elegant vigour, adding another layer of sumptuousness to her impression. The fine cashmere wool of his jacket begged to be stroked. *Don't go there.*

"What's your specialty?" She appreciated his style—his gaze hadn't once strayed below her chin, and her décolletage truly was shocking. She liked his persistence, truth be told. A lot of men turned tail when confronted with her acerbic tongue.

He sipped his drink, drawing attention to his hand. Brown and scarred, reminding her of Niall, her sibling-in-law's hands. None of Hunter's scars looked recent, but the working-man's hands reassured her as the expensive clothes and dynamic looks hadn't. "I'm an architect by training, although I spent a lot of time on building sites growing up."

"Commercial, residential, industrial, sustainable or conservation?" Excitement rippled through Anna. Maybe his arrival was an omen. "Architect" was her magic word.

"Hard to chat freely in this crowd." The twinkle in his eye hinted at a humour hidden until now.

"I'm interested in designs for a childcare centre." Anna abandoned subtlety. He stared at the ceiling and looked around the room before bringing his gaze back to her face. *Truth or dare?* She had only his word he was an architect. She took a punt on the history written on his damaged hands. "One drink. Downstairs bar."

"Shall we go?" He might have been pleased or indifferent; his expression didn't change.

"I need to say a few goodbyes. I'll meet you there." She glanced at her smartwatch. "Ten minutes, tops."

Anna finessed her way through the press of people to reach Bea's side. "He's an architect. I'm having one drink, downstairs, and picking his brain. I'll text you when I leave."

Bea caught her arm, held her long enough to brush a cautionary kiss to her cheek, and whispered, "Make sure you do. Or I'll come after you." Her friend's citrusy shampoo carried the scent of girl-next-door reliable.

"Yes, Mama."

Anna gathered her jacket and spoke to a few friends, all the while edging toward the door, then took the stairs. Hunter was crossing the last few metres to the bar's entrance when she hit the bottom step. For a big man, he moved quietly. *Avoiding attention?* Impossible, given the controlled power emanating from him. She'd accepted a drink, nothing more, so she shrugged into her jacket and zipped it closed.

Hunter rose to his feet when Anna walked into the bar, his survey taking in the thigh-length jacket ballooning around her dress. "What can I get you to drink?"

"Hot chocolate." She smiled at the waiter who'd approached. "Please."

"I'll have coffee. Black. Can I start a tab?"

"Certainly, sir."

"Thanks."

Hunter waited until Anna sat on the low sofa before taking the seat beside her. His body was angled toward her, but the distance between them told her he wasn't making assumptions.

Smart man.

"Why a childcare centre?"

Soft rock played in the background, giving the bar a friendly, rather than intimate, vibe. The spill-over of escapees from the cocktail party talking business was a further vindication of Anna's choice of venue for this "almost-business" chat. She had backup, if needed. She didn't do casual hook-ups. *Ever.*

A hot chocolate, a little conversation, she'd be out of here in twenty minutes—tops.

"The company I work for has been growing in recent years. We've recruited some incredible young women, and if we want to keep them, we need decent childcare."

"Providing your own childcare is unorthodox. Wouldn't it be easier to pay for places at another centre, or subsidise employees to choose their own?" Leaning back, he slipped the button of his jacket. His stylish T-shirt was the palest pink, more subtle than his pickup line, while his assessment was incisive.

"Been there, done that." She allowed herself to relax a bit, wriggling further back on the leather couch. When he stilled in response—his focus entirely on her—her stomach did a slow roll. She breathed through several heartbeats before she continued. "My boss Antonio's a lateral thinker and a good man. A number of my fellow employees are single parents. Having their children nearby and having a say in how the centre runs gives them a greater sense of security."

"And an employee who feels listened to works harder." He spoke with the authority of someone who'd been both employee and employer.

Who are you? How did you get from architecture to marketing? And who do you work for?

"Establishing your own centre is a lot of work."

"It would be, except that's not our plan." She lifted her head, wrinkling her nose. "Coffee smells so much better than it tastes."

"Says the woman who's about to drink a chocolate bar." He nodded at the waiter. "Thank you."

"Look at it." She pointed at the frothy milk topping her mug, sprinkled with yet more grated chocolate. "Decadent and delicious. Yours is inky evil."

"You obviously don't write the jingles," he said drily.

"I started as a graphic designer, however, I'm currently strategic manager of promotions," she admitted. "My job description includes creative thinker."

"Could have fooled me." He pushed a hand through his hair, mussing it. The hunter had loosened up in the last few minutes and dropped some of his emotional distance. Anna sensed his confusion that she'd used some trick to relax him. "What's your plan?" he asked.

"We've got preliminary agreement from an existing reputable childcare provider for them to handle recruitment, staff registration and legal protocols." She'd sold the plan to Antonio in parts. "We supply the premises and join the management board."

"Your boss plans to be on the board? That's quite a commitment."

Had he inched closer? His scent was too elusive to identify—beguiling, and she bet he knew it.

"I'll be on the board."

"As I said, a big commitment. Love or money?" He stretched his legs under the table, angling his body more toward her.

Another practised move?

"Voluntary, but that's hardly relevant to our conversation." She wrapped both hands around her mug of chocolate.

"You should get time in lieu."

He'd surprised her. Anna glanced at his bare left hand. In a just world, he'd be single. *Pity they didn't live in a just world.*

"Juggling charity work with full-time employment and raising a family is challenging."

"Are you speaking from experience?" She sipped her liquid chocolate bar, impressed by the smooth segue. He'd asked about her marital and family status without uttering the words *married* or *children. Did that mean he took the institutions seriously?*

"Observation." His gaze rested on her mouth, the light in his eyes hotter than her drink.

"To answer your earlier question, I'm not married or a parent."

"What do you want from an architect?"

"I've found a suitable site." She channelled Antonio's positive thinking that they'd be able to negotiate a lease with the new owner. "It's nearby, was an operating childcare centre until about eleven months ago, and with some refurbishment and a bit of creative thinking, will deliver exactly what we want."

"Creative thinking. That's where you come in, right?" His focused study suggested he wanted to swallow her whole, while his beautifully sculptured mouth formed pertinent questions. The disconnect simultaneously teased her mind and set her insides quivering. "Are you purchasing or leasing it?"

"Leasing. We'll need the owner's agreement to make changes. But we're looking long-term—five to ten years—so that would give the owner a guaranteed income." She took another sip, just to feel his gaze on her mouth. A captive architect and hot chocolate—her day had improved.

"Possibly. Rents can fluctuate over a long period." He drained his cup, and it was her turn to watch his throat while he swallowed. "A locked-in lease might deny the owner future profits."

"Not everything is about money."

Bea was right. He could be an architect turned marketing entrepreneur. Ridiculous to be disappointed. Time to stop flirting and focus on her reason for being here.

"Almost everything." His baritone had dropped to a purr, but his focus on profits and returns had broken her mood.

"I'm not asking you about the lease but about modifications to the building." Anna lassoed her soaring imagination and set her empty mug on the glass tabletop. Her body had naturally responded to him. *Melting wouldn't do*. And she hadn't been tempted on such short acquaintance since her bad-girl teens. "We want to provide a sense of being outdoors in a multi-story property."

"Can I get you another drink?"

"One's my limit." *Although I was considering a second until thirty seconds ago.*

"Have you worked out your wish list? Does it have windows that open? Does it have balconies? Does it have access to a roof space? Are you looking at the top floor? I'm assuming you want the highest standards for accessibility—mobility and sensory-impaired children?" He rattled off questions with the urgency of a man who was genuinely interested in the topic, or her. "You said you'd found a suitable site. Have you closed the deal?"

"Not at this stage." She crossed her fingers in the folds of her jacket.

"But?" He looked at her. "There has to be a 'but.' A serious 'but' since you were edging toward the door before I approached you upstairs. Professional politeness demanded you give me a minute of your time. That's all you were going to give me until you discovered I was an architect."

"You *are* observant." *Anna Turner, where are your usual protective instincts?*

"And lucky." His lips quirked in unmistakable invitation. "A shared interest in architecture got me some time alone with you."

"As you deduced, tonight's not a good time." *Never on a first date, and much more rarely than people assumed.* "I've been negotiating on the perfect building for weeks. I was gazumped."

"Name a time. And we can talk about your questions and lots more." His answers had been concise, his scent alluring, and while his body had subtly shifted closer to her during their conversation, he'd played by her unspoken rules.

"Do you like fish and chips?" she asked. The beach was another neutral location, and she wanted to hear his answers to the questions he'd posed.

"That works. Can I see you home?"

"I brought my car." She rose, and he stood with her.

He packed enough appeal to tempt her to leave her ride share parked downstairs and accept a lift home. *Caution is your friend.*

He recited his number, and she sent hers.

Her phone pinged with the incoming message. She smiled, then looked down. "Hunter S. Thompson?"

"The S is for Samuel, not Stockton." He braced, legs apart, and answered carefully. "Although my mother chose Hunter S. for the American journalist and author. She was a fan."

"*You!*" She backed away, disgust surging through her even while the sane part of her mind was telling her to get out before she did something Antonio would regret. Her boss had said to sleep on it, not launch herself bodily at the man they hoped to negotiate with. "You knew who I was when you were watching me, you conniving bastard. What are you playing at?"

"My parents were married and, to my knowledge, faithful when I was born."

"Not funny." She shoved her phone into her pocket. "You know who I am, who I work for, and you had the nerve to flirt with me, to coax me into sharing my dreams when you're the sneaky wheeler-dealer who cancelled my impending lease without notice today."

"What's the address of the building you want?" He'd shifted from friend to foe in seconds.

"You know the address," she hissed.

"I asked a friend at the party who you were. I've never heard of Changing Minds." He scowled patiently.

How was that even possible?

"The managing agent told me H. S. Thompson insisted on vacant possession even though we were hours from signing the lease." She tugged her jacket more tightly around herself. "Do you enjoy lording it over people you've crushed?"

"I'd say we're finished for tonight."

"Tonight?" She slapped a hand over her mouth before she uttered "When hell freezes over." *Settle, Anna, you're the hard-headed twin.* And damn him to hell—she'd liked the snake a little, proving her taste was still lousy.

"Right move." He nodded. "I think we might both need to do a bit more fact-finding."

"Fact-finding!" She snorted.

"I expect you to use the intelligence you demonstrated in our conversation to examine all the facts."

She spun on her heel and strode through the door, across the lobby, and out into the night. *Damn H. S. Thompson!* She'd swallowed her worst insults, but she'd feel better if she'd matched a fraction of his cold detachment. She didn't look forward to telling Antonio about this meeting. Worse—she might have blown any chance they had to persuade Hunter S. to reconsider their lease.

* * *

Hunter sank onto the sofa when she stormed out. She'd spilled her dreams, believing she was building them— adding texture and colour to a project she was passionate about. When she'd twigged to who he was, Anna Turner had retreated to drama and disgust to disguise her despair.

She was a perfect stranger and another innocent victim of his father's, Nick Richardson, games. Hunter had been H. S. Richardson until his eighteenth birthday, when he'd taken his mother's family name. For more than a decade, it had kept Nick out of Hunter's life.

The waiter edged nearer.

"Lagavulin, please."

"Yes, sir."

"A double."

Anna Turner would hate the term "victim." He'd bet serious money she'd regroup and come at him from another angle. That made her ... fascinating.

The press release announcing H. S. Thompson was relocating his headquarters to a five-storey medium rise in Darling Harbour was a red herring designed to stop Nick Richardson. Hunter didn't want or need new headquarters. He did want to protect Raed Hariri, his best friend Casildo's father, from Nick's latest attack.

Hurting the people Hunter loved was Nick's party trick.

Nick's plan was to financially kneecap Hariri Senior, firstly by sabotaging the tenancies in The Hariri building with arson attacks and petty burglaries, then by spreading the word the building was overvalued and finally by instigating a hostile takeover of the premises.

Nick's true purpose was always to bring Hunter to heel. *Never again.*

This latest attack had followed Hunter's refusal to become Nick's junior partner.

Although, now The Hariri was temporarily in Hunter's name, he could see possibilities in the gracious, old building.

Architecture was a passion he rarely had time to indulge these days. In recent years, property investment had taken most of his time. But the power of architecture, the complexity and the simplicity, the utility and the beauty fascinated him—no wonder he'd taken the bait when Anna Turner had gone all soft and welcoming after discovering he was an architect.

His whiskey arrived. "Thanks. I'll settle up now." Hunter added a generous tip because someone deserved to finish the night happy.

Staring into the single malt for endless seconds, he let the peat smoke tease his nostrils. Peat, fruit sherry with a hint of vanilla.

Spontaneous combustion was a serious hazard around Anna Turner. The flame-red dress had marked her out as a risk-taker in a room full of pastels and black and white. The way she was poured into it had given his libido, which he'd feared was on life-support, a sharp jolt. Well-defined curves, legs stretching forever, and a sizzle burning clear across the room. When he'd agreed to accompany Casildo, whom he'd abandoned without a word, to the cocktail party, a mindless tumble with someone of a like mind hadn't been on his radar. Anna Turner had tempted him, until he'd worked out the word *unavailable* should have been tattooed across her forehead. Still, he'd been drawn to her, and until he'd told her his name, she'd been interested too. Irrelevant now.

Swallowing the amber liquid in three gulps, he welcomed the explosion of salt-and-pepper smoke at the back of his mouth. Sacrilege to gulp such a fine drop. The same might be said of Anna Turner. He didn't regret the buy, but starting tomorrow, he'd work out how to deal with Ms. Collateral Damage.

CHAPTER TWO

Restless, Hunter pushed back from his desk the following morning and crossed to stare through louvred windows. An ordinary suburban street, saved from mediocrity by the large memorial park opposite. Constructed to honour war dead, the park was repeated with variations across the suburbs and small towns of Australia. With its border of mature, small-leaved fig trees, a classical rotunda with a domed roof, and a brick cenotaph emblazoned with a number of honour rolls, flag staffs, and service commemorative objects, this was a particularly pretty version, popular for weddings and picnics.

The park had tipped the balance in favour of the decommissioned petrol station for his headquarters. The Thompson Corporation—a statement about his preferred lineage and his disinterest in creating a dynasty. Decontamination had been tedious and time-consuming, but once complete, the configuration of the site hummed as a hub for his various business interests. His apartment sat on top. Perfect work-life balance, if you worked sixteen-hour days.

"I need to see you." Hunter left the message on his friend's phone.

A bad night's sleep hadn't killed his curiosity about the compelling spitfire who'd slapped her hand over her mouth to stop herself from saying what she really thought of him. The Patrick Doyle theme from *Thor* broke the silence.

"Hi, Cas. Where are you?"

"Not far. I turned the car your way when I got your message." A car horn honked down the line. "Al'ama," his friend squawked.

"Problem?" The first time Casildo had muttered the Arabic oath, Hunter had celebrated an expletive worthy of school suspension, only to discover it meant "damn." Casildo was constitutionally unable to behave badly.

"A Great Dane plonked its backside in the middle of the street and is refusing to move." His friend sounded nonplussed.

"It could only happen to you." Hunter chuckled. "Coffee at Ya Habibi's?"

"See you in ten."

"Donna," Hunter spoke to his PA on his way out. "I'm with Casildo if you need me."

"Got it." The efficient, discreet forty-something woman in jeans and a sweater had joined his team shortly after she'd been widowed. "I text the word *panic* if it's something I can't handle."

"There's nothing you can't handle." She'd been with him since he'd started rehabbing houses on his own in his mid-twenties. Ten years, and she'd never once let Hunter down.

"Now you've jinxed me."

He ambled the short distance to the Lebanese patisserie. Arriving first, he ordered Arabic coffees and took a seat at the small table tucked behind the glass front door. Amused, he watched the sideways glances Casildo attracted as he sauntered down the street. His friend had the charm and athleticism of Virat Kohli wrapped around the soul of the Dalai Lama. Cas slid onto a chair as the coffees were delivered to the table.

"You call, I'm at your service. What's up?"

"You didn't tell me a company has been negotiating for weeks to lease the third floor in your father's building." So much for his due diligence. Hunter hadn't learned—or hadn't been told, which didn't sit right—about an almost-signed lease for one floor in the building he'd bought.

"The old childcare centre?" Cas spooned three sugars into his cup and stirred.

Hunter winced at the sugar overload.

"I didn't know that. And it's your building now. Who told you?"

"Changing Minds has spent quite a bit of money investigating the viability of the site as a new childcare centre for their staff." For reasons he didn't fully understand, Hunter didn't mention Anna.

"I saw you panting after Anna Turner at last night's cocktail party." Casildo shook his head in seeming despair.

"I don't pant." Hunter drained his inky-evil coffee, the kick almost as powerful as the desire to see Anna again.

"Not usually in public and not for far too long." Casildo leaned back with his fingers linked behind his head. "Anna works for Changing Minds. Just a guess here. But you and she disappeared early last night in quick succession."

"I went home alone." Hunter bared his teeth.

The enveloping jacket Anna had worn to the bar had quashed his fleeting fantasy. The hot chocolate rather than the Moet as a nightcap had signalled she wasn't the type to pretend alcohol had befuddled her judgement if she found him naked in her bed. Her absorption with natural airflow, the ratios of babies and children to toilets and beds, a ring collection that could double as knuckledusters, and her no-nonsense "I've brought my car" were red flags she wasn't looking for a one-nighter. Damned if he knew why, but she intrigued him.

Casildo jack-knifed to an upright position. "She's not your type."

"I don't have a type."

Since Nick's reappearance, Hunter had lost the freedom

for true intimacy with a woman. Getting close to him was as good as having a price on your head. Some of Casildo's concern was for the lady. "I wheel and deal. I'm a carbon copy of my *biological* father—a ruthless negotiator who doesn't give a damn about who gets hurt along the way so long as I make obscene profits. *And* a womaniser."

"Says some stupid wanna-be business blogger trying to make his name riffing on Greek mythology and father-son struggles for power." Casildo raised his voice, a sure sign he was pissed off. "I reckon it's suspicious that blogger only appeared after you refused Nick's royal command to become his junior partner. You should sue."

Heads turned toward them in the small café.

"Who? Nick or the blogger?" Hunter held up his water glass and pointed, receiving a nod from the waiter. "But I agree, Nick Richardson is the blogger's logical source for the most personal stuff."

"I know some people who could shut Nick up." Cas was half-serious.

"No, you don't."

"Well." Casildo dragged a hand through his hair. "I know some people who know some people who might know—"

"Ignoring him has worked in the past." But Nick's obsessions were becoming a bigger problem for Hunter. The attack on Raed Hariri was premeditated and brutal.

"You were a kid, then you were dirt-poor. Now you're competition. Helping us has put you in his gun sights."

"I'm not competing on a bloody thing." Hunter let his frustration show, but since Nick had re-entered his life, blog and media posts insisted Hunter was trying to sabotage Nick's business and seduce his women. The thought turned Hunter's stomach.

"Existing is competition," Casildo said solemnly. "The man's a sicko."

"Changing the subject, bro. Take me over the steps again."

"What steps? When you offered to yet again be my knight in shining armour—"

The name was an old joke from primary school days. Hunter had been cast as lead in a school play. In the final scene, the female lead had simpered and declared that he was her knight in shining armour. She'd married a few years ago and moved interstate. Hunter had been at her wedding.

"What happened to the Great Dane, Cas? Bet you got out of the car and walked it to the kerb." Casildo was more Sir Galahad than Hunter would ever be.

"Roads are dangerous for dogs." Casildo shrugged when Hunter raised an eyebrow "Changing the subject, *bro*. When you offered to buy the building, I called Dad. The lease freeze was in case Nick Richardson—I'm not going to call that pile of doggy do your father. I favour nurture over nature, and my dad and your uncle did the nurturing—"

"Not relevant to here and now." Hunter stopped him with a raised hand.

"Always relevant." His friend wrapped an arm around Hunter's shoulder to pull him in for a quick hug. "As I was saying, we halted leasing in case someone was snooping about. The story we've put out there is that you need more floors for your new HQ. If news got out that we were signing leases on those floors, it would blow our cover story. But Dad wouldn't have reneged on a promise, not even for you."

"Essentially, he did. He just didn't know it." Hunter waited for Casildo to absorb the hit. "So, what did we miss?"

"The managing agent was overzealous?" Casildo tapped the spoon against the side of his ceramic cup, a slow drumbeat of suspicion.

"The agent told Changing Minds H. S. Thompson demanded vacant occupancy."

Casildo hit a button on his phone. The call was short and in Arabic. "The agent was relaxed about a freeze, said they'd had some interest in one floor, but the tenant hadn't called for a few days and were unsure anyway."

"He lied." Hunter's life had become a cobweb of lies where Nick Richardson had crafted the web and was tightening the threads prior to cutting off Hunter's supply lines for his building jobs. Nick's invitation for Hunter to become his junior partner would help Hunter grow, or so Nick said. Given Nick's track record as a parent, Nick wanted Hunter to fill the role of dutiful, fawning, powerless flunkey.

In truth, Nick wanted to absorb Hunter's business and expected Hunter to be grateful.

Nick Richardson was a fantasist.

"To Anna, and my dad. He won't get the chance again." Cas made the vow. "Are you sorry you've bought the building?"

"It was a coup, making the purchase before Nick," Hunter mocked himself.

"*Says* the crappy blogger Bizgos. He's more malicious gossip than business commentator." Casildo scowled at a waiter who came too close.

"Forget the blogger. In six months, I'll transfer the building back to your father at cost price plus interest on my loan. We agreed." Hunter lowered his voice. Even a friendly café could trade in secrets if Nick Richardson or one of his minions made the right offer.

"Are you worried about the money?" Casildo and his father had exhausted all their options before approaching Hunter.

Hate was a destructive emotion, but Hunter could make an exception for Nick's humiliation of father and son Hariri. "If it starts snowing in Sydney, I'll start worrying about the money—"

"Don't underestimate climate change." Casildo visibly relaxed.

"My question is about what we need to do to sign a lease with Changing Minds without raising suspicions about my purchase of the building."

Hunter had twigged a moment too late he was the

unscrupulous buyer who'd cancelled Anna's lease. Her rage at the perceived injustice was incendiary, like her appearance. Whereas her attempt to control her temper was instructive—a hard-won self-discipline matching her intelligence and passion.

"We need a new story—a bit of fact, a bit of fiction to cover our tracks." Hunter studied Casildo. "I'm capricious. Now I own it, I've changed my mind. Or maybe I've over-committed myself. I want to jam as many tenants onto two of the vacant floors—"

"And you want to lease out the third floor to a nearby business to house a bunch of ankle-biters?" A wide grin split Casildo's face. "Capricious investors don't do good deeds, Hunt. Remember, you don't want to give Nick any more points to leverage."

"No one need know."

"What sort of rent are you planning?" Pretending to be a hard-headed businessman looked almost funny on Casildo.

"I haven't decided." But he'd balance Raed Hariri's needs with Anna's.

"I rest my case. Plus, I don't trust Bizgos not to still be sniffing around!'"

That blogger's a pain in the butt." The selling power of the father-son-battle-to-the-death story frustrated the hell out of Hunter. *What a bloody mess!* "Let's say I've seen a gap in childcare provision in the area." Hunter frowned, while he rearranged some ideas. "I'm converting the third vacant floor to a childcare centre, and I might, just might, be prepared to negotiate a long-term lease with a suitable client for part of it."

"Part of it?"

"The market's shifted. The renovation will cost money. I doubt Changing Minds will want to wear the full cost of refurbishment. I doubt they need all the places."

"Anna Turner will make mincemeat of you."

"I'm planning to offer her what she wants." A delicate

negotiation when he was curious to taste her. He'd shared an almost innocent flirtation with her over non-alcoholic beverages, parted on bad terms, and she fascinated him more than he wanted to admit. Curiosity was allowed.

"Mm." Casildo remained unconvinced.

Hunter shrugged. "The key point is—this was and, in six months, will again be your father's building. He needs to be happy with any building works I authorise and comfortable that the final rents and tenants will ensure his finances are ring-fenced from further raids."

"You're going to improve the building, bring in new tenants with long-term contracts for his benefit, then hand it back to him at cost plus interest?" Casildo stared into his empty cup. "Are you sure you don't want the partnership Dad offered?"

"I don't want a partnership. More than that, I don't want my 'sire' to bankrupt your father as payback for my perceived sins." Hunter had had years to fight his rage at Nick into a low voice and a relaxed body posture, making his anger invisible to the casual observer.

"'Sire' is a fancy word for pond scum." Casildo touched his arm in understanding. "You're not responsible for Nick's twisted ego."

Hunter's mother's death two years ago had brought Nick Richardson back into Hunter's life, and maybe Hunter should have handled that better, but he'd deal with what he had now. He'd learned to live with a lot of losses, but seeing Raed Hariri's good name tarnished while he was simultaneously beggared wasn't going to be among them. "Maybe we should have a rift in our friendship."

"I'm not going to like this."

"If I was heard badmouthing your dad, it might get Nick off my back for a bit."

"I told you I wasn't going to like this."

"If Nick hears your dad screwed me on the price—a sleeper clause in the contract that requires the buyer to pay for building defects, and I announce a heap of defects—

Nick might lose interest in his loser son."

"That's bullshit camouflage," Casildo muttered and ducked closer. "He ignored you for years. Your mother's death triggered this cycle of hell and his belief you used her money to bankroll your growth. He's been escalating since then."

"Because Nick believes he should have inherited Mum's estate, that she was nothing until Nick married her."

"Why don't you just tell him what you did with the money?"

"Because it's none of his damn business." The venom and persistence behind Nick's latest attack had taken Hunter by surprise.

"Does your uncle know your silence has unleashed Nick's inner prince of darkness on you?"

"Ben's out of the building game. He's no longer competition."

"He's running a charity funded by your mother's inheritance," Casildo whispered close to his ear, his frustration scorching the air. "I hope you buried those financial details in some secret impenetrable vault with a password known only to a Tibetan lama and a Swahili tribesman."

"Nick will run out of steam." Hunter was counting on it. "Soon."

"If you believe he'll give up whatever crazy revenge he's planning, you're clutching at straws."

"I just need to prove I'm not successful enough to be a threat." Hunter was juggling new initiatives and didn't have the time for this crap. Nick *always* ran out of steam.

"How do you plan to manage that when most builders in town would rather give you a discount than work with him?"

"I've overcommitted my resources." Hunter suggested a different approach. "I stay out of the property market until he loses interest."

"And if he doesn't lose interest? He's an emotional

vampire."

"There's no one else left for Nick to target. He thinks he's already squashed my uncle. Gina and I agreed we didn't suit. He's just had a go at you and your dad." Until Nick lost interest, Hunter had no plans to add people to his life who might become targets for Nick. "I'm safe, and I plan to live my life my way."

"I don't trust him, and I'm not disappearing. I won't tell any strangers or alert Bizgos that I love you like a brother. But don't ask me to bad mouth you either."

"You're my brother in every way that counts." Hunter signalled for two more coffees. "Which is why I'm talking to you about how we can do this."

"I know you." Casildo shook his head. "You've already decided the childcare centre's non-negotiable."

"She was cheated." Hunter's bones carried the scars of betrayal, and he wouldn't be party to another innocent's suffering.

"That's your only interest?" Casildo raised an eyebrow.

"You said she's not my type." Hunter shrugged.

"If it comes to a showdown between Anna Turner and Nick Richardson, my money's on Anna."

Anna wouldn't be in Hunter's life long enough for Nick to notice her existence.

"Come in," Antonio Perez beckoned Anna into the room.

Hunter's assessment didn't change when she stood in the open doorway. Anna Turner delighted in leaving clues to distract rather than inform. He'd seen other businesswomen wear charcoal pant suits and cream shirts. Anna's deftly applied minimal makeup and elegant silver necklace were further statements she was a professional. No knuckleduster rings in the office. The plum-coloured boots were probably a stock item for creatives. But her tousled gamine haircut looked like she'd tumbled straight from bed.

At five in the afternoon for pity's sake.

"Take a seat, Anna," invited Antonio Perez. "Hunter tells me you and he have already met." Perez's mouth had tightened when Hunter first mentioned it, confirming Anna had told Perez about their first meeting before Hunter had admitted it.

"I've had that pleasure." A pleasure akin to being nibbled to death by ducks from her steely glare. She sat with one leg crossed over the other, leaving him on the outer.

"Hunter's bought The Hariri building where we hoped to locate our childcare centre." Antonio rubbed his hands together. "He's discovered we were on the point of signing a lease with the managing agent and has a proposal for us."

"That's"—her throat moved as if she was swallowing expletives, then she moistened her luscious, water-proof, bruised-plum-lipstick lips—"interesting."

"I hope it's more than interesting." Hunter was beginning to enjoy himself. "In fact, my goal is a mutually beneficial business arrangement."

"He's offering us a deal on a childcare centre." Antonio came around to sit on the front of his desk.

Anna stilled, as if listening with her whole body. She had the quality of testing the air for the mood, of being able to sniff authenticity from error.

And I'm never fanciful.

"I've told Hunter you're the lead on this deal. I'll be guided by your advice."

"What's the deal?" She was still direct and prepared to pluck truth from an inferno.

"Once Hunter explained his reason for being here, we agreed you and he should continue the conversation." Antonio smiled, while creating the professional space for him to veto Hunter's scheme if Anna expressed any doubts. Any solid working arrangement earned Hunter's respect. Antonio and Anna's bond was diamond-hard.

"Should we make an appointment?" Anna stood.

"I'm free now." Hunter followed her into the hall.

"My office is this way—" she began.

He placed a hand on her arm, allowing him to steal a whiff of her perfume. Gardenia perhaps? He'd been unsure at the cocktail party. Too many fragrances in too crowded a venue. In the bar, he hadn't been close enough. Her appearance was a statement on so many levels, but he'd need to nuzzle her throat or hair to uncover this secret. "I saw a bar downstairs."

She looked pointedly at his hand. "It's a bit early to drink."

"They serve coffee and tea." He moved his hand, but her scent had fortified him. "Probably hot chocolate."

"This is not a reprise of the other night, Mr. Thompson." Her words were chipped ice.

"Call me Hunter. Your boss has suggested I run my proposition past you."

"Antonio used the word 'proposal.' Let's stick to that, shall we?"

"I didn't know about your lease when I purchased the property." He held up a hand when she opened her mouth. "More importantly, neither did the owner. There was a miscommunication with his managing agent."

She snorted.

"The previous owner is an honourable man who came to me as soon as he learned you'd been cut loose." Hunter figured he wouldn't emphasise the Hariri surname, given Anna knew Casildo.

"And you're going to kiss it better?" She was lemon tart.

"I'm happy to kiss any part of you better." He couldn't hide his grin. "It's more correct to say, I now have the facts and am prepared to negotiate."

"Are you negotiating with all pending leaseholders who've lost out?" She'd be brutal in a corporate boardroom, yet had chosen a career in the creative arts.

"Yours is the only outstanding lease according to the previous owner."

"What's the catch?" She continued down the hall. "Why

change your plans for us?"

"Suspicion is a terrible thing, Anna. And beneath your negotiating skills."

"What's your interest in honouring previous leases?"

"Raed has an enviable reputation in the business world. He was forceful in challenging me on this." Hariri Senior had agreed with Hunter, after Hunter presented the facts. "I'm offering you a different deal because while I appreciate his desire to keep his reputation, I'm not responsible for the error. However, I planned a childcare centre long-term." More importantly, Casildo's father was committed to having one long-term because he was a father and a grandfather, as well as a long-term supporter of a woman's right to work. "But I currently have only a few staff who need one."

She stopped, arms crossed. She hadn't forgiven him. "The press release said you'd be using that space for a new headquarters."

"Don't believe everything you read in the business pages." Hunter didn't like lying, but this secret wasn't only his to share. "I can achieve what I want with the other floors."

"How do I know you're genuine about a childcare centre?"

"You check the development plans I've submitted to council."

The plans included a childcare centre and drawings for a remodelled separate floor, which looked remarkably like a doubling of Hunter's existing office space. An elaborate ruse to throw Nick off the scent, but thwarting Nick Richardson was the main game. Targeting Casildo's father simply because Hunter regarded the Hariris as his family was—as Cas would say—the action of pond scum.

"I will."

"Wise woman." Hunter nodded. *Where had she learned suspicion?* He knew his teachers intimately. "Get everything in writing."

"I had everything in writing, was hours away from

signing on the dotted line, and still you gazumped me." She showed perfect white teeth, which would leave a scar if she decided to take a bite out of him.

"Old business, Anna. Prosecuting it won't get either of us anywhere."

"Your honesty is relevant to future business. You're asking us to enter a partnership."

"I didn't know about your lease until you told me." It took too much energy to worry about what strangers thought about him. Anna was a stranger, and his interest should be restricted to business, not uncovering the nuances of her shape and scent when she was wrapped around him. Impossible to mix business and a short fling. Impossible to consider anything else. After Gina, occasional sex between consenting adults seemed the safest option. "Take it or leave it."

"It'll take time to get the plans from council," she said. "I'll call when I have those."

"I took the liberty of getting a certified copy for you." He slipped an envelope from a folder he'd been carrying. "And sent an e-copy to Antonio while we were talking."

Her eyes widened in speculation. He'd be a fool to underestimate her.

"I'll call when I've studied those." She recovered quickly.

"I've got back-to-back meetings for the rest of the week." He held up his hands. *Hey, I'm innocent here.*

"I bet you have," she said. His envelope might have been contaminated the way she held it away from her body between her thumb and forefinger.

"What about a business meeting over a meal tomorrow night?"

She studied him, and he knew the moment when desperation for the centre won. "I choose the suburb."

"Fair enough. I pick the restaurant. Where?" He'd lower her resistance with fine food and wine, ferret out her secret passion for a childcare centre and, when she was distracted, engineer to take her home for a quick tumble. One of his new architects could handle the centre's design, and he and Anna need never see each other again.

"Bondi."

"Want me to pick you up here?" Was she inviting him to book the hatted restaurant hovering on the Bondi headland? Hunter had decided her outfit at the cocktail party was camouflage or a trap. A super fancy restaurant seemed out of character. But fancy worked as scene setting for a casual liaison.

"Text me," she said. "I'll meet you there."

* * *

"How's it going?" Her boss joined Anna in her tiny office the following afternoon.

Anna had spent the night before poring over Hunter's plans to council and couldn't find a flaw.

Anna had always joked there was room for her and no one else in her office. Since hosting a meeting with her tall, broad-shouldered now brother-in-law, his twin, and her sister a few years ago, she'd hung a collapsible chair on the back of her door for special occasions.

"I said I'd come up when you were free."

"I'm free. I like coming here." Antonio waved at her notice board with its collection of family photos, postcards, and old campaign promos. "How's Kate?"

"My twin is nearly as large as a small elephant. But disgustingly well and happy." Anna handed him the plastic chair.

"Good." He flipped the chair open and took a seat. "What do you think?"

Anna opened her eyes wide. "About maternity, my current project, or your delicacy in raising the subject of our childcare centre?"

"About Hunter Thompson."

She leaned back and audibly exhaled. "I'm still deciding about him." Her dreams were haunted by the wretched man. "The proposal seems genuine. His plans have been lodged with the council. Floor three is definitely designated as a childcare centre. A building compliance check has been completed. Much faster than I could have achieved, even with a lease."

"But?"

"I've agreed to have a meal with him tonight to discuss further details." She frowned.

"Dinner?" Antonio asked.

"Mr. Thompson claimed to have back-to-back meetings all week. Tonight was the best chance to answer my questions." She was a mess of nerves and realised she didn't want Antonio to veto the meal. She was looking forward to sparring with Hunter again.

"That's plausible." Antonio steepled his hands in front of his mouth. "I did some backgrounding myself. This will be the third development he's taken on in the last eighteen months. The first and third ones he's bought outright. He's in a partnership on the second."

"Are you concerned he's overcommitted?"

Even if she wanted to spar with Hunter, she wouldn't take a risk on this going belly-up. Or worse, that he preyed on businesses or people in trouble.

"My checks show he's delivering what he's promised; his partners, suppliers, and trades aren't complaining."

"You're happy for me to deal?" Relief made her dizzy.

"I've established that he's solvent and planned work on his projects is proceeding in an orderly manner." Antonio rubbed his chin, a sign of qualified praise. "Quite a feat in the building industry these days, with supply constraints, fluctuating costs and variable availability of materials and labour."

"That's a yes." Her heart raced. *Yes!*

"It's a maybe. He hasn't laid out the costs and specifics of what he's offering us." He touched her briefly on the arm. "The budget I gave you remains the budget. If the offer comes in within budget and delivers what we want, then we're good to go."

"I understand."

He smiled wryly. "Don't waste time on Thompson if the proposal won't work for us. We'll find another property."

"I won't let you down." She'd make this proposal work. The building was perfect. "Your research shows he's solvent. The council documents show he's serious. Honouring the previous owner's lease shows he's decent." Especially after her outburst in the bar. Anna respected decency.

"It's not a matter of letting me down. I know this is important to you. I don't know all the reasons why, and I won't ask. I can see the positive office and inter-office chatter it's generating. Delivering will boost morale. I've spoken to Nadia, offered to pay the difference between her current childcare and a centre closer to work for a few months. She's thinking about it." Antonio was also a decent, generous man. Widowed when his kids were in primary school, he understood the challenges of being a single parent.

"Thank you."

"I know we stand to lose her." He massaged the back of his neck. "Plus, you're right. My overall opinion of Hunter Thompson is positive. He didn't chat much, didn't set out to charm. Let's see the detail of what he's offering ..."

Anna spent the next hour rechecking the plans, developing a list of questions and reviewing her previous budget. Leasing part of the premises and sharing costs shouldn't cost more than her original plans, but that was one of her first tests for Hunter. Satisfied, she pushed back from her desk.

Solvent, serious and decent, making Hunter's game-playing with his father a puzzle as well as a turn-off. Anna had no patience for betrayal in any of its guises.

CHAPTER THREE

Hunter arrived at Bondi Icebergs Dining Room and Bar ten minutes early, accepting that he hadn't wanted to miss Anna's entrance. Battle armour or work clothes? Finding he didn't mind either way was a surprise.

Trouble lurked in the warmth of her smile.

Enough trouble that he'd finagled his way to dinner tonight when he should have done everything via phone or email. Keeping scrupulous records of all exchanges was Lesson in Caution 101. The best way to avoid misunderstandings or blackmail. Dinner meetings didn't allow for scrupulous records. *She's forbidden fruit.*

She smiled at the majordomo, answered the man's quiet question, and surrendered her light jacket before she turned toward the bar. A multi-coloured peasant skirt with what looked like one of those long-sleeved, button-down-the-front, black leotardy-type fitted bodysuits that followed rather than clung to curves. *Idiot!* His head was full of gibberish when it came to describing her outfits. More colourful than the charcoal suit she'd worn the other day, but she was here to deal.

"Hi." She slid onto the stool next to him and dropped a largish bag onto the floor.

"Thanks for coming. Would you like a drink here or to go straight to the table?"

"The table." She tilted her head. "But I can wait, if you'd like to finish your drink."

"Share some." He nudged it toward her. "Some sort of citrusy mocktail, but it's refreshing."

She sampled it without a word. Her lips might have rested where his had been, but who the hell paid attention to things like that? "A bit sweet for my taste," she said.

"Mine too. I'll order something else when we take a seat." Hunter signalled to a waiter and nodded in the direction of the table he'd been told was his.

The waiter appeared in time to pull out Anna's chair and flip open their serviettes, before offering them menus and wine lists.

"Thank you."

Hunter took the seat at right angles to Anna.

"Something to drink?" asked the waiter.

"Sparking mineral water, please." Anna gave the response Hunter expected.

"I'll have a beer. Is Peroni on the menu?"

"Yes, sir."

Anna put her elbows on the table, linked her hands, and leaned her chin on them to gaze out the windows. "I'd forgotten how good the view is from here."

"Come here often?" *Well, damn.* Maybe his choice of restaurant wasn't so impressive.

"Rare family dinner a few years ago when my parents came up from Melbourne." She grinned. "I'm not on expenses."

"Neither am I." He scowled. "Are you trying to piss me off to start the evening?"

"The food was delicious, the service excellent, while the view's stupendous. Thank you." She disarmed him.

"What would you like to eat?"

She studied the menu before giving him an up-and-under look. "Everything. I'm ravenous. But I'll settle for a green salad followed by the scampi."

With perfect timing, the waiter appeared at Hunter's elbow with their drinks. "Ready to order, sir?"

"Two salads, followed by two scampi," Hunter ordered.

"Gosh. Doesn't a working man need to eat more than that?"

"Not tonight. Because this is a working dinner, and we're keeping our wits about us." Which was why he hadn't inched closer to nuzzle her throat and parse out her scent. Different tonight but still Anna.

What's the matter with you, Thompson?

"Let's wait until after the salads. Just absorb the ambience for the moment."

"What ambience?"

"I'm a designer. You've got to give me some time to study the layout and eavesdrop on the conversations."

"We're tucked into this corner so no one will eavesdrop on our conversation," he said pointedly.

"Part of the clever design. We can be private in a public space."

"The space here is pretty box-like. The credit goes to the interior designer rather than the architect." He glanced around.

"There's my magic word again." She gave the waiter, who delivered the salad, a friendly smile. "Thank you."

The silence between them while they ate was comfortable. Another surprise. And maybe key to explaining why Cas had raved about her success at her job. Calm, composed, not the firecracker he'd encountered when she'd learned his name. Her calm suggested she had no qualms about their upcoming negotiation, that she wasn't personally invested in this victory. Tonight, she was giving a fine imitation of a poker player.

"Casildo said you've worked for Changing Minds for years."

"That's how you found your way to the cocktail party?" She hadn't asked around. Inviting her to Bondi beach's iconic Icebergs hadn't impressed her enough to bother stroking his ego. "I like Casildo."

"The feeling's mutual. How come after all this time you want a childcare centre? Are you planning to use it?" *Smooth, Thompson, ferreting out details on her relationship status when I have no intention of having a relationship with her.*

"We've lost two outstanding employees in the last two years because juggling divorce, childcare and a full-time job is hard work. Add domestic violence and the task becomes almost impossible." She wanted to shock him. "We're looking at losing a third. A centre nearby could make the difference."

"I didn't see you as a crusader." He studied her over his frosted beer glass.

"I'm not." She hunched a shoulder. "I act where I can. No big deal."

The childcare centre was a big enough deal for her to agree to dinner with him when she'd rather watch paint dry.

"Not buying that. This is personal." When she glanced away, he knew he'd stumbled on a secret Anna Turner didn't share easily. He waited for a prevarication.

"I've been in their position. A disloyal lover, a lover who breaks faith." She pinned him with her gaze—fierce, but unbowed. "Practical help is better than sympathy."

"Who?" Hunter barely breathed the word, not wanting to spook her into retreat. Her honesty sliced through his defences, terrifying and fascinating him in equal parts.

"I'll give you a cascading series of events from being the child of a philanderer to discovering teenage boys don't ask before posting naked pics or claiming they scored when they didn't. My sister was doxxed by an arrogant idiot who couldn't understand the word no. Men, who claim to be grown-ups, look at me as if I'm a collection of body parts and they're adding up the score." She stunned him with her anger.

"Explains your reluctance to share a quiet drink with a stranger." His conscience was clear, regardless of defamatory reports hidden under various social media rocks. *Why bother with facts?* "I apologise for my gender."

"Aren't you going to tell me it's my fault because of the sluttish dresses I almost wear?"

"I'm not big on blaming the victim." He leaned back in his chair. "I am in the you-can-say-no-at-any-point-in-the-proceedings camp. You're buttoned up to the throat tonight, confirming that the red dress—which was gorgeous—was a test."

"More a keep-off-the-grass statement." She picked up her glass, then set it down. "Okay, it's also a test."

"How'd I do?" His gut gave a nervous jump.

"Well enough for me to agree to a meal with you to close this deal."

"Did you research my business?" Better to know what he was dealing with.

"Antonio did due diligence on your business. I checked every line in your council application and their approval."

"What about before we met?"

"Nothing useful, and the council approval carries more weight with me."

"So, I passed, but you refused a lift here, and the venue is very public, should you decide to scream," he said, aware she was smarter and more vulnerable than his initial assessment.

"I rarely scream." She toasted him with her sparkling mineral water.

"Noted."

The waiter set their scampi before them.

"So, going back to our reason for being here …" Talking business provided a solid footing, when she'd just tossed him overboard in a storm. Wanting to discover more about her wasn't in his game plan. "I'm supplying the premises—"

"If we do a deal."

"You've just said you're here to deal. No reflection on the organisation you were looking at, but I'll also want to engage my own childcare provider, so that's recruitment, staff registration, and legal protocols covered."

"I'd want the childcare provider named in our contract."

"And you'll want to be on the management board," Hunter concluded.

"You were listening."

"I usually listen when I'm in a conversation." His heart rate settled. He was back in control. "Instead of leasing the floor, you'll be contracting for a set number of places in the centre."

"With the option to negotiate increased places every six months," she countered.

"Annual increases will work. Most mothers take some parental leave." He'd had this conversation with Casildo's sister when she'd been setting up her centre.

"If they can afford it or have family support."

"Option to increase the number of places annually, with an emergency clause for special cases." The quick-fire round of questions and answers helped relax him further.

"I can live with that. Set rate per place for five years."

"Now, you're trying it on, Anna. Annual review on place rates. You know that's fair. We're shouldering refurbishment and supply of all needs, provider costs including staff pay, benefits, insurance, plus utility costs, and the list goes on."

"*We're*—have you got a silent partner I should meet?" She was another good listener.

"A manner of speaking." Now wasn't the time to tell her she'd have a different owner by early next year. Her plan wouldn't suffer, so she didn't need to know before the rest of the world.

"I'll have to check with Antonio, but annual increases in fees, the capacity to increase or reduce places, and a minimum five-year contract might work."

He let her pretend Antonio would disagree with anything she negotiated. "Which brings us to modifications. How do you feel about a safe play area on the roof?"

Gotcha.

She lowered the fork she'd been raising to her mouth and simply smiled. "You were saving that, weren't you?"

"You've gone from ice to a puddle of warm water," he said. And she looked good all soft and happy with him.

"Your questions the other day—does it have windows that open? Does it have balconies? The answer's no. I've researched, and there are some outstanding designs in medium and high-rises, but fresh air is the cherry on top."

"Have to check local regulations, but it should be doable. It'll also allow more options for activities with mobility and sensory-impaired children." Hunter liked seeing her happy, and he'd think about that later.

"You have given this some thought."

"You might have ideas about colours." He threw that in to schedule another meeting with her. He was crazy. He blamed her luminous smile.

"Now I know you're playing with me. Architects consider light, colour and texture as part of their design work."

"True. But at this early stage, I'm open to constructive collaboration from a long-term tenant."

"You're assuming this is a done deal?" She tilted her head to one side.

"It's done if you say it's done."

"Have you designed a childcare centre before?"

"Yes." For Casildo's older sister, Maha. "I'm interested in sustainability, safety, non-toxic materials, and I'm a demon on storage spaces and the practicalities."

"Privacy and security are must-haves." She fiddled with her glass. "My sister and brother-in-law might have landscaping ideas for the roof, if it's accessible. Plants for the senses. I've read about that."

"This will cost less than your original plans. Antonio might like to have a garden named after him."

"A roof garden for me, a plaque for Antonio—you have spent some time identifying our weaknesses." She sipped her water, and he wanted her mouth on him.

He stifled a groan. "Not identifying weaknesses, Anna. Looking at what works for both of us."

"You're giving me everything I want." She paused, as if checking some internal list. "Timing?"

"What's your time frame? Had you lined up contractors to do the work?"

"I'd put out a few feelers. Hoping three months, but figured I'd be lucky to get it done in six."

"If all the ducks line up, three's a good chance. What?"

"I've been nervous as hell about this." She exhaled slowly.

"You don't show it. And the contract isn't signed yet."

"It will be."

Her conviction shifted something in Hunter. He'd done due diligence as well. Anna Turner's integrity was rock solid. Having her trust him on this mattered.

"I'm a stomach churner." She rested her hand on her belly. "How do you show you're nervous?"

"I'm never nervous." But she'd upended Hunter's assumptions about tonight, added humour and insight to simmering attraction, complicating his idea of a short affair.

She picked up his hand, turned it over to trace the prominent veins in his wrist. "Ice in your veins?"

Her touch heated his blood.

* * *

"Would you like dessert?" The waiter reappeared beside the table, menus in hand.

"No, thank you," Anna said.

Hunter was a private man. Little things gave him away. Although they were tucked in a corner, he'd kept his back to the room. Obviously wealthy men at nearby tables made a performance of calling for service and loudly naming the vintage they'd chosen. Hunter spoke quietly and hadn't tried to press her when she'd chosen water. Maybe that's why she'd blurted out her real reasons for wanting a childcare centre.

"Not even hot chocolate?" Hunter's dimple had its own charm.

"I've got a better idea. We'd like the bill, please?" Anna dismissed the hovering waiter, and her butterflies returned as dragons.

"I invited you for dinner."

"I accepted. But I'll buy dessert." Anna hadn't planned this next move, but Hunter's deal was more than fair, would save Antonio money, and set off a conga line of dancing employees at Changing Minds. Three months was a gift she hadn't dared hope for. *Yes!* She gave a mental fist pump. *This is for you, Helen.* Helen had always wanted children, and her dream had been brutally snatched from her. "I know a place."

"Your place?" His question was only half-hopeful because, whatever else he was, he wasn't stupid.

Anna shook her head. "Better."

Sharing some of herself in the hope he'd reciprocate was a tentative first step toward … friendship … something more? Hunter had made her consider more, even on the night she'd worn her *Killing Eve* dress. Hunter had exorcised some of the helpless rage that had driven Anna to buy it, after the creepy company executive's crude proposition had catapulted her back to her terrible teens when she'd been adrift.

Minutes later, she preceded Hunter from the air-conditioned splendour of the restaurant into an unseasonably balmy evening. A three-quarter moon hung low over Bondi beach, the Southern Cross constellation was spilling across the sky, and the air was soft and salty. Anna slipped her hand through his arm, his sudden stillness telling her she'd surprised him. Her wide skirt brushed against his trouser leg, a tiny susurrus of sound.

"In Italy they call it *la passeggiata*. It's usually a stroll down the main street of a village to show yourself off and talk to

the neighbours. But it can be an after-dinner promenade."
She steered him toward Campbell Parade. "We're heading
for Mapo."

"Gelato."

He smelt delicious this close, all dry, ambery, smoky and
mysterious.

"Uh-huh. What's your favourite flavour?" She pushed
open the door to Mapo. The roughly rendered brick and
sanded-back plaster walls contrasted with the silver-lidded
pozzetti containers keeping the gelato at temperature.
Shelves were packed with plyboard boxes of ripe fruit,
berries, citrus, with some early mangoes. The sweet caramel-
like perfume of strawberries in abundance clogged the air.

"Pear, but it's a short season." He scanned the board
menu. "Pistachio tonight. Want me to snag a bench seat
while you order?"

"We haven't finished our *passeggiata*. I'll meet you
outside." Re-joining him on the pavement, she passed him
a cone. "For you." She linked arms again to guide him down
the hill to the walkway above the beach. "Let's walk on the
sand," she said, her gaze out to sea.

"Why?" He halted.

Anna offered one of her lower-wattage smiles, one she
saved for friends. "Because we're here. It's a lovely evening,
and I don't often get the chance."

"Let's finish our gelatos first." His pink tongue lapped
at the gelato, his gaze steady on hers.

She bit into her cone, and his eyes widened slightly,
making her take the last mouthfuls in a rush. He continued
nibbling small pieces off his cone. Turning away from his
seriously sexy mouth took monumental self-discipline. She
rested her back against the railing.

"Finish it, Duck. Swallow it whole."

"What did you call me?" He choked on the last of the
dry cone.

She liked off-balancing him.

"'*Duck*.' I heard it in an old movie. It's a term of

endearment. Although, I was thinking of the definitions of the verb duck—evade, elude, dodge, avoid and sidestep."

"I *am* not evasive. We've just agreed a straight-up deal." He looked so appealing, slightly bemused, burdened in a way. A man called Hunter S. Thompson, even if the S stood for Samuel, must feel burdened on occasion. "And, I'm not answering to Duck."

"Private, then," she amended before rummaging in her shoulder bag. She waved aloft the collapsible backpack she carried for shopping trips. "This makes us hands-free." Heeling off her sandals, she tucked them and her bag into the soft pack. "Your turn."

While he removed his shoes and socks, Anna tucked the bottom of her wide skirt into her bodysuit, creating a ballerina tutu-like short skirt. He turned his head to stare at her naked knees, then peered up at her.

"Are you going in the water?"

"We're strolling along the water's edge. We're going to get sand between our toes, and maybe you should roll your trousers above your knees. Haven't you ever played in the water?"

"Not for years."

"That's sad." Anna had the sense his expectations of women were pretty low. What was that song? "Desperado"—something about walking alone being a prison. She wasn't alone, but she admitted there were times she was lonely. "It's part of dessert. My treat."

Dutifully adding his shoes to the backpack, he rolled up his trousers before shouldering the pack, then stuck out an elbow. "Shall we stroll?"

"We can stroll or saunter or"—she giggled—"I might manage a sashay."

"You like words."

"I love words. I'm the daughter of writers and the sister of a writer."

"Hence your choice of the word *philanderer* rather than *cheat* at dinner."

More evidence he *did* listen, another tick in the column marked appealing.

"There's a difference. A philanderer doesn't necessarily lie to his partners. Both parties might agree to a casual sexual relationship. A cheat acts dishonestly or unfairly to gain an advantage." Although both were betrayal, and Anna didn't give second chances.

"Did your father cheat on your mother?"

"All of my father's partners knew exactly who he was. That was part of the charm. My mother was also aware of what was happening. She described that period as one of 'creative differences.'" Anna tasted again the bitter disillusion of that discovery.

"What did you call it? he asked gently.

"Hell."

* * *

"My father is a philandering cheat."

And where the hell had that confession come from?

Hunter was scrupulous in not commenting on Nick. In trying to pretend Nick Richardson wasn't his father. Because then he wouldn't have any of the evil bastard in him.

She unlinked her arm from his. Guess he'd killed the moment. Moving closer, she took his hand, her fingers warm where they threaded with his.

"Like I said, hell. Brian Ferguson's my father."

"The playwright?" *Had she changed her name?*

"An Australian national treasure, but we digress." She patted Hunter on the chest.

"He's the philanderer?"

"A simple search of the World Wide Web will detail his sins."

I believe you.

"Tell me. I wasn't watching much theatre as a teenager." Hunter had been breaking his back working for his uncle and trying to figure out how to be a man.

"I call it his my-ego-needs-stroking period—the early heady years of his critical success when he couldn't say no to any fangirl, actress, model, passerby."

She'd meant it when she'd said "hell."

"How did your mother feel?" Hunter's mother had been devastated and determined to win her husband back.

"My mother, Rosamunde Turner, a novelist, gave him an ultimatum on her fortieth birthday: monogamy with her or divorce." She sighed. "His period of disbelief was short, but dramatic, and from there, we moved to the doting-family-man stage."

"Is that why you're called Turner?"

"My surname is almost an accident." She leaned closer, giving him a whiff of her spicy scent. Close was better than abandoning him on the beach. "My parents agreed that *a* girl would be named after my mother and *a* boy after my father. I use the indefinite article deliberately. One child was the plan. Instead, they produced the Turner twins."

"Do you see them?" He'd seen too little of his mother at the end, still angry at how easily she'd danced to Nick Richardson's tune.

"Whenever I'm in Melbourne, or they're in Sydney. We talk regularly. We don't agree on many things, but we've made peace. Do you see yours?"

"Seeing Nick wasn't an issue when I was a kid. He worked seven days a week, long hours, establishing his own real estate business. Empire—he always planned to have an empire." The power of that one word "hell" kept Hunter talking. Lots of people couldn't compute its endless, depthless darkness. "I've often thought part of Mum's appeal was her brother, Ben. He was a builder. Nick met him first. 'Found him,' he used to claim." Hunter had to give it to Nick. He recognised skill, and Ben had been a genius on a building site.

"Your uncle did the rehab on properties your father sold."

"Smart girl." He should have expected her to join the dots. "Nick got the loan for the property, paid Ben for labour, materials, and twenty percent of the profit on resale. He kept the rest."

The theft from his uncle still turned Hunter's stomach. Ben had refused every compensation offer Hunter had made, until Hunter had had the idea about the charity.

"Does Ben still work for your father?"

"He did sixteen years, stopped around my fourteenth birthday." Another milestone in Hunter's life.

"And you wonder why he stayed so long?"

"He stayed because of Mum." Hunter had spent countless hours on the puzzle. "Maybe because of me. Ben and Ellie couldn't have kids. We're close." And that had become one of Hunter's most carefully guarded secrets.

"The question has to be asked."

And yet few people ever had.

"Why did Ben stop?" Anna was smart, observant and, at this moment, Hunter didn't feel he was making a mistake confiding in her.

"Mum walked in on Nick screwing his secretary in their bed." Hunter didn't add he'd been close behind. In time to see tits and ass, and humping, and hear Nick's guttural groans and a saccharine sweet voice say "Oh baby, oh baby." Nick's secretary's scent had overwhelmed his mother's light floral fragrance. Heavy exertion carried its own smell, giving the scene a gritty immediacy missing from the blurry images on mates' pirated porn videos. The real-life fuck had replayed endlessly in Hunter's head—titillating torture.

"What happened?" She spoke with the caution of someone who knew the next step wasn't straightforward.

"He wanted a divorce. Even more, he wanted to sell the house. But it was in Mum's name—a tax dodge he'd done a few years earlier. She mistakenly thought keeping the house would bring him back to her."

"What about you?"

"I went from being a kid, whose father was absent because he worked all the time but demanded adulation and total obedience when he was home, to a kid whose father was absent because they were divorced." *WTF, I've just spilled my guts to Anna Turner.*

"I love the moon on the sea. Classic cliché, but moonlight on water spells romance." She was letting him off the hook—wasn't demanding more details or offering psychoanalysis.

Her perfume slid into his consciousness above the salt in the air and the roasting garlic and chilli from nearby Thai restaurants.

She upended him. Hunter figured he had a sense of her, and she tucked up her skirts and became a sprite on a moonlit beach, quiet and as easy to be with as an old friend.

"I told you my sister was doxxed. So, while I have to have a social media presence for work, she and I prefer as far as possible in this connected and dysfunctional world to keep our private lives private."

"I didn't check."

"I did." She made an apologetic face. "I gave myself ten minutes. You don't appear to have personal social media accounts. Any gossip about you is all second-hand."

"Work's my excuse. No time. I do have business accounts, managed by my tech-savvy secretary. They don't include shots of me."

He wasn't sure where Anna was heading, but she'd run a few checks. *Everyone checked.* Ridiculous to feel flattered, but going beyond the business bloggers, beyond the due diligence showed a personal interest.

"I'm telling you because I don't make my judgements about people based on social media. If I have a question, I'll ask you, and I expect you to do the same."

"Fair enough."

She released his hand. "Race you." Then took off, her long legs sprinting across the packed, wet sand.

One hundred metres later, he tapped her elbow. "Tag."

She slowed, finally coming to a halt, barely puffing. She stepped forward until they were toe to toe, her gaze on his, assessing him, weighing her next step. Hunter held his breath. He wanted to touch her, but she'd sprinted past the moment when they could have had a mindless hot and heavy coupling. When she smiled, Hunter knew she'd reached a decision and questioned his sanity. Her hand cupped the back of his head, and she rested her fingers on his other cheek.

Hunter had a split second to react before her mouth brushed against his. He opened his arms to wrap her closer. Like holding sunshine and joy. She lifted her head, her eyes dreamy and smiled.

"Your turn. Wanna kiss me, Duck?"

"I just might." He scanned her face to imprint her features on his mind. Clear eyes, barely-there makeup, flawless ivory skin, and he wanted to kiss every freckle scattered across her cheeks. Because something told him he shouldn't do this twice. Kissing Anna Turner was dangerous. "And I hate that name."

The moonlight on the water, the crash of waves at his feet, the tang of salt in his nostrils and mouth, and her impish grin—absent any kind of fakery—tempted him to recklessness. She caressed his ear and anticipation roared beyond temptation to blazing need.

"I promised myself I wouldn't do this, despite the little hum we've got going. You talked to me. Really talked. Honesty, and not leering down my blouse, are my Achilles' heel." She rose onto her toes, leaning against him in innocent provocation. Her smile faltered. The tip of her tongue moistened her top lip, then touched his.

"If we're only doing this once, we'd better do it right." He breathed against her lips. She tasted sweet and tart and strong, with a hint of the salted caramel from her gelato, and the combination packed a bigger punch than he'd expected—and he'd expected a flashfire. Once was already not enough.

Bracing his feet in the sand, he was aware when her body trembled before settling more certainly against him. He teased her mouth open, deepening the kiss because he craved the closeness as much as the taste of her. She moaned—an enticing, involuntary sound—then lifted both hands to cup his face. She held him while her kisses became more demanding and the press of her body against his more insistent. He traced the fine bones around her neck, then slid urgent hands down her flanks to grip her butt. *Got to keep your balance* said a voice in his head, while another asked why he cared.

A wave broke over his ankles, chilly water slapping at his knees.

"Oh." She sprang back, looking as befuddled as he felt.

For a few moments, he'd forgotten where he was, what day it was, forgotten his own name. And hadn't given a damn. He hadn't let down his guard down like that since … forever. Had never felt so completely safe in a woman's arms.

Maybe I've been on the metaphorical wagon too long?

"You kiss like Sam-I-Am."

"Can't be any worse than Duck."

"Like a man who's resilient, who tries again after a knockback." She laughed, a joyous, musical half-giggle, half-guffaw. "Sam-I-am got sixty-nine rejections before he got a taker for his green eggs and ham."

"You can tell all that from a kiss?" He was a man dying of thirst, and she was cool, clean water.

"Strong yet flexible and durable. Durable's important." She untucked her skirt. It tumbled down to cover her bare thighs. "You gave me more than a kiss tonight."

Dangerous, alluring, risky—too risky with Nick on the warpath? Hunter never gambled with the safety of people he loved, like his uncle, or Cas and his family. He'd already circled the wagons to protect his own.

"Thank you." She smiled.

"What for?"

"For sharing an ice cream, for a walk along the beach. The restaurant was a treat, but this is for every day."

Taking a risk wasn't a gamble—uncertainty was a natural part of life. Right, Sam-I-am, and you're hoping to get lucky with a woman who compares you to a children's cartoon character and makes you fantasise about ice cream and beach walks every day. "Want a lift home?" he asked.

"I've got transport." She held up her phone, tapped the ride share app, and organised a pickup.

"Do you always arrange transport?" He was curious, and she was being as cautious as him.

"Always." She turned to walk up the beach, her fingers tangling with his. Her warmth seeped through him, so that he couldn't find it in himself to be offended by her brush-off. She valued herself, which meant he had to value her too. "I don't always use it." She gave him a hip bump.

"The childcare centre I designed belongs to Casildo's sister. Her name's Maha. I'll give her your number. Suggest you have a look." He was insane to entangle his life with her any further. Any decision had a domino effect, including unintended consequences, which might blow up in his face.

And I'm thinking with my gonads, not my brain.

"Maha." She rolled the name around her tongue. "I'll have to look up the meaning. My sister's pregnant and is collecting names."

He laughed. "According to one source, it means beautiful eyes, like those of a wild cow. Maha waited until we were in bed one night and threw a bucket of ice water over us for sharing that."

"Sounds like you've known her a long time."

"Since childhood."

"See, durable."

A car drew level. After confirming it was her ride, she took her sandals and bag out of the backpack. Placing a hand on his shoulder, she lifted onto her toes to kiss him. Soft, memorable, addictive.

"I'll collect the backpack later. Thanks for dinner and

the walk."

Was spending time with Anna a risk or a gamble? Not a gamble—he barely knew her. Neither of them was looking for anything deep and meaningful; they were just following the buzz. Except she thought he was durable, an unorthodox compliment he wasn't sure what to do with. He watched the vehicle disappear around the corner.

"Sheesh, you're agonising over a kiss." A calculated risk, not a gamble. Nick didn't know Anna, and based on Hunter's history in recent years, Anna wouldn't be around long enough for Nick to shift his interest from Hunter's business to his personal life.

CHAPTER FOUR

What on earth was I doing? Anna never flirted with the clients. Okay, Hunter wasn't a client. Not in the usual sense. She flopped against the vinyl back seat of the café while she waited for Beatriz.

But he was complicated, and complicated men were trouble. A property developer in competition with his "philandering cheat" of a father. One blogger, Bizgos, in particular, fanned the flames. Hunter Samuel Thompson was also giving her the childcare centre she wanted, sooner than she'd dare hope. A roof garden. *My giddy aunt.*

A friendly kiss—she'd owed him that, for the inspiration of the roof garden, for sharing the story of his fractured childhood. Barefoot in the sand and wearing a bemused smile, he'd been a different man. She'd stepped closer until his scent drenched her senses, daring her to take a chance with a man she barely knew, but who tugged at her in ways she didn't fully understand.

Bea appeared at the door to the café, placed her order, then joined Anna at the table.

"Sorry I'm late."

"I haven't been here long myself."

"Sooo?" Bea let the word stretch and hover in the air,

while Anna got her story straight.

"He's offering a very good deal."

"Personal or professional?" Bea waggled her eyebrows.

"He's given me the name of someone operating a childcare centre he designed. I've called to organise a visit."

"Mmm." Bea leaned on her fist. "Is the person a friend? Maybe they'll exaggerate his skills."

"Maha Hariri, Casildo's sister. That's why I'm visiting. I've checked out enough centres in the last two years to know a good design from an off-the-shelf one. Have you ever heard Casildo talk about a sister in childcare?"

"Nope. And I didn't see Casildo with Hunter at the party. But it was too crowded to keep track of everyone. What's with Hunter's name?"

"He was christened Hunter S., although the S is for Samuel. He said it was his mother's idea of a joke."

True to form, Bea maintained a discreet silence while the waitress delivered their meals: salad and juice for Bea, a sandwich and water for Anna.

"Odd sense of humour. Must have been hell at school." Bea studied Anna's lunch order before lifting her tomato juice in a toast. "Congratulations, Anna. You've got your centre."

"I kissed him." Anna put her uneaten sandwich back on her plate. Toasted cheese and tomato—her go-to lunch when she needed a calorie hit to smooth out her mood.

On a moonlit beach, his cheek had been warm, despite the slight breeze, smooth even. He'd been unsmiling, focused on her next move. He hadn't smelled or felt like a corporate raider. *Who am I kidding?* She'd wanted to kiss him anyway. *Just once.*

"Before or after you resolved the contract?"

"What difference does it make?"

"It's better if business is complete before you start on dessert." Bea fanned herself with her hand. "Bet he was hot."

"He was"—Anna raised a hand and let it drop—"I don't

think he'd like me talking about how he kissed."

Her friend shovelled another mouthful of her kale and traditional grains salad into her mouth.

"I think he saw me as a hook-up for a night, then changed his mind."

"Shows he's got some smarts."

"I love what I've seen of his designs. And I didn't expect to. I expected utilitarian, regulation compliant, and—honestly—bog standard," Anna admitted. "Shame on me."

"Are we still talking about his kisses?" Bea fluttered her eyelashes.

Anna laughed and picked up her sandwich. "No."

"Did he flash his designs while you were in this clinch? Was it a full-body kiss?"

"What's your sudden fascination with a kiss?"

"I've been fascinated by kisses since my cousin's best mate offered to teach me when I was twelve." Bea tapped her mouth demurely with her napkin. "Today's fascination is with you. How long has this drought been?"

"I've kissed."

Bea looked at her.

"Okay. I've dated occasionally. Done some heavy breathing—"

"Is *that* what you call it?"

"I haven't had sex with a man since—" Anna did a calculation in her head.

"Let me help you. You haven't had sex with a man since Kate told you she's having a baby. My guess is that subconsciously you're expecting a niece and are already modelling good behaviour."

That's not"—she frowned—"a conscious decision." Kate and Liam didn't want to know the gender of their baby.

"It's a mothering kind of decision." Bea checked her smartwatch.

"That's warped."

"I assumed it was an identical twin thing. You're looking

out for your niece before she's even born; don't want any shonky characters in her life. And I'm going to have to go." Her friend pushed back from the table.

Anna glanced at her uneaten sandwich.

"Stay. Finish that." Bea passed her and rested her hand on her shoulder. "You have lots of lovely, honourable male friends, many of whom you've known since long before you met me. You just never fall in love with them. Call me."

Anna bit into her sandwich and started chewing. She redid the mental calculation. Bea was right. She wasn't even vaguely promiscuous, but she was young, healthy, and hoping to find someone she could love, so of course she dated, had occasionally extended or accepted an invitation to stay the night.

How on earth will I know it's Mr. Right or even Mr. Possible if I don't sample the wares?

Except she hadn't sampled anyone's wares since Kate's early ultrasound.

Pop psychologists would probably have an explanation, but she wasn't going to ask. Bea was right. Trusting herself was her biggest issue. She took another bite of her sandwich and scowled at the plate. Was Hunter shonky or, more importantly, unreliable?"

Her head said "the jury's still out," but her heart wanted to disagree.

Anna had learned suspicion at her father's knee. The lesson had been reinforced in her teens. If it had been hard to trust before Helen was sexually assaulted, it became almost impossible after Helen's death.

She'd coaxed Helen to join her on what should have been a one-night job—the rebellion of eighteen-year-olds. Burst naked out of a birthday cake, hang around for a few minutes, and then disappear with enough cash to fund a long weekend at the music festival Splendour in the Grass.

Except it hadn't worked out like that for Helen. Helen had tried to live with what had happened to her that night. Instead, shame and hurt had paralysed her. She'd forgotten how to do basic tasks, like wash herself, dress, even eat in the weeks leading to her suicide. Helen's innocence had been betrayed. Anna still raged at being unable to hold Helen's attacker to account.

Anna had itemised her disillusion for Hunter. He'd *shared* her rage, which marked him out as what? One of the good guys? A liar? Unusual?

Anna rejected the victim label. Having a twin was part of that—together Kate and she were stronger. Anna had reached a truce with her father. She'd told herself every teenager picked dud partners from time to time, and forgiven herself those mistakes. She'd also finally forgiven herself for being so overwhelmed by grief when Helen committed suicide, that she didn't see fast enough that Andrew Levin was a control freak intent on destroying Kate.

Okay, I set tests for people, like my outrageous outfits, the fact I rarely drink alcohol at public venues, and arrange my own transport.

She'd been doing well until that company exec threatened to get his company's contract cancelled. She'd fought hard to be strong and resilient, then one guy with a Madonna/whore complex had made her question whether all her wounds had healed.

Anna liked Hunter S. Thompson, but in listing her disillusions, she hadn't told him about Helen.

* * *

Five days, a mere three working days later, Hunter had expedited the legalities with the local authority and lined up a team to start on the rehab. He had rough drawings, some colour and fabric samples and, crazily, couldn't wait to show them to Anna.

Financially, it didn't matter if she signed or not, although he'd had the contract drawn up and emailed to Changing Minds. Hariri, father and son, were sold on the concept. The next step was pointing out it was the perfect stepping stone for Maha to expand her business, and it gave him a kick to realise he—family, but not family—would provide the chance for the Harisis to help each other.

But a part of Hunter he'd fought into a box, the part seeking praise from someone he cared about, wanted to see Anna's face when he showed her the possibilities of the space. Someone who wasn't part of the extended Hariri or Thompson tribes.

Hell! I don't care for her. He was attracted. The edginess he felt around her hadn't subsided in the past five days. Impatient to see her, but he wasn't going to drool or grovel. She'd made no move to contact him except to send a text thanking him for Maha's call. Maha had been equally tight-lipped.

Your friend called in. We chatted about kids' needs, about space, about activities, about colours, about diet, about sleep, about kids, about security. You know what it's like.

He had no clue what it was like.

"Hi, Anna, I've got to be at Sydney University for a meeting. Can you do Newtown for lunch? I've got some designs and ideas to show you, and we can chat about any problems with the contract." He had thirty minutes, max. *I'm mad.* Because he wanted to see her smile at him, and go all gooey, like she had when he'd mentioned a rooftop garden.

"You moved fast," she said, leaving him unsure if she was surprised or pleased. "We've got copies of the contract."

"You want fast on this. There's a café near the hospital, if that suits? It's on a bus route from the city."

"You've arranged transport for me?" *Now*, she sounded pleased.

"Seemed like the thing to do."

Hunter was waiting when she stepped off the bus. "Thanks for coming here, when you've probably got back-to-back meetings of your own."

"This is a priority. I can work later." She fell into step with him as they passed the hospital entrance. She was wearing a skinny trouser suit, her jacket ending at mid-thigh. Rich burgundy, with some sort of lemon concoction for a shirt. She looked professionally delicious. Leaning closer, he caught a whiff of flowers and citrus. Different to their night out, still, it made him want to nuzzle against her throat to untangle her scent and taste.

"Hey, you."

Hunter heard the guttural demand before he saw the speaker. The owner had a craggy, beaten-up face atop a wizened body. Perched in a hospital wheelchair, he was parked beside the stone fence bordering the hospital grounds. His carer, if he had one, was nowhere to be seen.

"Hey, you." The voice was louder, deeper, more intent on catching his attention.

"You mean me?" Hunter pointed toward himself.

"Yeah," the man said. "Come here."

"Excuse me," Hunter said to Anna. "What's up?" he asked the patient as he drew closer.

"I've dropped me cigarette. Pick it up for me. Please?" His cigarette had fallen between his legs and rolled under the wheelchair.

Hunter bent, picked it up, and handed it to the old man.

"Thanks." The man's ears were scratched raw. Age or experience had dug deep caverns around his mouth. He was missing a few teeth, which hampered clear speech. The guy could easily be an old bricklayer. Hunter had met a few in his time—one injury away from poverty. His Uncle Ben's charity had a few on their books. "Take me to the Seven Eleven." The man pointed about fifty metres down the street. "I need to get something."

"Sure." Men like this delivered the profits for people like Nick Richardson … and for Hunter. With their bodies. Uncle Ben had made sure Hunter understood that. No one who'd worked their entire lives should have to accost a stranger for help. Hunter turned to Anna. "Is that okay?"

"Sure." She had a twinkle in her eye.

"Flip the brakes off," Hunter said. The old man obliged, and Hunter started the slow journey to the shop. "Brickie?"

"Thirty-five years. How'd you guess?" The guy grunted.

"I've met a few." Entering the shop required careful navigation, but once indoors, Hunter stopped. "What do you want?"

"A cappuccino." The man gestured at the automatic coffee maker on the side wall. "Small."

Hunter was last in a queue of five. Ten minutes later, he set up the cup and pressed buttons. "Sugar?"

The man held up gnarled fingers. "Four."

"Do you want a lid?"

"Yes." The man dug in his wallet and extracted a dollar. "Mind you give that to the boy behind the counter."

Anna choked on a laugh. Hunter guessed an old-timer might consider a man in a Brooks Brothers suit could only be a shyster. He offered the man the Styrofoam cup.

"No. You carry it 'til we get back."

Hunter pushed the old wheelchair back to its original position, Anna ambling silently at his side, as if the loss of twenty minutes made no difference to her day. Hunter had just blown his chances of showing her his drawings today. "Don't forget the brakes," he said.

The man flipped the wheel brakes into place.

"All set, mate?" Hunter placed the coffee on the stone fence within easy reach and added a business card. "This might come in handy."

The guy scanned it, then tucked it in his pyjama jacket pocket. "Thanks."

"Have you still got time for lunch?" Anna asked when they were out of the man's hearing. "Or would you like me to pick up a sandwich for you and deliver it to your next meeting?"

"I blew that date." He checked the time. "Should have waited until I had more time."

"Your definition of a date needs work." She studied him, and he couldn't read the expression in her eyes. "If you were so tight on time, why didn't you wait?"

"I thought you'd like to see the drawings." And he'd like to see her face when she first saw them.

"What was on the card?" She was a noticing kind of woman, but not in a bad way. Hunter had expected her to be pissed off or impatient or indifferent to a battered old man demanding attention. Instead, she seemed more relaxed. "And don't embarrass us both by saying 'what card?'"

"The name of a charity that supports injured building workers and their families."

"No time for lunch, yet you should eat." She beamed. Cross-examination temporarily over. "That's a monumental dilemma for a man who needed help deciphering the instructions on an automatic coffee machine."

"I've never used one before." He shrugged. "What can I say? I'm a coffee snob."

"You're a sweetie." She patted his lapel. "Does roast beef and salad work?"

"Go easy on the salad." He rather liked the idea of being her "sweetie."

"I insist on tomato and lettuce at the very least."

"I can live with that." He could live with having someone concerned about his well-being. *And that's a weakness you can't afford.* The only people who genuinely cared about whether he lived or died were his aunt and uncle, his maternal grandparents, Casildo's family, some workmates and a few school friends. "I'm sorry about this. I wanted to show you those drawings."

"Don't be sorry. I learned a lot. I'll walk you to your meeting, so I know where you are, collect a sandwich, and drop it off. I can also drop by your office later today?" She let the question hang.

Hunter hadn't invited her to his office. His office downstairs from his large comfortable bed. It wasn't that he didn't trust himself.

I don't.

"You're about to start the rehab. I'd like to see those drawings before you get underway." *Was she wheedling?* Her expression was neutral, her outfit business-like, but this was the first time she'd initiated a meeting.

"There's time. We're just clearing and cleaning at the moment. Checking the plumbing and the wiring. The original setup is good." Why was he putting her off when he'd been panting to show her his drawings earlier?

"And you've decided to ask Maha to take on management."

"What do you know about that?" The Hariri family kept his secrets almost better than he did himself, yet Maha had let Anna in on a few.

"She said you sounded her out. I liked her. Liked her partner. Liked their mission statement, liked what I saw of her interaction with the kids and her staff. She wants to expand. She's ready to expand." Anna worked some special magic everywhere she went. What had she said? *"You talked to me."* Anna was the one who talked to people and listened to their answers—spoken and unspoken.

"Yeah." He brushed his lips across hers. Her eyes widened in surprise. *Good.* "That's for the sandwich."

"So, can I come and see the drawings after work?" She meant architectural drawings. Anna Turner wasn't the type to use 'can I see your etchings' as a shield.

"I'll be finished by six. You've got the address? I'm out in the sticks."

"Not that far, and—"

"You've got transport. I know."

* * *

Anna had practically begged to meet him at his office. He'd pushed for a quick lunch, *then what?* For some reason, he didn't let people get to know him. Too late. That little interlude with a sick old man, who'd looked more hobo than patient, had reinforced her assessment at the beach: strong, flexible and durable. The durable quality was the lure for her. She knew her weaknesses, and if a man was only interested in her body, she walked away. She hadn't found enduring in a relationship yet, but it had to be possible.

Does Hunter regret sharing his secrets with me?

He certainly regretted introducing her to Maha Hariri. But his relationship with the capable childcare director played to the same weakness. Sam-I-Am was loyal and won loyalty in return.

Anna arrived at six. Actually, she arrived at five-forty, time to wander around the park opposite and admire it and the view of Hunter's unusual office from across the street. A converted service station was a creative use of space with plenty of parking for the work crews who passed through.

She was in time to see six employees depart, including a casually dressed woman with a munchkin who might be eleven or twelve. The kid yelled "Night, Hunt" as they exited. The woman tousled his hair, then chased him to their car. The other departees included two suits, a man and woman in paint-spattered overalls, accompanied by a girl in a school uniform. Work experience student or family? Hunter employed a mixed bunch, but she didn't spot anyone who looked like they needed a childcare centre. If she'd come a bit later, she wouldn't have known.

"I think I can hear the church bells tolling six." He smiled.

"Is this a test? Were you standing there watching the clock?"

"Looking forward to your visit." He stood back to let her in.

"Smooth, Hunter. Actually, I arrived earlier. Got to see the stragglers depart. Who's the kid?"

"My secretary Donna's son, Gareth, after his father. Refuses to answer to Gary."

"Donna's your secretary?" she asked. Donna looked

wholesome enough to be the chair of the parents and citizens.

"Problem?" He raised an eyebrow. "Why don't you come in?"

Anna turned her head as she passed him. "Been with you long?"

"What's with the questions, Anna?" He sounded wary.

"Just trying to get my bearings."

"This way." He gestured to a corner office. "I've got the contract and the drawings ready for you."

"Not those sorts of bearings." On impulse, she leaned forward and kissed him. A quick brush of the lips, except his mouth opened in surprise. He'd recently had coffee, sharp, dark. "Am I with the very private—I won't say Duck—or Sam-I-am?"

"You said Duck." He swung her around and kicked the front door closed. Her back was against the wall, and she'd never felt safer in her life.

"I don't want you to pretend when you're with me." Anna rested a hand on his chest, his heart racing beneath her fingers.

"You don't know who I am," he said harshly.

"I know bits. I want to know more."

"Donna's been with me a decade. She's my right hand."

"Married?"

"What the f'"—he dragged a hand through his hair—"widowed."

"Makes sense."

"Not much around you makes sense." Exasperation looked good on him.

"You're stingy with personal information. Makes it hard to have any kind of relationship."

"Maybe I don't want a relationship." He scowled.

She hooked an ankle around his calf to draw him closer. "You want a hot, sweaty fuck that short circuits any functioning brain cells, then you want me to leave so you can get some sleep. You might run to flowers the next day."

"Sounds like a good starting point. Although hand-made Belgian chocolates might work better for you."

"Not going to happen. But you've already worked that out." Anna patted his chest and unlinked her ankle, although the stirring of his cock against her was a nice boost to her ego. "You give, I give."

"Give what?"

"A piece of yourself."

"To repeat someone in this room—not going to happen."

"Some of it happens without you. Casildo is your friend. I've known him professionally for years. He's an angel."

Hunter grunted.

"Maha is another friend of yours. I saw what she's built, is building. She said you helped her, and no one was twisting her arm. You were ordinarily kind to a hospital patient today. No grandstanding for your audience of one—me."

"I'm a saint. Maybe you should write the business blogs." He cocked an eyebrow, all bashful embarrassment. "I forgot. They wouldn't accept copy from you, because you're a creative thinker, not a realist."

"Ask my family. I'm the pragmatist and the solution seeker. There's another thing." She sauntered toward the middle of the room, glancing over her shoulder to see where his gaze settled. "For a man only interested in sex, you spend no time ogling my bits."

His gaze dropped from the ceiling to her.

"My tits, my bum, my legs. You actually look at my face when you're talking to me. It's a dead giveaway that you're decent."

"I can look at your tits and bum."

"Don't forget my legs." Anna grinned. "It's too late to start now. I'll know you're putting on an act."

"Are we discussing the contract or my seduction style?"

"I can multi-task."

"I've got water, or we do fresh juice. Today we've got orange." In response to her raised eyebrow, he added,

"Water's in the cooler. The juice we make on-site. Buy the fruit at the local market. Saves food miles."

"Water thanks. Where do you want me?" She giggled. "That came out wrong. You said something about an office." She scanned the large open space.

"Yeah, I have an office, although we're mostly open plan. We have meeting rooms if anyone needs silence. This afternoon, I want the flat, clean space of a large table." He collected glasses of water and led her into a small meeting room. As light and airy as the central area, temperature-controlled via a mix of natural and artificial methods. The bank of solar cells she'd spotted on the roof and the batteries testified to off-grid. "Have you got your copy of the contract?"

"Right here." She patted her bag.

She'd done her research. Background checks on Maha Hariri, even though she'd liked the woman on sight. Probity and child protection checks, any complaints. The place price compared favourably with other centres she'd checked. A little on the high side, but the quality and the ability to participate in decision-making balanced that out. She had facts, figures, scenarios before she'd talked it through with Antonio.

"What's the decision?"

"Antonio's authorised me to sign the contract. I'd like a preliminary Board of Management to be established immediately. Obviously, we can't get parent reps yet, but I want to know what's happening at each step of the way. To be able to drop in and see developments."

"It's not your money," he said.

"Not my kids either."

"You're treating it as seriously as if it is."

"So are you," she countered.

"My work has my name on it."

"Duh! So, does mine." Anna glanced through the glass windows of the meeting room to the well-designed space beyond. "This looks like it was custom-designed as your headquarters."

    "I'm expanding. That's why you're here."

    "Do you live upstairs?"

CHAPTER FIVE

"Want to see?" Where the hell had that invitation come from? She befuddled him. And Hunter was growing to like the sensation.

"Perhaps we should finish our business first." The childcare centre was her priority.

"Fine. Preliminary Board of Management. Regular visits to check progress."

"So, what's in the other drawing cylinder?"

"Some ideas about colours and textures I thought you'd like to see." Anxiety trickled down Hunter's spine, a line of cold doubt because he wanted her to like his ideas. He didn't need her praise to know he did good work, so what was with the jitterbugging butterflies?

She treated the samples with care, going through them carefully. Ridiculous to be holding his breath.

"They're fabulous. I like the lot." She gave him one of her sunshine and laughter smiles.

"Thanks." But something inside him settled.

"You can show me upstairs now."

What the hell did that mean? I want to see where you live? I want to jump your bones?

Yes, please, but unlikely.

Anna defied predictable.

Hunter's heart was thumping. Not a noise he was familiar with. His hands were clammy. Hell, this was ridiculous. Unlocking the disguised door in the rear side wall of the building, he gestured her to precede him.

She strolled toward him. She used all those *S* words she loved when she walked—stroll, saunter, sashay—and a few others—amble, meander, occasionally she hurtled. "What's that?" She pointed to the facing door.

"There's a separate entrance from outside."

"So, you could sneak me up here without the staff noticing?"

Her grin relaxed him. "I doubt it. People look at you, Anna. You draw eyes."

"Not sure I like that."

"I've been trying to work it out. It's a vibe, a positive energy, as seductive as sunlight after a long, cold winter."

"That's a lovely thing to say."

Hunter gave her a complete tour. He'd only just moved in when his mother died. His ex-girlfriend, Gina, was the only woman to have spent a night here. His PA Donna and his aunt Ellie had taken charge of the soft furnishings and stocked the kitchen, so he had two large sofas and a few comfortable armchairs in similar colours but not identical patterns. The cupboards had enough plates, glasses, and pots and pans for a standard cook. He was standard—thanks to his aunt. A casserole, a grill, a bake, a few pasta dishes, one at least vegetarian, and a few salads. Dessert, he always got in, if he had warning.

"This is nice." She stepped into the main bedroom and crossed to the big wrap-around window he'd installed. "The angle's great. You're not directly facing the street, but you still get an edge of the park. I didn't notice this tree down the side from the front."

"I cheated on it. There was nothing growing on the

property—too contaminated. The old petrol station had been here for decades. I only got to see the full impact of the windows at the front of the building when the huge old canopy for the bowsers was removed. Anyway, we replaced dirt, and then I lashed out and bought a mature eucalyptus so it filled half the window."

"Who's we?"

"I know a landscaper."

"And he helped you fix up your place?" She sat on the window ledge facing him.

"Problem with that?"

"You always assume there's a problem when I ask a question." She tilted her head to one side. "I'm asking questions about you because I'm interested in you. But it's like digging for gold in a clapped-out gold mine."

"You think I'm gold." Hunter's mouth stuck on a smile. "He helped me, and I gave him some design tips on his place."

"This place suits you. And don't withdraw into your shell like a turtle intent on protecting itself."

"A gold turtle? Duck, turtle, you sure pick weird analogies. Would you like a drink?"

"What have you got?"

"Coffee, tea, mineral water, wine, whiskey, beer." He gave her the drink menu, although he'd never seen her drink alcohol.

"A glass of white wine, please."

"New Zealand Sauvignon Blanc suit?" Hunter swallowed his surprise, leading her back to the living area.

"Great." She sat in the middle of one sofa.

"I've got potato crisps." For watching games with Cas.

"How'd you guess I'm an addict?" She grinned. "Notice how I'm modelling sharing information."

"What! We've got potato chips and Sav Blanc in common."

"It's a start. Thank you." She accepted the glass of wine and toasted him with it. "Do you have something planned for tonight?"

"What did you have in mind?" His pulse raced. *Was she planning to stay?*

Forgive me, Cas, for what I'm about to do.

"An early snack and some chat. My brother-in-law tells me there's a must-see game on TV tonight. He's got half a dozen friends joining him at his place. I'm keeping my sister company."

"Sprung. Cas is coming by later."

"I said early and some chat."

"What's your definition of chat?"

"Not what you're thinking." She took another sip of her drink, her gaze meeting his over the glass.

She was an honest temptress. If they bedded each other, it would be because she liked him and wanted to be intimate with him. And—inspiration struck—it wouldn't be rushed. *Thank the heavenly angels.*

"Take it or leave it."

"Sheesh. You drive a hard bargain. What are we eating?"

"I chose the venue, you choose the cuisine."

"And you've organised transport home."

"I love a man who pays attention to what I say." She'd come into his territory, was sharing a wine, opening a door he'd nailed shut after Gina.

"Pizza?" He inclined his head.

"I like artichokes and chilli."

"That works with pepperoni." He pulled out his phone and pressed a button.

"You've got pizza on speed dial?"

"Doesn't everyone?" Hunter hunched a shoulder. "Should be here in fifteen to twenty. Their son earns his pocket money with local deliveries. And in the interests of sharing information—they vet who he delivers to."

"I like this pizza already."

"Let's eat in the dining area."

"I also like the way your living area goes from front to back. Lounge at the front and dining at the back, leading onto a deck." She followed him from the front to the back of the space. "Nice flow."

He snorted.

"I've been reading the notes with your architectural drawings," she confessed, "I've learned a lot."

"So, you've already noticed I can shut off each room." He gestured to the folding glass doors between the two rooms for temperature control."

"Not yet, but I would have." She grinned. "Are you responsible for the mature trees across the back of the property?"

"Most of them are in the neighbours' backyards. They wanted screening from this place when it was a service station. Now, we all get the benefit of privacy. Although I, or rather, my landscaping friend, is responsible for the deck plants and discreet external lighting." Hunter wandered through to the kitchen, returning with plates, cutlery and some table mats.

"You like light, and you like nature." She'd been staring through the glass doors onto the deck—closed tonight to keep out the chill—but she turned when he reappeared.

"Don't you?"

One night over a TV basketball game, after Cas and he had downed enough pizza and beer to fell a bull, Hunter had confessed he loved this place. Liked what he'd created, liked what he'd established, especially liked his office being nestled in the middle of a suburban backwater with windows that opened, kids screaming in the background as they dangled from climbing bars, and local shop owners who knew his name.

Now he discovered he liked the way Anna looked in his home.

* * *

"A question," Anna said, smiling into her drink. "I'm impressed. I like nature and light in this form." She turned a circle to encompass the apartment. "I'm a city kid. Born and bred in Melbourne. Followed my sister to Sydney for university at eighteen." Right after the disaster with Helen and the party. When she was young and stupid and thought Helen was recovering.

Not tonight, Anna.

"I've had more exposure to the country in the last few years. My brother-in-law and his twin started their lives on a farm up in the northern rivers area."

"Started? Did they move because of the big floods and bushfires in the last few years?" His phone beeped. "Hold that thought. Roberto's downstairs with the pizza."

Anna heard muffled voices from the stairwell, the sound of a door being closed, then Hunter reappeared with a large box. He set it on a table mat in the centre of the table and arranged two places beside each other, looking onto the deck.

"Please, sit down."

Anna sat and continued her story. "The farm belonged to their mother's family. Ultimately, her siblings wanted it sold so they could get their inheritance. Niall and Liam moved to Newcastle with their parents."

"And now they live in Sydney?" He transferred a slice of pizza to her plate.

"Yum. I love melted cheese." Holding the slice high above her plate, she nibbled the bottom tip, then saw him watching her. Her pulse picked up. "What?"

"For a moment, I had the weirdest fantasy. I was a slice of pizza, and you were nibbling at my edges." The heat in his gaze held her spellbound. "It's okay. Gone now. Keep eating."

My giddy aunt—the images he created. She couldn't stop thinking about kissing him, nibbling around his edges, swallowing him whole. Rattled, she lowered the remainder of the pizza slice to the plate. "I'm not sure I can."

"Good. Now you know how I feel." He picked up his slice. "Keep talking then."

"Liam and Kate are in Newtown." She cut her slice into mouth-size bites. "Niall's currently in an old warehouse in Concord."

"What do they do?"

"Liam's in environmental law. Kate's a researcher and a romance novelist. Niall's the resident artist—a woodworker extraordinaire."

"How'd you meet?" He smiled at her over his wine glass.

"Don't think I don't know what you're doing."

"What am I doing?"

Innocence be damned.

"I'm not fooled by the bashful smile after the sexy-mow-me-down smoulder." Anna popped a mouthful of pizza into her mouth, chewed it until it was dead, then swallowed. "You're asking me heaps of questions."

"I thought you wanted conversation and some food."

"If you want a good night kiss, you have to share."

"I'm an only child. No cousins. I met Casildo at school. We've been friends and blood brothers since we were eight, when we came off our bikes at the bottom of a hill. We were bloody. Cas said that was a good moment. He's squeamish, wouldn't subject himself to a random cut, even to become blood brothers." He toasted her with a piece of pizza, and she smiled at the sweetness of the memory he shared.

"I moved out of home before I turned sixteen, couch-surfed between my uncle's place and Casildo's. Rented a room in a boarding house at eighteen."

Sharing a not-sweet memory was a truer sign he wanted something more from her than a hard, fast fuck. Anna simply liked him. Liked his home, his smell, his caution in sharing pieces of himself, the way he made her feel special by telling her that he and Casildo became blood brothers after a bike accident.

"Damn," Hunter muttered when his phone launched into the theme music from *Thor*, shattering the intimacy of the moment. "The blood brother's early."

"I'll stay to say hello." She leaned forward and pressed

her lips to his, the trace of chilli on his providing an extra lick of heat. "Then you can see me out."

"Bet on it."

He disappeared down the stairs again. More muffled voices, but this time Casildo appeared in the doorway first.

"Hi, Anna." Casildo stepped forward with a smile. "How are you?"

"On my way out." Anna smiled in return. "I have to be somewhere."

"Don't leave on my account."

"I really have to be somewhere." She glanced at Hunter hovering at Casildo's shoulder. "I'll just call a ride share."

"Sure," Hunter said easily. "I'll wait with you downstairs."

"Don't mind me." Casildo picked up the last slice of pizza and stared at the ceiling. "Pretend I'm not here."

"You were supposed to bring beer and pizza." Hunter frowned at him.

"I'll call in a while." Casildo waved the remaining slice of pizza in their direction, before sauntering back toward the lounge area and the remote.

"You don't need to wait with me," Anna said. "The car won't take long."

"Let's see what we can achieve in a short time." He preceded her down the stairs, stopping when he hit the bottom step and turning toward her. "Did I do enough to win a kiss?"

"You know what?" Her face was level with his. "I like you."

"Against your better judgement?"

Anna moved closer, placed her hand on his cheek and touched her forehead to his. "I like you. No conditions. Deal with it."

"I want to kiss you."

"That's a modest goal."

He laughed. "Okay. I want you in my bed until we're both exhausted by the loving."

"Loving? Good choice of verb. Sam-I-am might get his wish." She leaned back, keeping her hand on his cheek.

His mouth widened into a smile—warm, open—holding nothing back. Private and intimate. He cupped her cheeks with his hands, the calloused fingertips unexpectedly tender against her skin. His scent, muted at this end of the day, held the earthiness of sage with a hint of smokiness, its mysteriousness a match for the man. Endless seconds before his lips touched hers, the anticipation killing, the reality a coming home.

That shouldn't be possible.

That was her last coherent thought before he gathered her in, one kiss easing into another. Hearing a moan, she realised it was hers because he'd drawn back infinitesimally. But she wasn't done yet, so she wrapped her hand around his neck. "More."

He kissed with a focus that wiped her mind clear, kissed as if there was nowhere he'd rather be, nothing he'd rather do. She'd thought—hoped—assumed her uncharacteristic gooey befuddlement after his kisses at the beach had been the result of a balmy evening, a shared ice cream, and her excitement in taking him out of his comfort zone. He'd been unfazed, in command even as she'd melted into a puddle at his feet.

"I want to kiss every square inch of your body," he said, slipping the top button of her shirt.

"That might be my ride." Reluctantly, she pushed back in his arms, resenting the arrival of her lift.

"How does anyone resist you?" he murmured, confusion in his gaze.

"Most people don't get the chance to even think about it." She patted his chest, her heart galloping.

"I've been invited to a party on Saturday night. Come with me?"

"You were saving this up for the penultimate moment?" Anna glanced over his shoulder, recognising the plate number on the car approaching them. She tilted her head to the side, unsure of her next step. "Did I pass some kind of test?"

"I wasn't planning on going," he admitted.

"And now you are?" She started along the path to the ride share.

"If you'll go with me?"

"What's the party?" She'd thought she'd caught glimpses of the man behind the mask tonight. The sudden invitation to a party he hadn't planned to attend reawakened all her cautious instincts.

"Posh. Eastern suburbs. Marygai Renouf, a friend of my mother's."

"Will your mother be there?" Meeting his mother would be a … step into new territory.

"My mother died a few years ago."

"I'm sorry."

"So am I." He leaned forward to double-check the ride was hers, and his concern for her safety cemented her decision.

"Yes," she said. His mother's friend lived at a posh location, and he'd been couch-surfing at sixteen. Was he dropping another veil or adding a new one?

"I'll pick you up." His expression didn't change.

"I'll meet you there." Anna slid into the car. "Text me the address."

He leaned forward to brush his lips across hers. "I'll call."

* * *

"What are you doing?" Casildo demanded when Hunter returned upstairs.

"Negotiating a long-term lease for part of a floor in The Hariri building." Hunter essayed an innocent grin. He didn't know what the hell he was doing, just that every time he left Anna Turner, he started counting the minutes until he could see her again.

"Bull dust, my friend."

"Any objective observer can read Bizgos and see I've bought a new building and am leasing floors."

"Did you feed that blogger, who I'm convinced is Nick's gossip pigeon, the line that you've overstretched resources and might have been summoned to see your bank?"

"Not directly." Hunter looked down his nose at his friend. "I finessed him through a third party."

"As a cover for your seduction of Anna." Cas stood hipshot.

"Am I trespassing?" The flash of knowledge he'd fight for her unsettled Hunter. *Fight for what?* A few kisses, time with her?

"Al'ama." Casildo threw his hands in the air. "No, you're not trespassing. I've seen her at work functions for years. If I'd been interested, I'd have made a move before now."

Cas was as cautious about women as Hunter.

"I like her but know nothing about her other than what she chooses to share."

"So, she's a private person." Hunter breathed out the tension that had hit like a sucker punch.

"She's capable, loyal and the dress was—"

"Battle armour," Hunter said, and headed for the fridge. "Designed for some lust-addled idiot so she could point out she was a person, not a body."

"You were lust-addled." Casildo took the beer he was offered.

"Ah! But, fortunately, I didn't behave as if her body was all she had to offer. She asked about architecture and saved me from myself." Hunter snagged another beer. "Cheers. Are we watching the game, or spending the night gasbagging?"

"The game." Casildo topped his beer. "Can you trust Gina?"

"What's my ex-girlfriend got to do with anything?" But he understood where Casildo was heading. "I haven't seen Gina for nearly two years." Not since she'd stolen and crashed his car, then uploaded photos to Insta with the caption *Guess what happened to me?*

"Can you trust her not to resurrect the lies about her car crash that she splashed all over her socials if she hears you're interested in someone else?" Casildo's hand hung loosely at his side, the bottle swinging gently backward and forward. "Can you trust her not to accept Nick's money to stir up trouble for you again?"

"Gina called me. Said she'd never intended people to assume the injuries were the result of a beating." Hunter repeated Gina's unconvincing excuses offered forty-eight hours after the accident. By then he'd weathered the police knocking on his door to tell him Gina was on her way to the hospital, and asking him to accompany them to the local cop shop.

"Her feed didn't mention she'd crashed your car either."

"She removed the photos when the commentary got stuck on a loop around when she was going to charge her shit of a boyfriend with assault."

"She started it." Casildo had been furious about the dubious posts. Seemed he still carried the anger. "And my tech mate insists Nick fed the trolling."

"Gina apologised. She was pissed off at me for ending things. Never expected it to get out of hand." But Hunter knew the records were being tumbled by the vast algorithms in the internet of things waiting to be found.

"Gina never corrected the record."

Hunter put his hand on Casildo's shoulder. "The hospital took the shots with a police officer present. There's an official record of interview explaining she was upset because we had a fight and stole my car while I was calling a taxi. Her injuries are consistent with the seatbelt bruising her and bumping her face on the steering wheel. I have a certified copy."

"You never told me whether Nick screwing Gina was the reason for your breakup?"

"Gina said it was just the once." Once was enough to

make Hunter sick to his stomach. "And Nick told her the money was a 'gift.'" She'd been too distracted at the time to be disgusted, but the insult was targeted at Hunter.

And Hunter had absorbed the humiliation.

"Yet you nurse a guilty conscience when you did nothing wrong." His friend stomped into the other room. "Gina's accident was not a mirror image of your mother's."

"They tested Gina and me for alcohol. Both clear. That's also in the report." Hunter's mother had died while driving drunk. After another fight with Nick. Hunter's fight with Gina had been about Nick. "Look, I haven't thought of Gina in months."

"Be careful."

"Are you saying I'm a womaniser, like Nick?" The idea hurt.

"Don't make me laugh. You've never dabbled in the dark arts of seduction, and we both know why. But Gina and Nick did a number on you, so now you're limiting yourself to occasional consensual liaisons."

"Liaison exaggerates their importance." And Hunter's cynicism showed how unsuited he was for a relationship with any woman.

"There's that cynicism creeping in. Gina's the reason for your largely monastic lifestyle. Anna doesn't do liaisons, for want of a better word."

"Sheesh, Cas. Leave it alone." Hunter flopped onto a sofa.

"I'll call through another pizza order." His friend jutted his chin in the direction of the table, where he'd finished what Hunter and Anna had abandoned. "What's with the artichokes?"

"Anna's choice." Hunter knew the risks he was taking becoming involved with any woman, knew the war chest of grievances and accusations Nick was hoarding. *Stuff it.* Anna made him feel alive for the first time in a long time. And they hadn't moved far from flirtation.

"If you get serious about Anna, you'll have to tell her

about Gina, because someone else will be only too happy to dish the dirt." Cas remained standing. "She's got zero tolerance for men who mistreat women."

"We're not serious." They weren't about to have a one-night stand either, and Hunter could admit in the dark reaches of his soul that if he were ever to consider becoming serious with a woman—a remote hypothetical—Anna was the one.

"You don't have to tell your life story to everyone you meet." Casildo wasn't letting this go. "But sometimes you need to explain yourself to the people who care about you, share what's in your heart."

"I haven't got a heart."

Casildo took a swig from his bottle as answer.

"Before we abandon the conversation about the childcare centre, how do you think your dad would react if I said I wanted Maha to manage it?"

Casildo's shoulders slumped, and he dropped onto the second sofa. "Another good deed?"

"Maha's always planned to open her own centre when the time was right."

He kept his voice neutral, because while he'd had the credit record with the bank to get the loan to buy The Hariri building, Cas had handed over every cent he had to his father first, money Cas had been saving for years to start his own business.

Hunter continued. "Maha and her friend set up the first centre together because neither could afford to do it alone. You know they planned a second, when they had more experience and resources behind them, so they could each manage one."

Hunter liked matching the right people to the right project. A skill he'd discovered in himself that he hadn't observed in anyone else in his family. Claiming it for himself gave him enormous satisfaction, enough he was realigning his business interests to operate more as broker—assembling a team with disparate skills, then placing them in made-to-measure projects. Maha was right on so many levels for this project—not least because she'd see it as standing up for her family in a time of need.

"You think they're ready?" Cas asked.

"Maha thinks she's ready. She's not so sure little brother and Daddy have noticed she's all grown up, running a successful and expanding business and ready for new challenges." Hunter put his feet on the coffee table. "You dope. She's the one who hung on your father's every word about business at the kitchen table. You're the dreamer."

"Has she asked you?"

"I was the one raising hypotheticals, but she spent a lot of time with Anna showing her around her place and essentially auditioning for the role."

"I'll talk to Dad. Get him to suggest it to you." Casildo wore a proud grin.

"Now can we watch the game?"

Casildo's answer came in the form of punching buttons on his phone, followed by "Pizza in thirty. I don't rank as highly as you."

CHAPTER SIX

Anna's ride share delivered her to her sister's home twenty minutes later, and Anna had spent most of that time with a goofy smile on her face. Hunter's kisses could melt ice sculptures, and despite some gossip to the contrary, she wasn't made of ice.

"The boys are already here," Kate explained, although the male laughter coming from the living room made her comment redundant. "I'll show you what we've done in the nursery first," she said, "and don't you dare say I waddle."

"Wouldn't dream of it." Anna hid her smile because her sister definitely waddled.

"What do you think?" Her sister remained leaning against the doorjamb, while Anna wandered the room.

"The buttery yellow feature wall is gorgeous," Anna said. "Perfect for my niece."

"I finished it today. You're as bad as Niall, only he's expecting a nephew. He's bringing his cradle by tomorrow."

"Oooh, I can't wait to see the finished product." Anna clapped her hands.

"Okay. We're in the sunroom tonight. And I am so ready to roost." Kate led the way toward the back of the house. "I'll apologize in advance. I'm not very hungry, and I'll probably be comatose in an hour."

"Suits me. I spoiled my appetite by sharing a pizza with Hunter."

"When am I going to meet him?"

"Mm. Not sure." Anna's heart skipped a beat. Introducing a man to Kate was another one of Anna's tests.

"You like him?"

"More than I expected to. I was distracted by the buzz between us." A chemical cocktail of pheromones that disarmed her defences. "The buzz complicates what else we might have."

"A buzz is good."

"Says the professional romance writer. He was following the buzz and tripped over himself." The care he'd taken with their kiss in the darkened hallway had seeped into her soul. He claimed he wanted a one-nighter, but his actions betrayed him.

"You make a kind of sense. He only wanted the buzz, but you're making him wait."

"At this stage, I think we're making each other wait." The anticipation was a backbeat to every encounter. Anna was aware of him now, picturing him on one sofa, Casildo on the other, a pizza between them.

"Ah." Kate sank into an armchair and lifted her feet to a footstool.

"Maybelline, you're looking like a matron." The southern belle nickname was more suited to the svelte, unpregnant Kate, but Anna teased her anyway.

Kate's eyes narrowed. "I'll remind you of that when your time comes. Now fetch." She pointed dramatically at the door. "There's a platter of goodies on the top shelf in the fridge and a jug of non-alcoholic mint Mojitos."

Anna did as instructed. And fetched.

"A drink first?" She held the jug with its aromatic sprigs of mint aloft.

"Please," her sister replied. "I've been waiting all day for this one bit of decadence."

"You are so ready to have this baby." Anna dragged a side table to her sister's armchair and placed the drink within easy reach.

"That's my line. I am soooo ready to have this baby. I've got a few weeks yet. At this rate, if she's a girl, she'll be a quarterback." Kate took a slow sip of her drink. "Yum."

"I'll hold up items of food, and you nod if I make the right selection."

"Deal."

"Half a hard-boiled egg." Anna placed it on the plate, then added some cherry tomatoes, some avocado segments, and a thin slice of multi-grain bread sliced in quarters.

"That's enough for now."

"I'm guessing the mixed berries and yoghurt I saw are our dessert." Anna's hand hovered over the platter before choosing the rest of the avocado and some bread.

"Real men only eat yoghurt with curry."

"Didn't Dad use that in his last play?" Anna sipped her own Mojito.

"To mixed audience reaction." Kate giggled. "He asked me if he was losing his touch?"

"He *did* not!" When her sister nodded, Anna started to giggle, then laugh until she brushed tears from her eyes. "When did Mr. Romance Is Crap start seeking your opinion on his writing?"

"When my last book made the *New York Times* Bestsellers list."

"And you kept his grovel a secret until now?

"You've been busy, I've been busy." Kate waved a hand in the air. "To be honest, I forgot until now."

"I love Liam."

"He's already taken."

"I love him because until you met him, you never fully believed in yourself as a writer. You never stopped writing, but you're freer now, bolder." Anna wanted that for herself.

Her sister's smile was that of a woman deeply, happily in love. "Tell me more about Hunter."

"H. S. Thompson. So much about him doesn't make sense. For a start, he lives above his current headquarters. He's designed the place to suit his every need, but the story is he needs a new headquarters, only now he's devoting a floor to a childcare centre."

"Does he have a plausible explanation?"

"He's expanding. But he was doing that before this latest purchase and kept his HQ in the same place."

"Are you sure you're not overthinking this?" Kate paused long enough to select a ripe tomato. "He's bought a medium rise in a prime location. If his business is growing, it makes sense to join the monied class closer to the heart of the city."

"There's something wrong." Anna frowned. "I haven't worked it out yet."

"Will you ever be able to take a man at face value?" Kate asked gently.

"Maybelline, can you hear the rubbish coming out of your mouth?" Anna jumped to her feet and circled the room before her pacing brought her to a halt in front of her sister. "Caution is our middle name."

"My next female lead will be called Prudence, and she'll be anything but." Kate bit into her tomato, her teeth snapping shut on the hapless fruit.

"Sarcasm doesn't suit you." Anna plopped back into the opposite armchair, letting out a long sigh. "I fancied him on sight. Then I discovered he was the enemy and wanted to despise him. Except, everything I've learned about him makes me like him. He doesn't have a fake lifestyle. He doesn't have fake friends …"

"I trust your judgement."

"You have to. You love me. But I need these little signposts. Dad is so plausible. He was plausible even at his philandering worst."

"So, what happens next?" Kate eyed her plate before selecting a toast triangle and smearing it with avocado.

"I've accepted an invitation to a party on Saturday night

at Rose Bay. An old friend of his mother's."

"And?"

"It's our first real date, and he sounded weird about it." Weird in that he'd implied he'd only attend if Anna went with him. Not a date then. An ambush for one of them?

"Wasn't tonight a date?"

"I made it a date. We had a business meeting, and I asked him to show me his place."

Her sister stayed silent.

"Okay, then I suggested we have something to eat and a drink."

"I imagine there was no—" Kate circled a hand in the air.

"I kissed him goodbye." Anna crossed her arms, then uncrossed them. "Okay, he kissed me goodbye too. It was only then he asked me to go to this party."

"Rose Bay's the top end of town. Maybe he wants to show you off."

"I'm not a trophy." *But he has a reputation as a womaniser as well as a corporate raider, yet he doesn't act like either.*

"Scars of your misspent youth? He's not Dad; he's not about to state in an interview that his current mistress is the muse for his latest play. Do they even have muses for childcare centres?"

"Hunter's nothing like Dad, but he's reputed to be at loggerheads with his father, although I think Hunter would have told me if his father would be at the party." Anna tapped her mouth with her index finger. "His mother's friend means people in their fifties and sixties. Rose Bay equals serious money and tycoons—whatever their background—mix with celebrities these days. I hate parties littered with 'the cream of Sydney society.' And Rose Bay is a little too close to Point Piper for my taste."

"It's his mother's friend, not an all-male birthday party in a penthouse in Point Piper. More to the point, you're not newly arrived in Sydney and eighteen anymore." Kate knew Anna's demons. "Or do you think you might recognise someone?"

"I didn't pay much attention to faces; I was too busy avoiding roving hands." Anna shivered with revulsion. "Although I remember the birthday boy."

"You're overthinking again," Kate objected. "Your work involves social events. You attend theatrical events when Mum and Dad are in Sydney. The other party-goers aren't the issue. Showing you off can mean 'Hey, look at the lovely human being at my side.'"

"Right. And that's a line you're going to give your next hero." Anna stared at the ceiling for a few moments, then brought her chin down.

"Uh-oh. You've got that look in your eye."

"What look?" Anna opened her eyes wide and battered her lashes at her sister. "I'll wear a steampunk outfit to Hunter's party. Bea's sister has this gorgeous dress I've been dying to wear. The online promo called it bordello western."

"Is that as over the top as your red cocktail number?"

"Bea calls the red dress my *Killing Eve* dress. Bordello western might get a more dramatic reaction."

"Are you wearing it to test Hunter's reaction or as payback for a party more than a decade ago?" Kate's perceptive question made Anna squirm, but something felt off about the late invitation to a party Hunter hadn't intended to go to.

"Maybe a bit of both."

"I'd like to see photos, especially reaction shots," said Kate, who hated paparazzi, hated photos taken without the subject's knowledge, and frequently lifted a hand to cover her face when a camera turned her way. "Maybe you should wear a bodycam."

"You're serious, aren't you?"

"If I'm going to call my next book *The Exploits of Prudence*, I need settings. Riot at Rose Bay party sounds like the perfect exploit for my Prudence."

"We're not in a romance, Katie." Although the more time Anna spent with Hunter, the more time she wanted to spend. But she had binding rules for any relationship. "Hunter's got secrets."

"We've all got secrets. Why don't you tell him some of yours first?"

"There was a time I had no secrets," Anna whispered.

"Not true. There was a time when you gave up any right to privacy. When you acted as outrageously as you could. I was never sure if it was to deflect Dad's attention from my romance writing or to shout at them both 'Look at me, I'm living in this house too, in case you've forgotten.'"

"A bit of both."

"But you always had secrets."

Her sister was right, and Kate had been hurt by Anna's secrets.

"They weren't all mine to tell." Anna shivered remembering the night of Helen's sexual assault. She hadn't told Kate about the attack on Helen until Helen's suicide.

"They're yours to share." Kate pushed to her feet, her hand pressed to her pregnant belly. "At the right time. Not with me. If I'd been the right person, you'd have told me by now. Don't forget the bodycam."

"Having you made all the difference when Helen died." Anna's fury at the injustice of Helen's death had compounded her grief. That's when she'd made her vow never to ignore a woman's call for help.

"Then I got mixed up with Drew, and you blamed yourself for not seeing the signs he was a control freak. Men who manipulate or regard women as personal property don't walk around with warning signs flashing above their heads."

"They often have some behaviours in common." Anna defended her position.

"You tried to warn me to go slower. I—we—were smart enough to outwit Drew in the end. I'm happy, healthy, have a kind, smart, sexy husband, and am looking forward to what comes next in my life. You need to forgive yourself, not that there's anything to forgive.

"I could have been Helen. The scumbag who assaulted her might have tapped me on the shoulder. Drew might have gone after me." Anna half-wished she'd been the person targeted because she would have fought dirty.

"Your antennae for scumbags, if not stalkers, was well-developed before that."

"I hate feeling helpless. Convincing Antonio to sponsor a childcare centre, helping make it real, being able to see the relief in women's eyes when they know they have options makes up for those other failures."

"Hunter seems to understand that."

"What do you mean?" Anna asked, intrigued by Kate's response.

"He could have given you your lease, let you do the work. Instead, he's taking an active role and will offer his own staff and others the same opportunity. Whether you have anything to do with him after the centre is up and running—and he's smart enough to know you might walk away—he's building something to last."

"You're saying you like him."

"I like what I'm hearing about him."

"So do I." And, for Anna, the heartfelt "thanks" from a sick and battered old man on the street was a more reliable guide to Hunter's character than the business columns.

The bar was one of a string owned by an eastern suburbs socialite and entrepreneur. Anna had been in a few others, each unique, tastefully designed, the ambience welcoming. This Rose Bay celebrity hangout was a rendezvous and about a block from their final destination. Anna met Hunter outside, as arranged, the evening chill justifying her balloon coat. Hunter's gaze dipped briefly to her knee-high black leather boots, then lifted to her face.

"Did you park closer to the house?" Anna peered around him. She hadn't seen a car pull up.

"I don't drive."

"What's with offering to pick me up all the time?"

"Cabs and ride shares can pick up and drop off at more than one location."

"Thanks for explaining that." She tucked her arm through his. "Anything I need to know before we arrive? Fill me in on the main players."

"The hostess, Marygai Renouf, is wealthy, divorced, available, and claimed to be a friend of my mother."

"Do you have reason to think she wasn't a friend?"

"A story for another time—we're here." Stopping outside a gate in a two-metre-high wall sporting triple garages and security cameras, he pressed an intercom on the side. Static, then a request for a name. "Hunter," he said.

"I guess there aren't many guests called Hunter." Anna noted his saturnine expression, a stiffness in his posture, infinitesimal signs of withdrawal a woman not schooled in the dramatic arts might miss. A childhood spent around directors, producers and actors taught you to watch for non-verbal signals. "Just guessing, but this isn't your first visit."

"Marygai's lived here since I was a kid."

The gate popped open, and Hunter gestured her ahead of him.

"I feel like I'm about to enter Aladdin's Cave," she said, then stepped through the gate and into a golden-coloured courtyard. "Provencal, as in Provence, France. I'm a fan of hanging vines and pots full of colour. Does Marygai have a gardener?" Anna trailed her fingers across a lavender bush before holding them to her nose.

"Yeah."

"I'm going to have a gardener when I grow up."

"In the meantime, keep moving, Anna."

"I'm on my own here, aren't I?" She walked her fingers up his chest. His suit had been a surprise, far more formal than his outfit at the cocktail party when this was supposed to be a gathering of old friends. "No background briefing notes."

"I won't abandon you."

His bleak response didn't reassure her.

The floodlit courtyard narrowed to a path leading down the side of the house. A security guard stood discreetly to one side of the entrance while a dark-suited majordomo type ushered them inside. "Madam, might like to take off her coat?" He spoke with old-fashioned formality.

Madam couldn't wait.

Shedding her coat, Anna stifled a giggle at the muffled "hell" from the majordomo.

"The dress tells me you're upset. We can leave now." For the first time ever, Hunter focused on her body. His gaze travelled from her booted feet, over the ruched-up emerald skirt revealing her knees and the lower half of her thighs—sheathed in fishnet stockings—to the black bustier. He finished at her face. "I'm sorry."

Anna was studying him. "I might have misjudged you. *I'm sorry.*"

"Don't be. My fault. You're not under attack. I thought I might be."

She glanced at the majordomo, who was still grinning. "The style's steampunk. Derives from steampunk in science fiction. The fashion came later. Victorian romanticism mixed with the Industrial Revolution."

"I repeat, I'm sorry." Hunter held his hands up. "I don't think I've ever seen a dress like that before. It has to be said. You look incredible."

"But it's not really a fancy-dress party." She stood hipshot.

"I should have explained. You're not here for my ego. You're here for moral support." He leaned closer. "Your scent settles me."

"I change my perfume almost as often as I change my clothes." Something that had annoyed the hell out of Anna's last date.

"I know." He took a step closer, then rested his cheek against hers. "They all settle me."

He was sweet. A rock-hard shell covering a gooey melted

caramel inside. Hunter's acceptance of her quirks eased Anna's doubts. Whatever happened, he had her back tonight.

"Why are we someplace you'd rather not be, Hunter?" she whispered against his ear, not a conversation anyone else needed to hear.

"Exorcising a ghost."

"Hunter." A cloud of too much Dior preceded the woman. "You came."

Anna read relief and a hint of calculation in the woman's coy smile.

"Marygai, this is Anna." Hunter stepped behind her, sliding a warm hand down the back of her neck, before he rested firm palms on her bare shoulders.

A caress with enough intent for her knees to go weak, a warning to their hostess, who'd been puckered up and ready to pounce? Anna stepped hard on his foot, a protest for putting her in the line of fire.

"Hi"—she stretched out a hand, the charm bracelet Helen had worn at that long-ago party dangling from her wrist—"lovely house."

"Thank you." The older woman's welcoming smile faded.

Marygai's appraisal of her outfit made Anna wish she'd worn the bodycam. She'd struggle to describe her hostess's expression to her sister. Disgust played a part, so did envy with a soupçon—a French word seemed appropriate—of admiration. Marygai looked to be in her fifties, a hard-lived fifties. Too much sun and booze, not enough contentment.

"Welcome. Anna probably won't know anyone, but"— Marygai turned to Hunter—"a number of your mother's friends are here tonight. Your father's coming. Why don't you go through?"

Anna plastered a smile on her face and headed toward the noise. The place was *House and Garden* magazine magnificent. Graceful rooms opened into each other, and the building was angled for maximum sea views. A double living area opened onto a patio, a parallel kitchen dining living space opened to the same patio. Beyond that was a manicured lawn broken by a translucent blue, double-lap pool, and more lawn ending in a stone harbour wall.

Hunter was behind her, his steps matching hers, his scent settling her as he claimed hers did him. Safe, an unexpected sensation. Her favourite male fragrances were those worn by her brother-in-law and his twin. Knowing they were nearby was always a reassurance. Hunter offered more—a reassuring challenge.

Waiters, trained to react to the slightest gesture or nod, circled the room with trays of drinks.

"Sparkling water, please?" Anna said.

"A beer."

"I'll be right back, sir."

Was Hunter making his own statement with that request? The waiter had offered red and white wine and champagne—all French. As anticipated, Anna's dress was attracting a few second looks.

"You weren't expecting your father," she stated.

"His sperm gives him biological rights to the title. That's all."

"Ouch!" Anna came to a decision and turned to Hunter. "There's a lot of history in this room. We're going to have to split up."

He accepted the beer from the returning waiter before answering. "I might not agree with your reasoning."

"Ghosts won't approach you with me hanging around." She pressed a finger to his lips, the bracelet slipping down her arm. He nibbled, surprising her. "Plus, the dress won't be a proper experiment if you're standing at my shoulder looking like a dog guarding a bone."

"What if I don't want to talk to ghosts anymore?"

"You said it's why we came. You should have explained that to me. How long do you need?" she asked.

"An hour's as much as I can stomach."

"I'll find you in an hour."

Anna spun on her heel and headed toward a couple standing near the open patio doors. Marygai's generation, but so were most of the guests, at least the male guests. Hunter was the youngest man present. Anna had feared she might be the trophy tonight, but from Marygai's welcome, Hunter was probably right. He was supposed to be tonight's trophy?

What was the game?

Anna moved from group to group, a smile fixed on her face. She introduced herself, answered questions about her work, how she'd met Hunter and how long she'd known him—long enough to want to know him better. She offered the last with a shy smile to contrast with her late-eighteenth-century naughty up-thrust bustier.

Tonight's neckline was marginally lower than the one she'd worn when she'd met Hunter but was more secure. It also separated the lechers from the men it might be interesting to get to know with no effort on her part.

Following a waiter with an empty tray, she found herself in the kitchen. Sleekly old-fashioned wooden cupboards, granite benchtops and top-of-the-line appliances. She coveted the clear glass roof—a morning sky with her first cup of tea was an indulgence she'd happily include in her routine. The caterers were skilled and near invisible.

"Where can I get a dress like that?" a soft voice whispered, while offering her a tray of tiny crab pastries. The waitress was in spotless black and white, but her eyes twinkled.

"I borrowed this from a friend," Anna confessed. "She bought it online."

"It's fabulous. I want one."

"Give me your number, and I'll send you the site."

"I'm not supposed to fraternize," the woman said sadly, offering her a serviette instead.

"My name's Anna, and I have an incredible memory for numbers."

The waitress murmured a number. Anna repeated it and

turned away. Discreetly, she checked her phone, noting the time and entering the waitress's number. Returning to the main room a few moments later, she scanned the crowd.

No Hunter.

That left the garden, and Anna spotted him in a corner, his back to her. His body language screamed discomfort, while the man facing him stood legs braced, crowding the space. A frisson of apprehension skated down Anna's spine. The older man looked familiar. Not because of any particular resemblance to Hunter. Although given the tension, the man was probably his father. Another person whose discontent had ravaged his features.

Anna recognised him, an older version but the same man; a man whose ego arrived ten feet before him. For a second, she froze, before forcing herself to move forward. Turning tail and running wasn't an option.

"Hunter, can you take me home, please?" Anna slipped her hand into the crook of Hunter's elbow, Helen's bracelet falling over her wrist. She needed the physical connection to ground her, to enable her to manufacture an apologetic smile. "I'm sorry, but my head's killing me."

"Of course." He turned back to the older man. "If you'll excuse us."

"Introduce me," the man commanded.

"Nick Richardson, Anna Turner."

"You can do better than that. I'm Hunter's father."

"Hello." Anna kept her smile in place with an effort. Her heart, no, her whole body roared in protest.

I will not give this man the power of seeing me upset.

"Sorry. I can't stay."

CHAPTER SEVEN

Hunter's fingers curled into a fist. Easy to drop Nick Richardson where he stood. His gaze on Anna reminded Hunter of a slobbering, rabid fox. He'd never have brought Anna here tonight if he'd known Nick would be here. Seeing Marygai in her sterile home ground had eased some of the nausea in Hunter's gut from his last sighting of her in his mother's home—the nightmare of waking to find her in his bed with her hand on his cock. He rolled his shoulders, old shame shifting to disgust. Laying ghosts was how he'd seen tonight.

Anna tugged on his arm. "I need somewhere with dim lights and quiet."

Nick leered, rocking back on his heels, tucking his hands in his pants pocket so his jacket was open and his hips thrust forward—a practised aggression move. Impotent rage was a familiar feeling. Hunter's nostrils were clogged with it.

Marygai had ambushed him. Or maybe it had been Nick's idea, like finding Marygai in his bed all those years ago had been Nick's idea.

"We're gone." Hunter steered Anna toward the door.

"Nick Richardson is a dirty old man," she said without inflexion.

Hunter hadn't known he'd been holding his breath. He stumbled, but her grip tightened, propelling them in the direction of the entrance. Then, her request cut through his disgust and anger. Anna Turner of the carefully planned getaway had asked him to take her home.

"Nearly there," she murmured. "Eyes on the prize."

"What's the prize?" he managed.

"Fresh air." She was gooseberry tart, her astringency an antidote to the cloying bullshit he'd been listening to for the last hour. The majordomo must have been watching her, because he had her coat ready and the front door open. Within seconds, they were outside. She picked up speed, dragging on her coat as she moved.

"Where are you going?" Hunter asked.

"The bar around the corner."

"Where you'll arrange your own transport?" Ridiculous to feel disappointed. But he wasn't surprised. He'd let down his guard, allowed himself to think he could spend some time with Anna untainted by contact with Nick.

"Where we'll have a quiet drink and discuss what in blue blazes just happened." She stopped and spun to face him. "Then we'll discuss transport." She grabbed his hand, her fingers linked with his for the next block, her bracelet brushing against his wrist, only releasing his hand when she pushed through the door of the bar.

Once inside, Anna scanned the room, then settled on a quiet and secluded booth in the back.

"You don't have a headache?"

"I have a low tolerance for fakery."

"I'll get drinks, then you can tell me why. Hot chocolate?"

Her smile sizzled down his spine. The kind of smile you never tired of seeing.

"Yes, please."

Ten minutes later, he set two cups on the table and slid in beside her. She peered at his "inky evil."

"Seems fitting," he muttered.

"Sorry for the bum's rush, but the atmosphere in that house was poisonous. I had to flee or disgrace us both." She sniffed her cup. "I'm being unkind. Remember I told you my father was a philanderer."

"Yeah."

"The fooling around was bad." She hesitated. "The lying was worse."

"A house of horrors where every door you opened sickened you more." Hunter surprised himself with the confession.

"I wanted to throw up. But my need to rebel was entrenched. I moved out when my sister enrolled at university in Sydney, not Melbourne. I'd been going through my own ego-needs-stroking period and needed a circuit breaker." She turned and pressed a kiss to his upper arm, making a friendly connection.

"Dad said my sister, Kate, was the fantasist because she believes in love. At first, I wanted to distract Dad from her. He humiliated her when she was eleven by reading her romance story aloud at a dinner party. I started staying out, drinking, smoking, the usual rebellions. Making sure I was found out."

"Did your parents notice?"

"You're not just a pretty face." She grimaced. "I think they noticed, had an adult conversation about adolescent defiance and decided it was normal for a high-spirited, intelligent young woman to act like a rebel without a cause. They turned a blind eye."

"So, you upped the stakes." Hunter hadn't wanted to act up; he'd wanted to be so boring no one would notice him.

"I started imitating him. I thought, what the hell? This is how it works. In the early days, I flashed my boobs to boys behind the toilet block, then lifted my skirts to give them a look."

"Is that how he operated?" Hunter signalled a passing waiter for two more of the same. "Dropped his daks at the back of the toilet block?"

She was mid sip, so his words made her swallow too quickly, choke, then laugh aloud. "I must ask him some time."

"Were you always angry?" He hadn't known what to do with the cocktail of rage, shame and lustful curiosity.

"Not always. I was about fifteen when I fell for a guy— *thought* I fell for a guy," she corrected herself. "I decided he was the one. He wined and dined me."

"Maccas?"

"Guzman y Gomez. Pleeeze, grant me some class." She nudged him with her shoulder. "Then it was the back seat of his parents' Toyota."

"Romantic."

"It had reclining seats."

"A deal maker at one point in my youth. I'm guessing you're carrying a few bruises"—he eased the frown away from her forehead—"otherwise, you'd still be with him."

"I'm taking that as a compliment." She sighed. "I read the news on his social media feed the next morning that my boyfriend got laid."

Her kind of honesty meant she might not have forgiven herself. And she was filling in the details of what she'd told him at Icebergs at Bondi.

"I'm guessing he never got lucky again."

"Not with me." She smiled smugly. "Or anyone in our school."

"He deserved the punishment."

"It's a learning experience I'm reluctant to repeat." Was she warning Hunter they weren't going to make it to bed, or demanding he keep it a secret if they did?

"I didn't want to be anyone's first," Hunter admitted. "Certainly not someone who might be in love with me, when I sure as hell wasn't in love with them."

"Loyalty always matters." She threaded her fingers through his. "Anyway, I'm taking a long time getting to the point. I was getting wilder, angrier. When I was eighteen, and new to Sydney, a bloke I knew said he'd get me and a friend good money for an hour's work." She paused, staring into her chocolate.

"Drink it while it's hot, Anna."

She took a fortifying sip before continuing. "I was a naked cake surprise." She paused briefly to give him time to respond. "What? No questions?"

"You're talking, I'm listening."

"The deal was burst out of the cake, circulate a bit, smile. The bloke promised no touching. No serious touching. Maybe a boob squeeze, a crotch against my butt, a kiss, but that was the limit. There were rules. He specified them. The punters knew them. The bloke organising it would be with us all the time."

"It didn't work out as he promised?" Hunter had witnessed parties like that in his family home.

"Later he told me he kept the bond. For damages. Offered to split it between us. I gave my share to my friend. Blood money." Her hand fisted on the table, her anger barely contained.

"Why are you telling me this now?" He had a second to guess.

"Nick Richardson was at the party." She lifted her head to meet his gaze.

Hunter's stomach wanted to rebel at Nick seeing her naked. Maybe touching her. Briefly, he closed his eyes, and his heart stopped.

"You think he recognised you?"

"No. I was eighteen, wore a wig, and had enough makeup on for vaudeville. But I did that, and you need to know before we go any further. You need to decide if you can live with that."

She was so solemn. What was the religious crap—*hate the sin, love the sinner*. Hell, his plan had been a brief fling with Anna. It was still his plan. He wasn't made for permanence. And why would she want anything to do with the son of a "dirty old man" anyway?

"I don't know where we're going." *I didn't just say that.*

"Fair enough."

He blamed himself for the caution that had replaced the fearlessness in her voice.

The waiter approached with fresh drinks and took his time removing the empty cups, and all the while Anna sat silently beside him.

"You don't use his name." She was assembling facts, and she'd need the *I*'s dotted and *T*'s crossed before she'd begin to trust him again. "Did you reject your father's name?"

Anna had told him about her encounter with Nick when she didn't have to. She deserved honesty in return.

"When I turned eighteen, I took my mother's family name. One of my easier decisions, although I copped a lot of ragging adding Thompson to Hunter S. It was Mum's joke when the surname was Richardson. I played it up. By that time, I rarely saw my mum but was close to her brother. I was proud to take his name, whereas I was ashamed of my own."

He hadn't revealed that reason to anyone other than his uncle and aunt.

"Nick joined the wrong dots. He thought I did it to become the beneficiary of her will. Her final demand to pay Nick back for divorcing her."

"Did she influence you?"

"She was as angry at me as Nick was." His mother had accused him of trying to kill her chances of reconciliation.

"You said she was dead?"

"Yes." Hunter liked the directness of Anna's questions. Non-judgemental. Maybe her misspent youth gave her that ability? "She died in a car crash. Drunk, driving away from Nick after a fight."

Nick Richardson had always won.

"Why did you wear that dress to the party, Anna?"

"It's battle camouflage. You know all about camouflage. You use it yourself."

"I know what it's for. Why did you decide you needed to protect and distract tonight?"

"I got the sense it was an occasion that needed this sort of dress." She'd expected an ambush, and he'd been so focused on expunging old memories he hadn't twigged. "I checked out Marygai. She has a reputation in social circles for taking-no-prisoners."

"She eats debutantes for breakfast," Hunter agreed.

"She must go hungry a lot. Can't remember the last time I met a debutant."

"But I think we can agree, tonight's ambush was for me."

"I was led astray by the last-minute nature of the invitation and your reluctance to go alone. I thought I might be food for the lions. I read you wrong. I'm happy I was wrong. I shouldn't have worn the dress."

"Not every male was drooling."

"Always a relief."

Hunter's hand covered hers. She'd made mistakes as a teenager but refused to be ashamed of her body. Maybe, there was a lesson in that, but whenever Nick appeared in Hunter's life, shame became his running mate.

* * *

Anna held her breath. Telling Hunter that Nick Richardson was the actual birthday boy was cruel, and she didn't need to do it to make her point. Hunter was as uncomfortable with his father's history as she was with hers. Or, Anna hoped he was.

"Why did you want the conversation here, Anna?"

"To keep it out of our personal space. Yours and mine." She hesitated. Hunter looked as rattled as she felt. "Maybe you could organise that transport to take me home now?"

"I'll do that."

He hadn't made a lewd joke. Hadn't laid a disrespectful finger on her. Hadn't recoiled in disgust knowing his father had seen her naked. Anna's stomach turned over at the memory.

Knowing who his father is, can I take Hunter to bed?

Hell, will he still want to take me to bed with this knowledge between us?

Anna sat silently, while her mind jumped from one half-idea to another. She'd become a punching bag, dizzy from the forces buffeting her and unable to find her balance.

Speak to me, Hunter. Don't send me home alone in a ride share.

"Ready?" he asked. "The car's on approach. Fare covered."

Standing, she let him help her back into her coat. Hell, she couldn't remember being this nervous. Crazy to feel that the next thirty minutes were the most important in her life. When his hands cupped her shoulders, she waited for him to kiss her. She'd welcome the lightest touch. Yet, when he tucked her into his side in the back seat of the car, his arm around her shoulders, his mouth against her temple, her heart leapt into her throat, because all she sensed was his uncertainty.

"What are you thinking?"

"X-rated." His chuckle was off-key.

"Because Nick Richardson's still in the room?"

When he withdrew physically and emotionally, Anna cursed her need to dissect silences between people until she'd unearthed absolute truths. They'd become two people occupying a space, which was too small to hold them.

Stuff it. If this thing developing between us is going to blow up tonight, I'll go out with a bang.

"I've got another question," she said, as the car pulled into the kerb.

He rolled out, while she slid across the seat to stand in front of him. "Ask," he said.

"Cancel the cab."

One beat passed, then another, before he leaned toward the driver. "I'll get out here too."

Taking his hand, Anna led him around the side of the building, backing him against a wall. "No prying eyes here."

"In the interests of keeping dirt out of your home."

Bitter resignation shaded his voice.

"Go with me on this. Is Raed Hariri related to Casildo and Maha." Anna was giving him a second chance, a chance to share more of himself with her. Something she never did, but she'd be damned if they'd part with Nick Richardson poisoning what they'd started to create.

"It's a common Saudi surname." He was quick with a reply.

"Kate and I have used that line about Turner to pretend we're not related."

"Does it matter?"

"You didn't want to be at that party tonight before you discovered Nick would be there." She poked him in the chest. "You can explain that another time. But if you want to share my bed, we have to get past Nick seeing my eighteen-year-old body naked."

"You're entitled to change your mind."

"You're the one getting a second chance." Anna wrapped her hand around his tie and tugged it out of his jacket. "Because for some stupid reason, I like you." A light snapped on in an upstairs apartment, allowing her to see Hunter's face. "Casildo's dad owned the building you just bought."

"Yeah."

Some of the tension left her. She'd breached his first barricade. "I'm not psychic. In checking your contract, I re-checked the original lease. I'd been focused on the managing agent, and his name was in bold print. Antonio called it The Hariri building, but you mentioned Raed. I didn't join the dots, until I found his name in the small print."

"I knew you'd check every word." He smiled, his first genuine smile since the bar.

"And you admire my caution." Anna inhaled, a deep breath she released in small huffs of air. "We're finding our balance, Hunter." His scent was part of the balance. Away from the crowd, here in a shadowy garden, no one could find them or pursue them. "Nick's worse than a lecher."

"He's a grade-A bastard. Ruthless in his personal and professional acquisitions. And if that's too polite for you; he enjoys destroying people—friend and foe alike. Specifically, he preys on women." Hunter sounded like he was releasing years of disgust with the words. He rested his hands on her hips.

She looked up at him from under her lashes. "And you're working hard at emulating his success in both fields."

"You'd have kneed me in the balls by now if you believed that." He braced in case she opted to punish him for taking so long to come clean.

"Another digression when you haven't finished the original story." Anna kissed his chin.

"Your courage blows me away, you know. You're not interested in revenge or punishment. You walk away or stay."

"Remember that." *And thank you for understanding what matters.*

"You're right. Casildo's dad owned the building. I spent a lot of time in their home as a kid, which is enough reason for Nick to target father and son Hariri. Casildo's dad is the opposite of Nick. He caught us one night looking at some porn. He asked us about it. Sheesh, it was mortifying.

"Who did we think was having the most fun?"

"Who got to choose the moves"

"Did we think they liked each other?"

"Had they both agreed?"

"Cas has two sisters. We both upchucked when his old man asked if we could picture one of them in the scene?"

"Are you trying to distract me?"

"Is it working?"

"No."

He gave a loud sigh. "Casildo's dad is a good man. With a few floors vacant, he wasn't making enough to cover all his repayments."

"How did Nick discover that?"

"While I wouldn't put it past him to have informants in places where he shouldn't have them, I'm guessing he keeps an eye on friends of mine."

"You meant vicious when you said ruthless earlier."

"Yeah." He brushed the back of his hand down her cheek, relief in his gesture. "You have soft skin for a woman who pretends to be tough."

"So, what's the deal?"

"What do you mean, what's the deal?" Clearly, he was playing for time.

"Did Casildo's dad decide you were less hostile, and if he had to be humiliated, he'd rather it be you than Nick?"

"Wow." He huffed out a half laugh. "There's honesty, then there's blowing my entire cover."

"We're dancing around here, Hunter. There are some fairly high stakes at play. You're interested in some horizontal tango—"

"Doesn't have to be horizontal. I'm open to experimentation."

"And I have certain unbreakable rules." Anna slid one hand around his back and squeezed his butt. "Rule one—talk first, touch later."

"You're confusing me."

"This is encouragement."

"You're a tough negotiator," he said, when she brought her hand back around his hip to brush the bulge behind his trousers.

"Part of you is happy to say hello."

"I'm a placeholder. In a few months, I essentially transfer the property back to the Hariri family and recoup costs."

"Won't Nick guess what you've been up to?"

"He might. But it'll be too late."

Her caress was a little bolder, making him suck in a swift breath.

"Do that again. *Sweet heaven.*"

Anna repeated the action, her pressure a little firmer.

"How did my lease get caught in all of this?"

"Collateral damage." He groaned. "If Casildo's dad signed a new lease just as I made my offer, it would look dodgy. The managing agent was overzealous, claimed you weren't really serious."

"Your 'father and son, two peas in a pod' reputation— where did that come from?"

"I bought a building." He sighed. "Didn't even know Nick was interested. Some up-and-coming business blogger called Bizgos wrote it up as a competition. Then I did it a second time."

"*And* coincidences like buying businesses your father might have an interest in is impossible." Anna moved her hand back to his butt, her squeeze nudging him closer to her.

"Well, I may have been approached by someone being threatened by Nick. Nick fed Bizgos the story he wanted published, then it gained a life of its own. It was complicated by the fact Nick approached me to become a junior partner in his business."

"You refused, when you were supposed to be pathetically grateful to be part of his orbit." Anna put the puzzle pieces together. She gave a little wiggle against his crotch, pleased when he went rock hard.

"He lives in his own reality."

"I know the type." She scrunched up her forehead.

"That blogger doesn't understand Nick's brand of insecurity. My refusal to deal triggered payback, so the third story was about The Hariri. The blogger is accepting Nick's insider gossip as gospel."

"I'm going to require serious compensation." Ending her caress, Anna wrapped both hands around his neck, pulling herself into his body.

"A longer lease, a reduced rent, anything," he muttered.

"I was thinking something more personal." She cupped his cock with her hips.

"While we're together, there's no one but me," he said.

"That's a given, and I'm sorry you felt you needed to state it," she replied.

"I'm not an innocent. I could hurt you."

"We could hurt each other." Anna offered her sexy-intimate smile.

"I don't want to."

Maybe he'd specified monogamy as a condition of their relationship to protect them both?

"That's the right place to start," Anna said. "And I'm betting you've seen enough of sex as a weapon to choose a different path yourself."

She was sorry that after all their truth-telling and inching closer, he'd be unsure of her, himself, or both of them enough to have to state his position. She was running on instinct. Instinct telling her that he needed to be held tonight. Despite the risk to her heart.

Another secret she'd keep.

In the second before she flipped the light switch in her apartment, she did a quick assessment of body, mind and spirit. She knew what she was doing. She had no doubt they'd both enjoy the encounter, and Anna was prepared to take the risk.

"Make yourself at home," she said.

"Show me." He linked his fingers with hers, his hand warm.

"Bedrooms are off this hall. So's the bathroom. I'll show you the living room. It's why I bought the apartment." When they reached the bottom of the hall, she pointed, her pulse racing. "Ta-da." The large picture window revealed the distant arches of Sydney Harbour Bridge with street lights highlighting its elegant curves.

"Nice view. Do you live alone? I've never asked."

"Kate's been a flatmate from time to time. I've been alone since she married."

"Can I help you with your coat?" he asked, his lips curving into a smile. "You won't need it."

"This isn't going to be a furtive coupling in the dark."

Mimicking her, he shucked his jacket and hung it on the back of a chair, before tucking his tie in his jacket pocket. "Candles or fluorescent tubes?"

"Bright LEDs," she insisted.

"I want to see you, Anna. Every gorgeous inch of you. Thinking of you keeps me awake at night," he growled, flipping open the top buttons of his shirt.

Her eyes were drawn to his fingers, to the slumberous slowness of his movements. His journey down his chest was unhurried, a measured slipping of each button, a leisurely reveal of bare skin. The light dusting of hair on his upper chest matched his dark locks. Relaxed, intent, invitation in his un-rushing.

"I've imagined you in my bed." She was close enough to detect the base notes of his fragrance, finding courage in his sage smokiness.

"We'll get there." His shirttails dipped to his hips. His fingers shifting to unbuckle his belt before dropping it on the chair behind mesmerized her.

"Am I stripping too?"

"You could change into something more comfortable. Say jeans and a polo top, and we can start the evening again."

"I appreciate the offer, but I haven't got the patience."

"Nice to hear. How does stripping work?" Snapping the button of his trousers open, he toed off his boots. "Do you pop a button and the dress falls at your feet?"

"You're interested in the way things work?" She lifted her hands to the leather bow between her breasts. "This is a sophisticated item of clothing, not a burlesque outfit. It's not held together with Velcro."

"For the record, I like burlesque." He stood hipshot, his trousers hanging on his hips, his boxer briefs—a teal green—riding higher, teasing her with the promise of what was to come. "Your turn to make a move."

"Have you planned the moment when you'll pounce?" Pulling the leather bow, she unwound the straps from the hooks down her midriff, enjoying the way his eyes narrowed, and his breathing quickened.

"We're a long way from pouncing." He sniffed the air, using the moment to take a step closer. "You smell like silk and satin and soft skin. Do you do that deliberately?"

Anna ran her tongue over her top lip, watching him swallow with a bit more urgency. "You said my perfume settled you."

"It arouses, it settles, it entices, it makes me smile." His voice rolled over the words, a growl, a rumble, a whisper. "I can't wait so discover what you taste like."

Anna drew both hands down her midriff, pushing the sides of the bustier wider. "What happens next?"

"I have no idea." He circled her, bent closer to brush a kiss to her nape, sliding a warm finger down her spine. A light touch, heat and encouragement. "The dress is in two parts. How does this work?" He ran his index finger down the length of the zipper from her waist to the tops of her thighs.

"I'll show you." With an added shimmy, the skirt slid to the ground, pooling around her boots.

"I like your taste in lingerie."

"What lingerie?" She held his gaze. The bustier made a bra redundant.

"I didn't pick you for a fish-net-stocking-and-suspender-belt kind of gal."

"They came with the dress. Or rather, Bea's sister insisted they were a mandatory part of the look."

His gaze drifted down her body. "The knickers are pure you, white cotton, a dash of lace and sexy as hell."

Stepping out of the muddle of fabric, she threw it in the direction of the sofa. "I'm not as neat as you."

"I'm betting you're better prepared." His trousers joined his other clothes on the chair. "I didn't plan for this, so no rubbers."

"Well, hell." She laughed. "That rather cramps our style."

"You weren't a boy scout?" He grinned.

"Girl guide. And no, I wasn't."

"A woman who takes care of her own transport doesn't leave contraception to any dumb male." He held his arms wide. Like his hands, his body carried a few scars, but he was broad-chested, and his muscles looked like they'd been earned.

Her mouth watered at the sight.

"You're not a dumb male."

"Have you got the chemist on speed dial?" His smile was hopeful.

"We won't need a delivery."

He stroked her chin with a calloused thumb and forefinger, bringing her lips to his, touching nothing else. The kiss was a slow, deliberate incitement, teasing all her senses and seducing giveaway moans from her. He was good at this.

"Can you hear the bells and whistles?" he murmured.

"What are we doing?"

Seduction should always be like this. A slow striptease, which was part seduction and all about finding balance. About moving slowly enough to step back, but fast enough for her blood to thicken and her juices to flow.

"I'm waiting for you to take the lead."

She laughed. "I might take off my boots first."

"I'm hoping you'll take everything off." He traced a finger over a jagged scar high on her thigh. "What happened?"

"Chasing Kate as kids. We were somewhere we shouldn't have been. I tripped and landed on an old car."

"I like it." He bent and put his mouth to it. "I like that we're doing this now that we know each other better."

"No slam, bam, thank you ma'am tonight?" Her stomach dropped. *Nerves?* But he'd raised the stakes, made himself vulnerable in a confession she hadn't asked for.

"We're going to be intimate, Anna. And that scares the bejesus out of both of us." He understood so much.

"You say the nicest things, Sam-I-am. We're in it together." Desire soared as a deeper tension slipped from her body.

"Let's do a few things together. Mmm." He cupped her face. "Kiss me, sweetheart."

"I believe I will."

He was smiling, filling his kiss with warmth and laughter. The jagged edge of passion pooled liquid in her lower body. A brush of lips before his tongue teased at the corner of her mouth. Her moan. His tongue slipping between her teeth to stroke and excite. She clung to him, lost in the magic of his taste. Anna had waited a lifetime for a kiss like this. One kiss eased into another, deeper, needier, straining to get closer. She forgot where she was, who she was, but not for a second who she was with.

"Anna?"

"Don't stop."

"An intermission. I want space, so we can take our time."

"Don't take too long." Reluctantly, she drew back just enough to focus on him. "And stop grinning."

"I'm happy." He sounded surprised, as if happiness eclipsed arousal.

"Me too."

"Unless you have an objection, I'm taking you to bed."

"Is that a euphemism?" Anna stroked the top of his ear. "Because I thought we'd already agreed you're not getting out of here until I've had my way with you."

"Bed," was all he said before lifting her into his arms, followed by, "Queen size. I spotted it in the other room. Soft mattress, warm covers, lots of room."

"That works." With one arm wrapped loosely around his neck, she squeezed his biceps. "I don't usually fall for big, strong, silent types."

"I don't usually play with soft-hearted sirens." He nudged the bedroom door open with his hip, then slid her to her feet, keeping her close. "I'm making an exception for you." Stroking two fingers over the gusset of her knickers, he flashed a wicked smile. "Damp. Let me help you take these off."

"Please."

Crouching in front of her, his nose was at groin level. "You smell of Anna."

He pressed against her, his hands on her butt. Slowly, he pulled the knickers down, lingering when they hit the tops of her thighs. He caught the front elastic between his teeth and tugged them low enough to glide his tongue down the crease in her lips.

Anna moaned at the touch, her knees sagging. With an edge of desperation, she tangled her fingers in his hair. "My turn. It must be my turn." Waiting was stretching the tension unbearably.

But he didn't acquiesce. Instead, he dragged the knickers to her ankles, and said, "Right foot."

Obediently, she lifted her foot.

"Left foot." He stood with his trophy in one hand. "Your turn."

Anna wasted no time. She was wet and wanting. Gripping the elastic on his boxer briefs, she dragged them down. "Atta boy." She planted a quick kiss on his glans, then tugged the boxers to his feet. "Take a step back." She pressed lightly against his chest, dropping him onto the mattress before straddling his lap. "Time to pounce, Hunter."

"If you insist." He fell backward, taking her with him, manoeuvring his way to the middle of the bed. "This might be the last time I can speak coherently for some time, so I'll just say you're gorgeous."

She laughed. "What about, *move, roll over, more*?"

"Starting now." He lunged up to take her mouth, his hands quicksilver, streaking fever everywhere they touched, and he touched every inch of her. A caress, a fondle, a brush of a single finger—lightly, then more urgently. Anna rose onto her knees, then lowered herself onto him. Holding his gaze, she watched pleasure shift his features, watched the control etched around his mouth—he was pacing himself to her needs.

A race they both wanted to finish, and neither wanted to end. Heat and damp and heady scents. An intensity that rattled her soul. Her body was separate, floating on an ocean of sensation, rising, reaching for her peak.

"Hunter," Anna half-sobbed his name as her body contracted around his.

His thrusts grew faster, more possessive.

"Yes." He roared, his body convulsing, before he collapsed, gathering her into his arms. "Let me hold you."

Yes, please. Forever.

But he wasn't ready to hear that.

CHAPTER EIGHT

The sound of running water coming from the bathroom stopped. Anna had passed on Hunter's offer to join him in the shower on the grounds that while the offer was tempting, he had to be at a game in an hour. Giggles, cuddles, lovemaking until the early hours—he'd woken her; she'd woken him. The last time she'd been this happy was when Kate announced she and Liam were getting married.

Stop it! she chastised herself. One night does not a summer make. Or was that one swallow?

After sliding two cheese and tomato sandwiches into her griddle iron, she turned on the kettle and coffee maker.

"Niall's shirt fits okay," he announced as he entered the kitchen, tugging her brother-in-law's long-sleeved T over his head, an appealing contrast to his suit trousers. "I'll wash it and get it back to you." He stopped beside her and tipped up her chin to kiss her. "Breakfast tastes good."

"We've already had breakfast. This is lunch because you've got an appointment."

"Yeah. Gareth's game. I don't watch them all, but this is the final. I'd invite you—"

"No." She pressed two fingers to his lips. "Your focus should be entirely on him on such a special day."

"Can't guarantee that." He grinned, watching her pour boiling water into a pot. "Tea?"

"I limit my chocolate consumption to after five o'clock unless it's an emergency."

"Thanks for the warning."

"I've got coffee for you."

"Can I see you tonight?" he asked.

"I'd like that." She'd been holding her breath waiting for the invitation. Silly, when she could have issued her own.

"I'll call when I get back to my place. Donna will drop me off, but whether we're celebrating or commiserating after the game will dictate exactly what time I get home. But before six. There are a few good restaurants within walking distance of my place, if that suits."

"Sounds lovely."

"What are you doing today?" he asked, then seemed to catch himself. "Don't answer, if you don't want to." Their first morning as lovers and already he was backpeddling on intimacy.

"Work. I need to catch up on some work. With the amount of time I've been spending checking out the renovations at the childcare centre, I'm behind on a project." She'd model sharing because if this was going to develop into more than stupendous sex, she needed him to lower Fort Knox type barricades and share himself with her.

Pot calling the kettle, Anna!

"While we're together, there's no one but me."

An icy bead of dread trickled down her spine. Anna was usually the one to make that stipulation. The one to state she wouldn't question, follow-up, or second guess what a lover did when he wasn't with her. She expected equal respect in return.

You choose to be with me. If you change your mind, fine, just say so.

Yet, when Anna walked him to the door, he was the one to wrap an arm around her shoulders, keeping her tucked in beside him. At the front door, he was the one to drop the bag she'd loaned him for last night's shirt and turn to face her. Tilting her chin, he gazed into her eyes for long seconds, then grinned. "Don't miss me too much." His mouth covered hers before she could answer.

Heat and longing and sensation whirled through her body. Still her lips clung.

"Just marking my place," she whispered.

He was the first to step back. "I'll call when I'm free," he whispered the apology.

She closed the door, rested her back against it and touched her fingers to her lips. "I miss you already."

And knew she was in serious trouble. She found herself wandering from room to room, following Hunter's scent. She even sniffed at the pillow on Hunter's side of the bed. When she moaned, she admitted things were worse than serious.

"You idiot." Thrusting her hands into her hair, she pretended to drag it out by the roots. "Go to work."

She forced herself to put in a solid three hours, and she had to force herself. Finally she pressed send. Antonio would be pleased when he opened his inbox in the morning. Settling into her seat on the bus home, she tried to bring her racing thoughts under control, and made a split-second decision.

"Can I come for dinner tonight?"

"Anytime," her sister replied. "Is something up?"

"Can I bring Hunter?"

"We'd love to meet him."

Anna snorted. "Maybelline, you can't fool me. You're desperate to meet him. You have to promise to be gentle."

"I'm crushed that you'd think we'd misbehave around your friend." Kate's voice held humour.

"He's gaining friend status." Time to stop procrastinating. "His father is Nick Richardson."

"Not *the* Nick Richardson."

Anna pictured her sister taking a step or two backward, her forearm across her eyes in true repertory style.

"I give up. Who's Nick Richardson?"

"The birthday boy when I made my first and last appearance as a naked surprise." Anna waited, then waited some more. "Say something."

"Have you told Hunter you were a naked surprise at his father's birthday?"

"He knows I was naked, and that Nick was at the party. It didn't seem necessary to rub his face in it by telling him it was Nick's birthday party." If Anna wasn't in a bus, she'd be pacing to alleviate her angst. This was a huge step, but she wanted her sister's endorsement—support—stamp of approval ... because? Anna did and didn't trust her own judgement.

"Is something worrying you?"

"No more than my usual paranoia." Except that wasn't quite true. Hunter had been ready to walk away last night. To end their relationship before it began, even though he was as attracted as she was. *Why?* Did it matter? "How are you and my niece feeling? I forgot to ask?"

"We're dandy. See you tonight. Niall and Lucy are coming too."

"Wow!" Anna whistled. "I haven't been able to coax Niall out of his cave for weeks. Will you be bugging the place for future fiction fodder?"

"As a creative, you know everything in life is fodder for creativity."

"Right. I'll let you know when Hunter accepts."

She was a kilometre from home when her phone rang. "Hi." She pressed a hand to her stomach. *Damn nerves.* This was a logical next step.

"Hi, yourself." Hunter sounded relaxed.

"Did you win?"

"Not only did the team win, Gareth scored the winning goal. Better than Christmas."

"That's great." Two more stops then she was home. "How do you feel about a change of plans tonight?"

"Your place rather than mine?" From him, the words

were beautiful and lightyears from the touch-and-go moment outside her apartment block last night. He didn't assume she was cancelling him.

"Dinner with my sister and her husband. At their place. Liam's brother's coming and bringing a friend. Informal." Her nerves were pinging like released elastic bands. "Very informal." She strained to read his silence.

"Is this like meeting the parents?"

"We don't have to." A stupid thing to say when she wanted Kate to meet him. And Liam, and Liam's twin, Niall.

"You'd like to?" Whatever reservations he was feeling, he was considering her wishes, and the crack in her defensive shell opened further. He was a honey.

"Yes. But it doesn't have to be tonight."

"Tonight's fine. Do you want to meet me there, or will I pick you up?" He wasn't making assumptions.

"They're inner-west. I can walk, but we can meet beforehand. Calllie's bar, Newtown, six-forty-five." She heard herself babbling. "I can background you about them."

"Have you backgrounded them?"

"They're literate, media-savvy grown-ups. As soon as I mentioned your name, my sister and her husband would have done their own research." No point in pretending otherwise. "We're close."

"I'll wear my flak jacket."

"Cute." She pressed the buzzer for her stop. "I'll brief you at the bar."

"I share, you share." He paused. "That's what tonight's about, isn't it?"

"That's how we move forward. Have I told you lately that I like you, Hunter?" Because he'd just been brutally honest about where they'd landed.

"The feeling might just be mutual."

* * *

The best sex Hunter had ever known one night, dinner

with the "literate, media-savvy" family the next, and Hunter hadn't uttered the slightest protest. He was even looking forward to seeing Anna in a different context because, like a diamond viewed at different angles in bright light, she revealed a different facet of her character each time.

I'm going crazy.

He'd seen her tousled and sweaty and begging in his arms, seen her as a self-aware siren at a party she hadn't wanted to attend, seen her as a professional advertising executive, a keen questioner on the intricacies of childcare centre construction, and at all times she displayed an integrity that left him in awe. He'd like to see her get down and dirty on a soccer field sideline, because while she'd be ferocious in support of her child, she'd also insist on fair play at all times. Kids understood fair play.

Her enthusiasm was irresistible.

At least to me.

But she was also vulnerable as hell and prepared to reveal that side of herself to him. He had the sense this was new territory for both of them.

Hunter pushed through the front door of the pub, a goofy smile plastered on his face, and spotted her instantly. She'd been watching for him, and his heart flipped over at the gentle smile curving her mouth. For him.

A popular pub, meaning he had to work his way through a cluster of people to get to her. She saw his dilemma and was ahead of him, already signalling the bar for drinks.

"Hi. You won, and winning makes the bruises painless, but was it a good game?" she asked.

"A high standard for their age group. And the final score was close. Gareth was carried off the field on his teammates' shoulders. His reward for scoring the winning goal."

"Before we go any further, can I say, Mr. Thompson, you look all easy rider delicious in your black jeans, dark turtleneck shirt and that weathered black leather jacket." She leaned closer, seeming to inhale him.

"If I can say, I had a hard time concentrating on the

game. I kept imagining that little shimmy you did when you stepped out of your dress last night." He stifled the moan accompanying the image.

"Don't tempt me. We're in a public place." But her gaze travelled down his body as if recalling with delight every move he, or she, had made last night, and this morning.

"Thanks." Hunter smiled at the woman who brought the iced mineral water, then drained half the glass. "I didn't realise how thirsty I was."

"I've watched enough boys watching football games to know they can forget to eat or drink when the game gets intense."

"You go to games? Where have you been all my life?"

"I went to a few finals," she clarified, "in my misspent youth, when I was trying to attract attention."

"Ahh. This was our first final."

"A big moment." She moved her stool closer, until her arm brushed his.

"It was. Now, quit stalling and tell me what I need to know to survive tonight."

"I already told you, my twin, Kate, writes romance and is a top-notch environmental researcher. Liam, her husband, is an environmental lawyer. They're besotted. Kate's pregnant with their first child, so talking babies will distract both of them."

"And they're very protective of you."

"Close doesn't always mean protective, but you're right, and both Liam and Niall see me as a little sister. I've joined an extended family, and I like it."

"And you're equally protective of them."

"Maybe." She drew a line through the condensation on her glass before glancing up at him. "I told you Niall, Liam's brother, makes bespoke wooden furniture. He's a genius, won a mentorship with a master craftsman in Ireland. Niall's got more of an Irish lilt. It's the one thing that distinguishes the brothers. With the market the way it's been for the last few years, it's been a struggle, but he's got an exhibition coming up."

"You sound proud."

"I am proud. We did classes together at uni. I've known him for years. I call him a carpenter. It's a running joke because he's so much more."

"You make friends with men," he teased. "You've adopted the Quinns."

"They're family. Families aren't just blood kin. You've adopted Casildo."

"Cas adopted me."

"Besides, I didn't have brothers, and it's important to have male friends, otherwise how will I know about men, what they're like, how they play? You need to see people in all sorts of situations to understand the underbelly of the beast. Don't you have female friends?"

"Clearly not enough. The underbelly of the beast is a closed book to me." Hunter thought of Marygai, Gina, even his mother and how they'd fawned over Nick Richardson.

"I can introduce you to women"—she patted his thigh—"who are only offering friendship."

"Jealous?" He drained his glass.

"I don't do jealousy. It's too destructive. I suspect you don't either."

She chose loyalty, and if Hunter couldn't offer the same, they had no chance of a future.

"You're right." But in his experience, too many people liked to keep their partner second-guessing about whether they'd stay or go, seeing it as part of the thrill of romance. In Hunter, it had bred a cynicism, which Anna was blasting away.

"You know my rules. We talk, we share, we trust. Reduces misunderstandings."

"Uh-huh. What about Niall's friend?"

"Lucy McTavish—an unknown quantity." Anna frowned. "She's his landlady. Maybe more."

"You sound disapproving."

"I'm reserving judgment. But I'll learn more tonight."

"Poor Lucy."

Sliding off her stool, she moved to stand between his thighs. "Hello, Hunter," she murmured before initiating a slow kiss.

Hunter anticipated sumptuous, because he was learning all Anna's kisses were sumptuous, but this one went deeper.

"Thank you for coming to meet my family." An "It Ain't Me Babe" ringtone sang out. "That's Kate."

"Why that song?"

"A family joke. Johnny and June Carter Cash. One of the first pieces of music Kate and Liam shared on a road trip." She stared at the message. "Oh."

"Something wrong?" He even found the pucker between her eyes sexy.

"Niall doesn't want us to discuss his exhibition tonight. I've sent Kate a thumbs-up emoji, but something's wrong."

"But you'll do what he asks because he's your friend." Hunter added this new proof of her loyalty to all the other examples he'd seen.

"Goes without saying." She hesitated, then added, "I saw him last week. I'm doing the exhibition promotion and have designed an extra page to add to his website. All the promotion should be live by now. He's running out of time to meet his deadlines."

"Any ideas?"

"Lucy." Anna scowled.

"I'll kick you under the table if you make faces like that at dinner. You look like a thundercloud on performance-enhancing drugs. Everyone will know something's wrong."

"Promise."

"You're serious?" Hunter asked.

"Niall's waited years for this exhibition. A few months ago, it was all he could talk about when we had a family catch-up. I don't want to say something I regret. So, yes, please. Kick me, step on my foot, spill a drink on me, kiss me if it's looking like I might disgrace myself and embarrass Niall."

"I'll distract Lucy. After all, she and I are fellow travellers. The outsiders under the microscope."

"You're here because I love my family and want them to meet you."

"That's what I said." He grinned.

They were assessing him.

I was expecting that.

Hunter wasn't expecting the absolute sense of unity between the two sets of twins. Liam and Kate were lovers, but Anna had the kind of relationship with Niall Quinn that Hunter had with Casildo. Siblings by choice, and Anna was concerned that Niall was besotted with Lucy and making all the wrong decisions.

Hunter understood what that was like as well. And despite Niall's almost total focus on Lucy, the carpenter had given Anna a hug, kissed her on the forehead and said "Keep safe" in parting.

Was Niall warning Anna to be careful about Hunter?

Good families, like the Hariris and the Turner/Quinn conglomerate, conveyed such complicated messages in a single glance, yet waited for the evidence to be in before judgment.

So, Hunter was unsurprised when the atmosphere subtly shifted after Niall and Lucy's hasty departure, when Liam Quinn ushered him into the lounge room and offered him a fine, single malt whiskey.

"I've been abstaining with Kate pregnant, but if you have one, I can have one." Liam tilted the bottle in Hunter's direction.

"Lovely." Hunter settled onto one of the sofas. "The last month to six weeks you're on tenterhooks." Hunter grinned. "And, in case you're interested"—*Liam Quinn was very interested*—"I'm speaking from second-hand experience. Someone I think of as a sister has two ankle biters, and I swear her brother and I had more Braxton Hicks contractions than Zahra did in those final weeks."

"It is scary." Liam handed him a drink, before staring into his own. "Although I'm being all manly and brave."

Hunter snorted.

Liam took the opposite sofa. "They'll be here in a minute. I have a feeling I'm supposed to interrogate you, but I can't think of a damn thing to ask."

"Really?"

"You look happy, she looks happy. Make sure it stays that way."

"That works as a threat."

"She's special."

"I agree. That doesn't mean that every relationship is headed for happily-ever-after." Hunter felt compelled to warn this man, who might have to help pick up any pieces.

"True. But, if it all goes to shit, tell her the truth. They've had a lifetime of lies with their dad. Truth's an absolute for the Turner twins, especially Anna."

"You must be a hell of a lawyer because I feel completely interrogated, and you're still smiling and swilling good whiskey."

Liam grinned back. "What can I say? It's an art form." He cocked his head to one side. "Sounds like we've got company.

Baby talk dominated conversation for the next hour, and Hunter was reminded again of Zahra's two pregnancies, of the late-night chats over coffee and Lebanese pastries with Cas, about how scary, yet thrilling, parenthood was. Before Anna and he left, or before they made their escape, because hell, he was as keen to get Anna back into bed as Niall had been to kidnap Lucy, Hunter was dragged off to see Niall's cradle. And he understood some of Anna's frustration. The guy did incredible work.

Hunter had pressed Niall on risk and reward at dinner, and the conversation was still swirling in his head when they arrived at Anna's apartment. He'd advised Niall not to risk something he couldn't afford to lose. Hunter was fast coming to the conclusion that losing Anna would destroy any good left in him.

"I like Lucy." He hung his jacket on the back of Anna's bedroom door.

"She's hard not to like." Anna was on the stool in front of her dressing table, her fingers unclipping her delicate earrings. The finely wrought strings of turquoise and silver leaves had danced for Hunter whenever he'd glanced across the table at her. They'd drawn his attention to the sparkle of her smile and the elegant line of her neck. "That doesn't mean I think they're right for each other," she said, tucking the baubles into her jewellery box.

"Do you always leap to judgement about other people's relationships?"

"Niall hasn't told her about the exhibition." She swung away from the mirror, a furrow forming between her brows. "Crafting the pieces for the exhibition was his major focus before he met Lucy, and now he won't talk about it."

"You blame her for distracting him from his work?"

An interesting idea, given Anna had distracted Hunter from his, distracted him from Nick. After years spent working with few rewards—and a bespoke woodworker plying his craft fitted that category as easily as Hunter did— a loving, lovely woman was a hard distraction to resist. Niall was risking his exhibition. Hunter was risking—what? Nick had seen Anna with Hunter. Time to keep a closer eye on Nick.

"It wasn't work on Niall's mind when he practically dragged Lucy out of the house before dessert." Anna sounded prim.

"As far as I could tell, the only thing on their minds from the second we sat down to eat was ripping each other's clothes off. I was surprised they made it past the first course." Hunter could understand Niall's urgency. Each time he'd made love to Anna last night, the tendrils of need had dug deeper.

"Okay. The chemistry between them is combustible. But I love Niall. I want him to be happy. I worry about their relationship if he feels unable to tell her what's important to him."

"He looked pretty happy when he left." But Niall, like Hunter, was keeping secrets from his lover.

"Sex isn't enough on its own."

Hell, she was admitting something Hunter was still denying. She and he had more than sex. He was the one placing limitations on what they might have. Permanence wasn't an option for him. Maybe he'd made a mistake thinking Anna was comfortable taking this one day at a time.

"I said happy, not randy."

"His craft is a core part of who he is. He's taken no pay to intern with major craftsmen. He's lost girlfriends because he wouldn't make cheap knockoffs." She raised her fists in frustration. "You can't stop being who you are and still be happy."

"You can't make it work for them." And that was a pathetic response, but her comment hit a nerve.

Hunter still had secrets, and while Anna would forgive him certain transgressions, there were others, like Nick's role in Hunter's breakup with Gina that he wasn't so sure about. She wouldn't be content indefinitely if all he offered her was sex—regardless of how good the sex was. He wasn't sure he could offer more. With her, he was beginning to want to.

"I can help, if asked. I can be there to pick up the pieces." She stood, flashed him an impish smile, and—what was that word she'd used—*sashay*. She sashayed toward him.

She wasn't just gorgeous. She was honest and generous and loyal. She didn't cross-examine him about his movements, who he saw, who he lunched with. She wasn't interested in his secrets per se—she expected intimacy, a sharing of hopes, dreams and fears, and he was denying her true closeness, denying *them* true closeness. She might hate him for it, but now he couldn't resist the light and joy she offered.

"Right now, I've got other plans." She patted his chest. "Want help getting out of that shirt?"

"I can manage my own." To demonstrate, he began pulling his shirt over his head.

She pressed her nose to his sternum. "You always smell delicious."

"Come on site with me one day."

She leaned back, giving a shimmy that shifted his arousal from a hum to a roar. "Do you wear a tool belt?"

"Boots, tool belt, hard hat, and not a stitch more."

"Surely you'd need a jockstrap"—she giggled—"for protection?" Her hand brushed over the growing bulge in his jeans.

"You're messing with my fantasy."

"Why don't we make one to share?"

She walked her fingers up his chest, and he'd swear the reverberations shot to his toes.

"I'd like that."

He slipped his hands under her knees and carried her to bed. Sharing with Anna was a kind of drug. While he might tell himself inviting anyone permanently into his life, with Nick Richardson circling, was asking for trouble, letting Anna go now was unthinkable.

CHAPTER NINE

Donna's message arrived within minutes of Hunter arriving at the childcare centre.

Panic. Nick!

The only time she'd used their silly little code, but it was the first time Nick had visited Hunter's office. All previous meetings had been in public places—at Hunter's insistence—although early on he'd been invited to Nick's palatial office in North Sydney. Nick had intended Hunter to be impressed by a flashy show of wealth. He'd been indifferent.

Like an itch he couldn't reach, Hunter sensed trouble coming. As a kid, fear had been physical—invisible walls closing in, pressing down on him until he couldn't catch a clear breath, then his head had popped off his shoulders under the pressure. Fear was loud, starting with a wind howling through a tunnel, then booming like cannon. You wanted your eardrums to burst so it would be over.

Later he worked out he'd been picking up his mother's mood. Years of living with Nick had given her a fine-tuned ear for when his tone turned spiteful, when he couldn't be jollied out of his mood with food or booze or sex, when he'd decided he hadn't got the adulation he deserved. She'd moved differently, her voice had held bewilderment as well as fear, even her perfume changed, the delicate floral fragrance becoming old-vase-water rank.

Never physical abuse. At least not in Hunter's presence. But emotional beatings left permanent bruises.

Hunter rolled his shoulders. He'd forgotten that period, when his mother had been his soft-hearted defender and companion. He'd spent too long living with the woman desperate to win Nick back. Desperate enough to mimic Nick's most promiscuous behaviour to encourage a bit of jealousy.

"Hi." Anna touched his arm, bringing him back to the present. "I'm looking forward to this run-through. You've installed the bathrooms." She rubbed her hands in delight. "I've never been so excited about a bathroom in my life."

"I can't stay." Her tiny withdrawal told Hunter he'd stuffed that up. "Sorry. Donna sent a message. Something unexpected has come up at the office." Hunter was dancing around the truth to avoid mentioning Nick's name. All he could think was Nick had seen Anna at the party on Saturday, and less than a week later, Nick was in Hunter's office uninvited and unannounced.

"I can wait to see the changes."

She was studying him as if he'd grown two heads. Not surprising, given he'd made this appointment wrapped around her in his bed this morning.

"No need." He signalled to his project manager, who joined them. "Kazim, you know Anna."

"Hi." The young man shook Anna's hand.

"Nice to see you again, Kazim," she said.

"I have to get back to the office. Can you show Anna where we're up to?" Hunter ignored Kazim's surprise. He'd just finished telling his manager he'd be here for about an hour.

"Are we still on for tonight?"

"Yes." He softened his blunt response with a smile.

Still, she hesitated.

"I'm looking forward to it. See you when you finish work," he said.

"Okay."

He didn't wait to see what happened next, already calling a ride, considering Nick's motives. Nick's visitations were never just a friendly drop-in.

Donna rolled her eyes when Hunter walked through the door. "He's in the green meeting room. I've given him a juice."

The green meeting room was located against the side wall of the property, was soundproofed, windowless, but one wall was filled with soothing Australian landscapes if you needed sedation.

"Thought I'd check out the premises before you moved on." Nick bounced to his feet when Hunter walked through the door. Edgy? Manic? Convinced he had the edge? Certainly the last.

"I'm keeping the site as a work depot." Given the suburban location, that had always been a plausible explanation if Hunter was seen here rather than in Darling Harbour.

"A little bird told me your apartment's upstairs."

Nick's interest was calculated to unnerve Hunter. Not Nick's knowledge. Anyone could get hold of building plans if they had the contacts. Nick had contacts, but he was snidely implying Hunter was under surveillance. An old tactic. Nick had successfully used that threat with too many people to need to follow through with action.

"It's convenient at the moment." Hunter shrugged. "Why are you here?"

"I was concerned about your girlfriend." Nick returned to a chair, smirk firmly in place. "Is she okay? She seemed unwell when you rushed off on Saturday night."

"Not relevant." Giving Nick any information about Anna would be a betrayal.

"But that's why I came." Nick drummed his fingers on the table, then knocked twice. "It's natural for a father to be concerned about his son and his girlfriend, especially when we're looking at a merger."

"She's a colleague interested in design. Wanted to see Marygai's house." A mistake to give Nick that much information, but Hunter saw the doubt he'd planted in the older man's eyes. "Thanks again for the merger offer." Gratitude was the last emotion he felt. "I prefer to run my own show."

"A merger would be good for your company." Nick added a lick of intimidation to his words.

"Is that a threat?" Hunter kept his voice pleasant, while cursing himself for taking Anna to Marygai's party, for putting her within Nick's orbit.

"I never make threats." Nick left hanging the implication that he translated words to actions pretty damn fast.

"Thanks for dropping by." Hunter held the door open. "I think we're finished."

Nick sauntered past him. He still wore the same cheap cologne he'd worn when Hunter was a kid. Hunter had long decided Nick liked to be associated with it—an olfactory assault before he opened his mouth. Menacing in the memories it conjured. At least for Hunter.

Watching him leave, Hunter left the door to the room open. It stank of Nick.

Donna beckoned him to reception, then pulled his favourite coffee from under her desk. "I got Georgie, the work experience kid, to go get it."

"I'm not sure that's on the list of duties we agreed with the charity." He accepted the coffee, and its sharp, inky evil helped banish Nick's odour. "Isn't that a bit sexist?"

"Fiddlesticks," Donna answered. "The junior on a work site is often sent to collect the lunch orders. Georgie spent the morning with Bernard on carpentry, and this afternoon she's going out with Meredith on a paint job. Besides, she's got a crush on the barista. Couldn't wait to go get the coffee."

"How do you know these things?"

"You pay me to know. Are you going back to the worksite?"

"No, I'll work here." But his mind kept circling back to the purpose of Nick's visit.

"Natural for a father to be concerned about his son and his girlfriend."

That was BS. Nick's only interest in Hunter's girlfriends was to entice them away from Hunter, then Nick dumped them.

Hell! If Hunter thought about it now, it had started in primary school, when Nick issued the invitations for playdate at home, then spent the visits offering the prettiest girls a piggyback ride, or making sure they won the best prizes. By the time Hunter was nine, he begged his mother to stop the parties, ashamed of being on guard all the time, but gut-sure his father was in some sort of bizarre competition with Hunter.

Hunter's friends were supposed to say Nick was more fun than Hunter. Anyone who put up resistance, like Cas, was on the receiving end of barbed comments for the rest of the party. Those snide remarks could add up. Even something as simple as "You're not as good as everyone else at that game," repeated multiple times, left scars on young hearts.

Foolish to think Hunter could keep his interest in Anna hidden.

Foolish to think Nick wouldn't be interested in any woman on Hunter's arm. He should have taken evasive action at Marygai's. Tried to protect her. Instead, she'd appeared warrior-like at his side to protect him.

Hunter wasn't prepared to stop seeing her. She was tart and sweet. She'd been at a party with Nick fourteen years ago and had read him in an instant. Witness her insistence on an immediate exit on Saturday night. She was too formidable for Nick to charm or manipulate or bribe.

Hunter had been taking careful steps, circling the wagons around his business, so that he had trusted contractors, trusted suppliers, and long-term tenants. From day one he'd built his business to be Nick-proof. Nick would lose interest. He always did.

He'd circled the wagons around family too. The Hariris were safe, his aunt and uncle were safe. That left Anna, but he made himself believe she was safe. He sucked in air, because he had to believe she was safe or stop seeing her.

Anna had told him about Nick. Not everything, but he had no right to know everything. And she'd told him the most important details. She'd jumped naked out of a cake at a birthday party where Nick had been present. She'd be here soon.

Damn, he was positive he could still smell Nick. A shower before he met Anna, and they'd come home via the external entrance.

* * *

Anna surveyed the crowd in the bar before bringing her gaze back to Hunter. "Did you sort out your problem earlier?"

"Yeah." Whatever his problem was, he wasn't sharing.

Suck it up, Anna.

He deals with commercial-in-confidence stuff or banal human relationships stuff. Just like she did. And she had no intention of downloading every detail of her working day on him.

"The bathrooms are gorgeous. You've even got one of those suites I saw at an airport one time. The adult/child combo." She savoured a sip of her Sancerre, a new wine for her, but the self-professed-sommelier cum bartender had convinced them both to try it.

"Airports are a place where you don't want to lose your kid when you have to go to the bathroom. But they can be useful in a childcare setting. Or so Maha tells me."

"It's really coming together."

"We're on track for completion within the three months." He toasted her with his untouched wine. "How's your team feeling?"

"There's only the one colleague I've been worried about. I've been showing her pictures," Anna confessed. "I was going to ask you if I could bring a tour group through one afternoon?"

"I'll check with Kazim when we're good to go with just basic safety gear."

A waiter appeared at Hunter's shoulder, pausing their conversation momentarily. "Your table's ready, sir."

The man wove his way through small tables and past booths lining the wall to arrive at the end booth.

"I like this better than Icebergs." Once seated, Anna nudged him with her thigh. "Cosier."

"I'm starting to learn that cosy is shorthand for telling you things."

"Is that a complaint?"

"A realisation that I'm starting to read your mind." He looked baffled.

"Not possible. I'm infinitely mysterious." She lowered her gaze to her menu. "I'll have the Mezze plate please."

"Infinitely mysterious in some ways and transparent as gossamer in others. You swap kisses for secrets. I'll have the Mezze plate too." He signalled the waiter and placed the order.

"I'm not asking for secrets," she said, fiddling with the stem of her glass. "To be blunt, I'm asking for intimacy."

"'Talk first, touch later.'" He repeated her words, and Anna couldn't read his mood. "I remember the rule."

"We've got a few minutes before our meals get here."

Intimacy mattered, sharing yourself mattered, and Hunter mattered to her.

"What do you want to know?" He propped his chin on his fist.

"Did you have any kind of relationship with Nick when

145

you were a kid?"

"Everything begins and ends with Nick." He sat back with a wry smile. "I was a loser. Born a loser. He started telling me that when I was about six and wanted to spend the day with Mum's brother Ben on a job."

"Working with Ben is how you got the scars and calluses." Anna turned his hand over and placed a kiss in the middle of his palm. "Bet Ben never called you a loser."

"Yeah to the scars. Ben told me I had skills and moves." He chuckled. "You have the damnedest ability to zoom in on the best bits of my life. Working with Ben was the best thing I ever did. Rehabbing was his skill. He took on more projects, cut me in. Trained me, paid me wages, and an increasing cut of the profits until it was fifty-fifty by the time I started studying architecture."

"Is Ben still building?"

"He decided he was getting a bit old, so he moved into crane hire. Started a partnership with a bloke. Sank all his assets into the business." To distract her or to drain the moment of its intensity, he held his wine up to the light, sniffed, then took a sip. "This is good."

"Very good," she agreed.

"Ben was doing well. They were doing well."

"I'm not going to like this, am I?"

"His partner got into financial trouble. Messy divorce, and he 'borrowed' money from the company. Ben lost his investment."

"And Nick engineered that?" she asked.

"Nick outed himself in Ben's partner's divorce. Although he dropped the woman as soon as Ben's partner declared bankruptcy."

"I'm sorry."

"You're sorry that I grew up with a man like Nick." He leaned closer to brush a Sancerre-flavoured kiss to her lips. "I love the hope in you." And then, as if he regretted the use of the word love, he hurried on, "I mean, despite all your experiences you still want to believe people are essentially good."

Some people are. You are.

* * *

A week later, Hunter arrived back at his office to find a limousine in the middle of his drive. The second time in as many weeks, and Nick's new interest in dropping in unannounced, had the hairs on the back on Hunter's neck standing at attention.

The flashy chauffeur-driven limousine currently blocking the driveway was an irritation, Donna leaving early today for a parent-teacher chat an unfortunate coincidence. Anna due in the next half hour flashed a code red.

Hunter pushed through his door. The young staff present in the office this afternoon lacked the experience to deny Nick when he was being charming.

"Hunter." Nick looked up from his position at the architect's elbow, bent close over the woman's arm and the drawings. A look seemingly innocent of industrial espionage. "I was waiting for you."

"Nick." Hunter headed for the meeting room, leaving Nick no option but to follow. Closing the door, he hit the button to lower the privacy blinds, then faced the man who'd sired him. His father. Even thinking of the relationship flooded his mouth with bile. "Next time, make an appointment."

Nick made himself comfortable in a chair. "I'm spontaneous."

You're unwelcome. "Make an appointment."

"Talented architect you've got there. Nice designs." Nick made the outline of a female figure with his hands. "Pretty too. Handy having a bed upstairs." Nick laughed. "You learned that from me."

"Did you come for a reason?" Disgust and shame roiled in Hunter's gut.

"I'm giving you a last chance to sign a partnership deal

with me." Nick kept his eyes on the table, his fingernails drumming on the wood, while he made his threat explicit. Trying to bankrupt Raed Hariri had been a preliminary skirmish. Initiated through intermediaries, Nick could claim plausible deniability for any hostile behaviour by overzealous lawyers and accountants. Nick was shifting to open warfare. Fuck him.

"Thanks for the offer." Hunter bared his teeth. "I don't want to trade on your name."

Nick's gaze lifted, momentarily curious. "You don't use my name."

So, that was part of Nick's grievance. Stupid not to have calculated the payback for erasing his obvious connection to Nick. Although Nick had shown no interest in him until Hunter had started making a name in property development.

"Same reason," Hunter said neutrally. "Can I see you out?" Staying polite made this his victory.

Hunter accompanied Nick to the door of the top line Merc Nick favoured. Not that Hunter was making sure Nick left the premises, more settling himself before he spoke to his staff.

Standing in the middle of the open space, he didn't need to lift his voice to be heard. "I know Donna usually handles this stuff, but when she's out of the office, I rely on the rest of you to show visitors without appointments into a meeting room."

"Sorry," the young architect said.

"He was pushy," Georgie offered from her desk in the corner. "No concept of personal space." She crossed her arms challengingly. In her shapeless dungarees, Georgie wouldn't have merited a second look from Nick.

"Sounds like the green meeting room was the right place for him."

Hunter scanned the young architect's face to see if he needed to apologize for Nick's behaviour.

"He said he was your father."

Of course he did. Hunter forced himself to smile. "No exceptions. Not even for the PM." He'd made his point. The current PM had stepped down pending investigation of sexual harassment allegations. Did the PM's kids feel as tainted as Hunter did?

A bare fifteen minutes later, Anna breezed into the office, and Hunter was grateful for her punctuality. She also lit up a room, and his off-key mood shifted closer to balance. He hadn't figured out if it was her smile, the positive energy she generated, or her warmth. He'd seen her with strangers and friends. People liked her. People talked to her.

With her hand on his shoulder, she pressed a kiss to the corner of his mouth. "Hi."

"Is that gardenia?" He rested his hand on her hip, letting the scent swirl in his head.

"Some." Her grin was intimate, mischievous.

Hunter understood his earlier dread. Nick could hurt her. Despite her tough outer shell, she was marshmallow on the inside, and not immune to the kind of taunts Nick had thrown at every friend Hunter had ever had, undermining their sense of self or badmouthing them to whoever would listen. Even Anna, strong as she was, wouldn't be able to withstand constant vicious jibes and attacks on her sense of self.

"I've got a few things to finish up." *I've got to get my head straight.* "You can work in a meeting room, if you like?"

"I'm going to add to your list." She threaded her fingers through his. "Can you give me ten minutes?"

"This is a pitch?"

He allowed her to lead him to the meeting room. Was it his imagination, or did the room carry Nick's stale, old-entitled-white-man odour?

"I'm asking for your help." She sank into a chair and pulled one around to face her. "Maybe you can sit down?"

At her request, they sat, knees touching.

"I'm listening."

She patted his knee. "I know you are. I'm just marshalling my arguments."

"Sounds serious."

Had she seen Nick leaving? And hated Hunter for dealing with a man she despised?

Stop trying to second-guess yourself.

"Here goes. Niall needs a venue for his exhibition. Preferably inner-west, ware-housie, industrial. Exhibition to start in two weeks and last a fortnight. Access in the days beforehand essential. Cheap rent."

"You want me to organise the space." Relief she hadn't seen Nick was his first thought.

"Lucy found out about the exhibition and blames herself for him cancelling it."

"You blame her."

"Yeah, well. It's more complicated than that." Her exhalation lifted her fringe. "Silly idiot also refused the bequest, and he'll be homeless within weeks."

"Unravel that for me."

"Niall had a twelve-month lease on a property Cam McTavish owned. Essentially a workshop at mate's rates. Cam's will left Niall another year free, if he agreed to be a mentor in a foundation set up in Cam and his wife's name. Cam knew about the exhibition. No exhibition, so Niall thinks he's unsuitable as a mentor."

"You want me to find permanent accommodation for Niall and his workshop?"

"Not yet." She smiled as if she expected him to solve all her family's problems. He didn't do family well. Witness his failure to manage one biological parent he'd had nothing to do with for most of the past decade.

"Lucy sent him packing." Anna whooshed out the air in her lungs. "He's trying to win her over with the exhibition."

"Last time I spoke to Lucy, she'd got her shit together," Hunter said.

Lucy had been desperately poor in her first ten years, and she and her mum had often been just ahead of debt collectors. Lucy had let those memories panic her when she'd inherited her grandfather's business. Juggling huge medical bills for her grandfather's care, the setup costs for the foundation Cam wanted established in his and his wife's name, the running costs for an antiques warehouse, and the family home, with Lucy's paranoia about debt had led to some unintended outcomes.

"Whatever that means." Anna rolled her eyes.

"I told you I saw her."

"How does she feel about Niall? Does she know her demands for him to restore furniture have stuffed his chances of an exhibition? Does she care about his craft, or only her blessed antiques?" She growled in frustration.

"It was a private conversation."

"Not when we're trying to prevent two people from stuffing up their lives." She leaned back, no longer touching him. "That's when you pool information."

"Are you jealous?" *Stupid question, Hunter.*

"I don't do jealousy. You're either with me or you're not." She waved a hand. "And I'm not asking whether you screwed Lucy."

"Did you screw Niall?" He was digging himself into a deeper hole.

"Whoa. This is getting way off track." She stood and walked over to the internal windows, then turned to face him. "We've had this conversation about sex and intimacy. I need you to share your thoughts as much as you share your body."

"I'm not sure I can always do that," Hunter said.

Nick's cologne lingered, a reminder of his legacy in Hunter's life.

Why the fuck am I goading Anna? Do I want her to tell me to take a flying leap?

"Niall and I have always been friends. Never lovers." She was more generous than him, offering reassurance when he was being less than open.

"I'm sorry. I shouldn't have asked." What Hunter

shouldn't have done was start a relationship with Anna when Nick Richardson was circling closer than he had in years. "I'll talk to a few people, see what we can do."

"Thanks. Maybe you don't want me to stay tonight?"

She didn't play games. "*You're either with me or you're not,*" making her the bravest woman Hunter knew. She didn't side-step tough issues. And he loved her for that.

Holy hell.

When had that happened? And what the fuck was he going to do about it?

"I want you to stay." He pushed a hand through his hair. "I'm sorry for being an arse. I'll make a few phone calls now. Are you okay on your own for thirty minutes? An hour?"

He needed to get his shit together, so he didn't spoil what time he had with Anna.

"Come and get me when you're ready." She walked back until she was standing in front of him, then dropped her forehead to his chest. "I want to stay too."

He kissed the crown of her head, then forced himself to return to the other office. He wanted to hold her in his arms and promise he'd always keep her safe. Except, knowing Nick's history of undermining the people Hunter loved, Hunter couldn't guarantee Nick wouldn't attack her.

CHAPTER TEN

Something had changed between Hunter leaving Anna's bed this morning and now. When he left the meeting room, quietly closing the door behind him, Anna scanned the room. The blinds were closed. She'd never seen the blinds closed. Whoever Hunter had seen before she'd arrived had warranted complete privacy.

Would he tell her if she asked?

That wasn't part of their deal.

Anna wanted to howl at the moon. She wasn't content with their deal anymore. She wanted more. Which is why she'd pushed. "Look where that got you."

Pushing to her feet, she pressed the button to raise the blinds. Then she sat at the table, her laptop open in front of her, while she surreptitiously scanned the outer office. No strangers.

Had he been trying to warn her? That made no sense. He'd been the one to spell out in inky-evil words that monogamy was condition number one for him. Having met Nick Richardson, Hunter's rule made perfect sense.

Nick Richardson—a man who saturated himself in cologne.

She sniffed the air. Faint, but possible that Nick had

been here. Hunter wouldn't have invited him. An uninvited hostile guest might explain Hunter's mood.

Trust was hard when you had a cheat for a father, although Brian Ferguson had been faithful to Anna's mother for a long time now. Trust was harder still when your father betrayed you. Anna's father's scorn for Kate's writing had scarred Kate and Anna. Kate had hidden her writing and fallen prey to the first man who'd pretended to encourage her. Whereas Anna had mimicked Brian Ferguson's promiscuous behaviour for a while, a stupid plan to make him look at her.

Instead, she'd reached the blindingly obvious conclusion that a lot of men make decisions with their cocks, not their brains.

Thankfully not all men. Choosing celibacy at university meant she had friends from those days, like Niall. She'd reclaimed space to rebuild her self-respect.

Brian Ferguson was no Nick Richardson. While her father hadn't supported his daughters, he'd never set out to beggar them and their friends. In recent years, she and Kate had both negotiated peace with their parents. Having the Quinns at their back had helped with the reconciliation.

Parents were supposed to love you unconditionally, and all the research said it made it easier to love others. Not uncritically—love wasn't blind acceptance. But knowing even one person loved you gave you a stronger base than someone who'd been belittled, criticised, and emotionally abandoned at birth. Anna had always had Kate.

Hunter was always on guard.

Yet he'd listened to her trashing Nick. And told her about Nick calling him a loser, Nick being unfaithful, Nick crushing his uncle Ben, and trying to bankrupt the father of Hunter's closest friend. Hunter was decent, and a decent man would be ashamed of such a father.

Disloyalty was the word she'd settled on to describe her parents' behaviour and the behaviour of boyfriends boasting of "getting lucky." Tricking two eighteen-year-old girls into thinking they'd be safe at an upscale all-male birthday party was treachery. By her definition, Nick was endlessly treacherous to Hunter. Easy to understand Hunter's reluctance to trust.

They'd never talked about Hunter's previous girlfriends; she'd assumed he'd never allowed anyone close.

"I'm getting close," she whispered. Just as well because she was three-quarters of the way in love with him.

Anna wanted to mend the tear in their relationship before it spread. More than anything, she wanted to make tonight light and playful. Opening her laptop, she brought up her slideshow of Niall's work, adding photos from exhibitions when he was in Ireland, photos of pieces he'd given friends or family.

"Hi, I already knocked twice."

Anna lifted her head to find Hunter lounging against the door jamb. "I can get lost in my work." She smiled.

"Tell me about it, but I've done what I can for now. Ready to go?"

"Sure," she said, slipping her laptop into her bag. "I'm guessing we're alone?" She stepped up to him, wrapped a hand around his nape and drew him closer. "I'm sorry for overreacting earlier." She pressed her nose along his. "That's a traditional Maori hello, in case you didn't know."

"I watch the news." He brushed a kiss to each of her cheeks—a peace offering. "I like the way the French say hello."

Holding hands, they crossed to the stairwell leading to his apartment.

"I keep meaning to cook for you," he said as he unlocked his apartment door. "Then forget to buy ingredients or run out of time."

"That's your subconscious sabotaging you. Or protecting you. You don't really like to cook."

"Not true." He shook his head. "What about the next free Sunday we have, we meet up here or at your place and each cook one dish?"

"Just to prove we can."

"I thought a creative thinker would be a good cook." He headed straight for the kitchen, dropping his keys in a gorgeous ceramic bowl. "That if I flung open any door in my pantry you'd be able to create a masterpiece. You know, like MasterChef—the box challenge, or the fridge challenge or the leftovers challenge?"

"I used my creative thinking skills to avoid cooking until I was living alone. I can cook, but it's not rave-worthy. We could eat at that place we didn't go to the other night?"

"Good idea." He glanced over his shoulder. "I'll make a booking."

"About an hour," she said. "And not for the reason you're thinking."

"You're a mind reader now?" He grinned. "Water or wine?"

"Water. I'll have some wine with dinner." Anna held up her computer bag. "Wanna see my designs for Niall's exhibition?"

He closed the fridge door, bottle in hand. "You know, I don't think I've ever seen any of your designs."

He grabbed two crystal flutes and followed her into the living room.

"These aren't finished. I'd like your thoughts."

She dropped her coat and bags on one sofa before extracting her laptop. When he claimed the other sofa, she kicked off her boots and curled close beside him.

"Here we go." Setting the laptop on the table in front of them, she pressed start. "These are shots of some of his pieces."

He watched in silence for a few minutes, then pressed pause. "He's very good."

"I told you that." She restarted the slideshow."

"Bowls, frames, furniture, and—what's he doing with— what do you call that piece of furniture?"

"A washing table, nineteenth, maybe late eighteenth century, but I'm guessing. Niall's repaired damage to the legs. See that marble leaning against it. I'd say he's using a piece as close to the original in origin and design as he can find. A wash jug and basin sit on it."

"It's like something Casildo's grandmother might have had."

"He's planning it as a gift to Lucy, I think. There's a jug and basin belonging to Lucy's grandmother in his storage unit, and the marble comes from her grandfather's stock. Niall's stitching it all together. But he hasn't admitted that, and she hasn't seen it."

"Are you running a slideshow on his website?"

"We'll do a slideshow, but we also want to choose a venue to suit what's he got. That's why I'm showing it to you."

"Makes sense." He nodded. "Gives me a better sense of the right space. Actually, the last bloke I spoke to tonight has a warehouse. White walls, high windows, polished cement floor, but with an interesting annex-come-foyer a creative thinker could use as a wow-you-can't-afford-to-miss-this-show moment."

"Sounds fabulous. When can I see it?"

"My friend's shifting the contents out next week. A day or two for cleaning, and then you and Niall can do your worst."

"Can't we have a peek in the meantime?"

"Doubt it, but I'll send the location, dimensions, costs, etc, and some indoor shots, and you can see if Niall's happy." His watch pinged, a reminder of their dinner booking. "We'd better start moving. It's about a ten-minute walk."

They'd had their first fight and come through it. She and Hunter were building durable. That had to be good. Right?

* * *

Two weeks later, Hunter stood in the large space where Niall Quinn was staging his exhibition, absorbing the ambience. The carpenter's work was cleverly showcased—Anna was a creative thinker after all—but the William Barton didgeridoo music, the flowers, the soft-voiced conversation added up to a successful night. Listening for the underscore, he noted the looks exchanged between Anna and her sister, with Liam, even occasionally with him—the conspiracy of support. Love flowed easily through this room, and the rich generosity made him want some for himself.

The invited art critic had just trapped Anna in conversation. She glanced in Hunter's direction and winked. She'd pushed him for emotional intimacy, and in return he was surrounded by new people, good people, who accepted him because Anna had.

The Quinn-Turner family with Thompson support had achieved as much as they could tonight. From here on, it was up to Niall and Lucy. What was the takeaway? Love was bloody hard work, but it was worth it. Tonight, he'd dwell on the joy of taking Anna home to his bed.

Hunter was the first to act, but they'd all recognised from the moment Niall had made his short speech and claimed Liùsaidh McTavish, not Lucy, as his inspiration that Niall and Lucy needed time alone. Liam and Kate needed time alone. She looked like she might drop her baby in the next ten minutes. Fortunately, Mrs. Quinn Senior was staying with them. Mary—she said to call her Mary. And Hunter hoarded every moment he got with Anna, storing up memories.

He moved around the room, quietly urging people on their way, making sure the catering staff started clearing plates and packing up leftovers. He'd got a surprising kick out his part in the night, and a few more ideas about different directions for his business. Maybe, a dedicated building for emerging artists to showcase their designs.

The art critic lingered, forlorn hope in his gaze. He'd like to be escorting Anna home, but Hunter had that privilege. She never tried to make him jealous, to boost her ego through having men brawl over her. She was simply gorgeous. Hunter knew he was a lucky man. He just wasn't sure how long his luck would hold.

"Roll over." Anna had been nestled under Hunter's arm and now took charge. When he rolled onto his side, she curved her body around his and wrapped an arm across his upper chest. "I want to hold you tonight."

Hunter breathed her in, not for the first time tonight, but this scent was mellowed by the desire and tenderness of their lovemaking. There was always desire, and whatever sex they had—hard, fast, playful, slow—the end was always tenderness.

"Thanks for organising that space by the way. It's stupendous."

"His work's stupendous. Thank you for my birthday present." She'd bought Hunter one of Niall's wooden burl bowls.

She giggled sleepily. "You still haven't told me the actual date."

"It comes around every year." He hooked his free hand over her thigh to keep her close.

"I'll ask Casildo."

"Blood brother. Sworn to secrecy."

The phone had barely beeped, but she was gone in an instant"— "That's Kate"—rolling to her side of the bed to answer it. "I'll be there." She sent him a look over her shoulder before diving for her clothes. "Kate's in labour. I've gotta go. Can you call me a ride share, please?"

"Call us a ride share." He was dragging on his pants. "RPA?"

"Yes."

The car was waiting when they reached the external door.

"Royal Prince Alfred," Hunter confirmed.

"I'm part of her birth team." Anna looked calm, but

repeating stuff he already knew showed she was rattled.

He slipped his hand into hers. "You and Liam are her birth buddies."

"Her waters broke just after they got home. They had a bag packed and were all set."

"Is this your first birth?" A question Hunter already knew the answer to.

"Yes."

"I'm ahead of you. It's my third."

"You dork." She giggled, before resting her head against his upper arm. "Maternity unit," she repeated for the driver.

With little traffic on the roads, they reached the hospital quickly and found a different world. Buildings were lit up, people were moving with purpose behind windows, and ambulances were arriving at and departing from the emergency ward. Anna knew the specific building she wanted, knew the floor, and headed for the nurses' station.

"Kate and I walked the corridors as a test run," she muttered.

"I thought I heard your voice." Mrs. Quinn emerged from a waiting room near the nurses' station. "You were fast."

Anna huffed out a breath. "Where are they?"

"Second room on the left."

"Hunter—" She turned to him.

"It's okay. I'll keep Mrs. Quinn company."

"Thanks." Her lips clung to his briefly.

Everything Hunter could ever want was in that kiss. *Now you're in la-la land.* Staring at her retreating back, frustration bit at him. It was a ties-that-bind kind of moment, and the ties that bound him to Nick Richardson would, in time, suffocate her. He couldn't bear to let that happen. Hunter rubbed his hands over his face. When he looked around, Mary was watching him.

"Is there coffee in that waiting room?" he asked.

"And tea—herbal and black, chocolate, milk, and a selection of biscuits. Much better stocked than when I gave birth to the boys. We agreed you'd call me Mary at the exhibition tonight. Follow me."

"Is Niall coming, Mary?"

"Liam wanted him to have tonight with Lucy."

"You don't sound convinced."

When Hunter held up two cups, she shook her head, so he made coffee for one.

"What do you think?"

"I think he and Lucy probably took less than fifteen minutes to make up." Old-fashioned term, but Hunter didn't know Mary Quinn well.

"I hope my boys devote longer than fifteen minutes to make-up sex."

Her grin was mischievous. Like him, she thought there was a good chance they were still rolling around someone's bed cementing their union.

"It's a no-brainer." Hunter's call to Niall was picked up quickly. "RPA—maternity ward. The baby's coming." Hunter closed his phone. "Niall said '*We're on our way.*'"

"I think you and I are going to get along well, young man."

"Hey, aren't I already your favourite person for finding the exhibition space?"

"There was a lot of helping Anna in that decision," she said shrewdly. "This is about understanding and valuing family."

Well damn! He'd been thinking of himself and Cas in the same situation. A guy wanted his brother to be part of the life-changing moments.

Niall and Lucy arrived a few minutes later, hands entangled. And that made four of them taking turns pacing the small space. Hunter wasn't sure the pacing helped, but none of them could sit down for long.

"Isn't she a bit early?" Niall finally threw himself onto a chair. "Kate shouldn't have been working at the exhibition."

"In my brief experience"—Hunter made eye contact with Niall—"you don't score many brownie points by telling the Turner twins what they should do."

"When did she go into labour?" Lucy flopped beside Niall and threaded her fingers with his, offering silent reassurance.

Hunter would welcome some silent reassurance from Anna about now.

"She was having a few contractions at the exhibition. They speeded up once we got home. Her waters broke about midnight," Mary Quinn said matter-of-factly. "And, hey presto, I'm going to be a grandma."

"How long have they been in there?" Niall asked.

"About twenty minutes longer than the last time you asked."

I'm still here, Anna, still willing everything to go well.

Hunter tossed his thoughts into the ether and magically, as if she'd caught them, Anna appeared in the doorway.

"The midwife suggested I take five."

Hunter was at her side in an instant. 'Sit down," he said, guiding her to a seat. "Want chocolate?"

"Please." She patted his cheek, before turning to the others. "Kate's doing fine. So far everything is exactly as planned." She huffed out a breath. "Liam's great. We're close to full dilation. I can't think of anything else."

Hunter handed her a cup and sat beside her. "It's not up to your usual standard," he apologised. Struggling to identify the emotions washing through him, he was conscious of a wish to hold her, to lift her into his lap so he could cocoon her from all harm.

"It's great." She rested her free hand on his thigh. "Niall. I'm so pleased you're here. Liam was worried about ..." She waved her cup in a circling gesture. "Who called you?"

"Hunter."

"Good call."

Her smile smoothed out Hunter's concern—for her, for Kate and her baby.

"I can't wait to tell Kate and Liam that you and Lucy are here." She drained her cup. "Time to go." She leaned against

Hunter, touching him almost from shoulder to ankle, then was gone.

Two hours later, a smiling Anna returned to the room. "Here's Lily. Mother and daughter are doing well. Liam held it together." She held up her phone to show them the video. "Okay, Liam cried like a baby when it was all over. And that's probably it for tonight, folks."

"It's six in the morning." Niall grabbed the phone to replay the video. "She's gorgeous. Look, Mum."

Hunter opened his arms and Anna walked into them. She had a whole smorgasbord of smiles, but this one held joy and relief, exhaustion, and exhilaration and love.

"We can go now." She leaned back, her impish grin back in place. "I could sleep for a month."

"Any idea when they're going home?" Mary asked.

"Maybe later today or tomorrow. They'll let us know and work out visiting hours." Anna yawned.

"Mum, do you want us to drop you at Liam's or come home with us?" Niall asked, one arm pulling Lucy close.

"Liam's," Mary said. "And I might sleep for a month too."

Fifteen minutes later, Hunter swung Anna's legs into the car and strapped her in before sliding in the other side of the ride share.

"I forgot to ask where we're going?" Anna slumped against him.

"My place." He put his arm around her shoulder, while she dozed.

Hunter held her. He loved her. He had no doubts. And he'd do anything to keep her safe. Keep her and her family safe because that's what Anna would do.

"Where are we?" she mumbled.

"My place." Placing his hands behind her knees, he lifted her into his arms.

"I forgot." She yawned widely. "You don't need to carry me up the stairs."

"You'd prefer a fireman's lift?" He swung her in a half

loop.

"No," she gurgled, settling back against his chest. "Nice."

The bedroom light, which they'd forgotten in their rush to leave, acted as a guide through the dark apartment. The bed looked like a bordello after an orgy, bedding and pillows strewn everywhere. He lowered her gently to the mattress.

"I'm going to undress you."

"I won't enjoy that as much as I should." She spoke with her eyes closed.

Shoes first, then her trousers, before he pulled her into his body to undo her bra. He hauled the bra and shirt off in a single move, then pulled a clean T-shirt over her head. "Say goodnight, Anna."

"Goodnight, Anna." Her giggle was ghost-like. "Thanks for being there."

"No problem." He pressed a kiss to her forehead before drawing the doona around her. *I love you.*

"Need to ring Antonio."

"I'll call Antonio."

He tucked her in and pulled the drapes closed before heading downstairs. She was where she was meant to be, and he didn't know how soon before he had to send her away.

CHAPTER ELEVEN

Even after six weeks together, and three weeks since Lily's birth, these moments, when Anna was curled into Hunter's side, after they'd made love, and when contentment seeped into her soul, were amongst her favourites of the day. Coming home to Hunter was as natural as breathing.

"I had an idea."

"You're always having ideas." He kissed the top of her head.

"Antonio has been hinting that he'd like to see how the centre is coming along." Anna traced circles around Hunter's bare nipple with her index finger. "Especially since I brought some of our mums through."

"Makes sense." He caught her wrist. "I won't be able to keep talking, much less thinking, if you keep doing that."

"I'll agree to a temporary pause."

Anna propped herself up. She wanted to see his face for her next suggestion. Family mattered to Hunter. Witness his call to Niall from the hospital, his cosseting of Anna after Lily was born. Yet, he'd only introduced her to one member of his family—Maha. Casildo didn't count because Anna already knew him. Maybe Donna counted, but Hunter's caution when Anna had thrown him into the middle of her extended family was a niggle.

"Tuesday. How about Tuesday? I'll ask him and Maha."

"Why Maha?"

"Because he's entrusting his staff's children to Maha as director at the centre." And Anna itched to get to know Maha better, to see how Maha interacted with Hunter.

"Aren't you delegated to be liaison?" Not a no, but a hesitation, and Anna had hoped they'd moved past awkward pauses.

"Antonio's interested."

"I'll have to check with Maha. See what her schedule's like." A frown had formed between his brows. "Does Antonio know anything about childcare?"

Anna smoothed his furrowed brow with her fingers. "His kids are teenagers now, but he was widowed when they were very young. He's familiar with juggling kids, work, life and grief, which is why he was so easy to convince on this."

"I didn't know that."

"He doesn't talk about it much, although the kids are regular visitors at the office."

"Okay. I'll talk to Maha. Fix a date." He threaded his fingers through her hair, part caress, part pushing it away from her face. "Any more ideas, or can you start touching me again now?"

"I have ideas about touching you."

He settled more comfortably. "Show me."

A few days later, Anna and Antonio walked the short distance from Changing Minds headquarters to The Hariri building, a building whose name, Anna now knew, would never change. For Hunter, the Hariris were family.

"Thanks for the invitation, Anna. I wasn't expecting it," Antonio said.

"You were sweating on it." She glanced sideways at him. "And you dropped enough hints."

"Did I?" He grinned. "Didn't know I was so obvious."

"If I haven't already told you, I respect and admire you as a person, a boss, and a friend, and I simply love working for you."

"Nice to hear. And it goes both ways. You'd hardly joined the company when I dumped a load on you. Beth was dying. The boys were devastated."

"It was a terrible time."

Anna had acted as a personal assistant and office conductor for a time, coordinating projects and timelines, mothering the teams that needed it, challenging the ones that didn't. Antonio had had a good staff even then. It was much bigger now.

"Your support probably saved the business from going under."

"Nice to hear." She elbowed him in the ribs. "Even if it's an exaggeration. Everyone pulled their weight."

"So, why now, Anna? Why do you want me to meet Maha Hariri? And I've been meaning to ask, is she related to the Raed Hariri, who previously owned the building?"

"Damn. Should have guessed your sharp eye for detail would catch me out." She linked arms with him. "She's Raed Hariri's daughter and Casildo Hariri's sister."

"Didn't twig to that one. What's the deal?"

"We're here." Anna stopped in front of the building. "I'll fill you in later. But for now, I'm using you for cover. Previously, I met Maha at her other centre. Our conversations were strictly business. I want to get to know Maha better."

"You mean pump her for info about Hunter?"

"I mean bring her into our world a little."

"Good luck with that. From my research on Hunter, his close associates are tight as clams." He waited for the front doors to slide open. "After you."

"It'll take a few minutes. I need to text Hunter so he can send the lift designated for construction activity."

"Makes sense. I like a man who puts safety first."

"Right on time," Hunter said when they stepped out of the elevator. "Maha beat you by a few minutes. She's already donned safety gear and gone through."

"Thanks for the invite, Hunter." Antonio stuck out a hand in greeting. "I'm looking forward to seeing where Anna spends all her spare time."

"Not all," she protested.

"She haunts the place." Hunter handed her the safety helmet reserved especially for her, before turning to fit out Antonio. He led them through a door plastered with safety and construction warnings, and shouted, "Maha. Coming, ready or not."

Maha popped her head around a doorway. "What happened to decorum, Hunt? If you don't behave, I'll tell them stories of your dissolute youth."

Maha wore the dark trousers that were the uniform at her existing centre, and the comfortable shoes Anna had noticed on her visit, but she'd changed the colourful uniform T-shirt for a blouse in crimson tones that flattered her olive skin. The fluorescent yellow safety jacket did nothing to hide her generous curves.

"Nothing to tell." Hunter shrugged.

"You knew him as a kid?" Antonio looked from one to the other. Anna had given him the relationship, not the history.

"You've blown it now," Hunter muttered. "Antonio will think I've hired you because you're family, not because you're the most suitable candidate."

"I'm the most suitable candidate." Maha turned a full-wattage smile on Antonio and stuck out a hand. "Hi, I'm Maha Hariri. I understand the contract is signed, so assume you did due diligence. This is just putting faces to names."

"It is," Antonio agreed. "It's also my first visit."

"Mine too. Hunt talks to me, but he's been keeping this place a surprise until now. Let's explore together." Maha turned to Hunter. "Antonio and I can handle this on our own. I promise not to stick metal objects into power points or throw anything off the rooftop."

"Are you sure you don't need me? I'm a regular visitor. I might be able to answer some questions," Anna offered.

Maha's arched eyebrows rose, and Anna was reminded of Casildo. Same dark hair, same almond-shaped hazel eyes, same straight nose. The features looked softer on Maha. "And here I thought you were going to pump me about Hunt." Maha sent Antonio a sideways look, half-conspiratorial.

"She was," Antonio agreed.

"I heard that," Anna said.

"You were meant to." Maha laughed, her eyes sparkling with mischief. "Don't get me wrong. I like you. A lot."

"You promised to behave, Maha." Hunter's warning sounded half-hearted.

"That's exactly what I'm doing. Follow me, Antonio. If we have questions, we'll note them down and ask when we get back."

Antonio winked at Anna before following Maha with a docility none of his employees would believe.

"Did you really plan to pump Maha about me?" Hunter leaned against a wall.

"She's family. You've met my family."

"I have. Lovely people every one. They haven't told me any of your secrets, Anna. Nor would they. They're all letting us fumble along and find our own feet."

"You're right." Anna reached up to plant a kiss at the side of his mouth. "But she confirmed something. She's loyal. To the bone. You inspire loyalty in your friends and in your employees. That's a big recommendation."

"I'm no saint, Anna." His brow puckered, revealing yet again his caution.

"I'm not looking for a saint." She'd found what she was looking for: a man who valued loyalty, who inspired loyalty, who made love to her as if she was the sun, the moon and the stars. She just had to convince him they could build a future together.

* * *

Two days later, Hunter sat alone in his office. Not yet five o'clock and he'd sent his team home. Donna had given him a bemused look, but had accepted his decision when he escorted her to the door. Now he slid the naked photos of a young Anna back into the envelope, leaned back in his chair and closed his eyes.

"You bastard!" he muttered, but he'd made the mistake, pushing Nick to the back of his mind in the weeks since Lily's birth. Anna adored Lily.

"Fucking bastard." Hunter pushed out of his chair, paced to the window, to the door, raised a hand, found it was a fist and hauled back to smash it into the wall. Stopping short of the wall, he dropped his forehead against it.

Hunter lived with the knowledge Nick could summon photos of Hunter's battered ex-girlfriend Gina from the internet sewer at will. Now Nick was threatening to broadcast naked photos of Anna. If Nick followed through on this threat, Anna would live in the same state of uncertainty as Hunter did.

Hunter's pervert of a father dirtied everything he touched. Now the manipulative bastard was trying to weaponize Anna's innocent adolescent rebellion. Anna was all that mattered, her peace of mind, her physical safety, and Hunter would sell his soul to prevent sleazy photos of Anna being splashed across social media.

New South Wales had laws about revenge porn. He'd checked after the fiasco with Gina, but Gina had uploaded photos she'd taken herself. The cops were obliged to pursue people who recorded and distributed original and altered images without the consent of the person in the image. It took time to lay charges. A successful prosecution was rare, and by that time the damage was done.

Snatching up the envelope, Hunter upended it, then peered inside. A white card was wedged in the bottom inside corner. Identification? Not that he needed confirmation to know the author of this threat. Still, he read the card and gagged.

"I don't believe it." Hunter flung the card across the room. "You bastard! You bastard! This time I'll kill you." A sob caught in the back of his throat. Nick Richardson's stories always held a fragment of truth.

Nick's note said he'd had his hands on Anna. More than his hands!

Reeling, Hunter grabbed the note and photos, jamming them back into the envelope, before slumping into his chair. The express post envelope sat in the middle of his desk, innocuous looking considering it had blown Hunter's life apart.

Think. Don't feel. It hurts too much.

But he was numb, unable to act.

Seconds, minutes, a lifetime later, Hunter pushed himself upright.

Nick had the kind of twisted mind that grew mentally sleek and fat on the despair of his victims, and he'd always demanded a particular sort of slavish obedience from his son.

Never going to happen, but Hunter needed to regroup. Fast. Work out why Nick hadn't lost interest in him or banished him as he had so many times before. More importantly, he had to work out how to keep Anna safe.

Stop seeing her?

That was one option. He'd always told himself it was the only option long term.

He scrubbed his hands over his face.

Nick's goal with every girl or woman Hunter had dated was to imply Hunter was second best. Hunter had let Nick count his separation from Gina as a victory because it meant Nick lost interest in Gina. Nick didn't need to know Hunter had been about to break up with Gina anyway.

Anna is not Gina.

Anna will never be like Gina.

Thank all the gods in the universe Anna had said she'd be out of town at a work function tonight.

Get your head together, Thompson. Make a frigging plan.

Would ending their relationship be better for Anna? The million-dollar question he'd known the answer to from the beginning.

* * *

The empty parking at five o'clock lot gave Hunter's offices a desolate feel. Anna pushed the front door open and shivered. At first glance, the office was empty. Hoisting her laptop bag with its incriminating evidence over her shoulder, she took a few steps into the office. Eerie, to find it deserted so early in the evening. Her pulse picked up, a sense of foreboding roiling her stomach.

On her regular cruise past the childcare centre yesterday, she'd assumed the crew were needed on another job. Today, she could see no work had been done in days. The final fit outs for the centre should be complete to meet their deadlines for opening. Had Hunter overcommitted staff and money? Had she pushed too hard for her starting date? He hadn't told her.

Although something more poisonous had driven her here.

"Hunter," she called, taking a few tentative steps.

"Back here." He moved into the doorway of the small office at the back, the one he'd claimed as his, yet rarely used. Tonight he'd drawn the blinds on the small internal space. Hiding?

Her sense of foreboding grew stronger. Work on the centre was at a standstill, and she'd received an express delivery envelope.

She crossed the room toward him, each step making her heart pound harder in her chest. "What's wrong?" She lifted a hand to touch his face.

"Nothing." He twisted away, and her hand dropped. "I

thought you had a work function."

"I cancelled." She wasn't sure he heard her.

"Sit down," he growled.

"I don't take orders from my lover." Instinct to throw up her barricades in response to his, but his voice was dead, coming at her from a distance, leaving her even more confused.

"Suit yourself." He shrugged, resuming his seat behind the desk, shuffling papers and pushing a large express post envelope to the bottom of the pile.

"I have a few things on my mind, but let's start with this." Dragging a chair to the front of the desk, Anna set her laptop bag in front of her, unzipped it, and extracted a large envelope. "I got these photos today."

At work, not home—and that had to count for something—the sender didn't know her address. She upended the envelope. The large glossy photos spilled across the table, one sliding past him and onto the floor. The photos showed a woman, mid-twenties, badly battered. Her face was covered in bruises, her shirt half-ripped off her shoulder showed more. The shots were taken from several angles.

He picked the escapee up from the floor, studying it for a few moments in silence.

"Your ex-girlfriend?" Anna asked, when the silence had grown painful.

"Yeah. And I beat her up one night when she pissed me off."

"That's what the message said." Anna put her elbows on the desk and bent her head, splaying her fingers into her scalp. At his continued silence, she looked up, linked her fingers to create a bridge, and rested her chin on it. "The message also made clear the photos were especially for me. Digital but published previously by the victim."

"I've got nothing to say."

Anna licked her dry-with-fear lips, while scanning his face for clues. "Talk to me."

He'd closed down. Locked her out, and his unyielding expression terrified her. Forget being lovers, he was putting their friendship on the line as well.

Anna picked up another photo, a closeup of ugly bruises on the woman's cheek. When she'd seen that one, she'd gagged, nearly losing her lunch. She slid it across the table.

"You're going to have to do better than that."

"I don't have to explain myself to you." Hunter's face was grim, his eyes bleak and implacable.

"No, you don't."

She scooped up the photos, tucked them back into the envelope, then back into her bag. Pushing to her feet took every ounce of energy and courage she could muster.

"Are you leaving?"

"Yeah." She gave him back his own monosyllable. Crazy moment to realise she loved him. How stupid was she?

"Do you think I did that?" He looked at her, then glanced away as if wanting to withdraw the question.

"What I think now isn't relevant." She hadn't believed—didn't believe—he'd hit a woman, but he'd trashed the friendship they'd created. "Remember rule number one, talk to me. If you won't talk to me, won't explain the photos, won't honestly tell me what you're thinking and feeling, we have nothing." Grabbing her bag, she remembered her other concern. "Have you stopped work on the childcare centre because of me, us?"

He stood to eyeball her. "I don't operate like that."

"You want me to take your word for that?" Except she did. Even with evidence of his lack of trust in her. "Goodbye."

She turned and walked away, keeping her back ramrod straight. The tears running down her cheeks were because she was an idiot.

* * *

Hunter waited until he heard the front door close. She

hadn't slammed it, but the soft snick of the lock hit like a bunched fist. He'd had a split second to adjust when she arrived, to figure out Nick's attack was a pincer move. Multiple scenarios and conversations flashed through his head in seconds. The result hadn't changed. So, he hadn't explicitly denied that he was responsible for Gina's bruises, because in a cack-handed way, he was—for not ending his relationship with Gina sooner, for not warning Gina about Nick.

Moving the people he cared about out of harm's way, out of Nick's way, had become Hunter's modus operandi. Tonight, it seemed like moving deckchairs on the *Titanic*. Fucking useless. He hadn't protected Anna. She had removed herself.

Anna's quiet exit when he'd refused to talk spoke of devastation rather than the rage he'd hoped to inspire. He'd hoped she'd shout, stamp her foot, and have his tantrum for him. Call him out for his cowardice in not telling her the truth.

He pinched the bridge of his nose. He had a killer of a headache coming.

She didn't know what Nick could do to her. What Nick's note had threatened to do to her.

God—he loved her loyalty and wanted it for himself.

Still, he'd used bloody-minded silence to kick her out.

Slowly, Hunter reopened his own envelope, spilling the contents across the table.

Anna was naked, as she'd told him weeks ago. She hadn't mentioned the wig was strawberry blonde, a mass of curls, and a bad impersonation of Marilyn Monroe. The fake cake was behind Anna, her arms were upraised, her body elongated, intended to be titillating. Holding the photo, he was reminded of Nick's parties from Hunter's teenage years. He could almost smell the fried finger food, spilled beer, and the cloud of alcoholic spirits signalling a crowd already out of control. Hunter had pushed those memories deep, but maybe he could find a weapon there, if he focused.

He wished he had the balls to burn them. He wasn't prepared to gamble on Anna's privacy, her reputation, her employment—hell, even her physical well-being could be under threat if a troll decided to track her. His set of photos and the note were concrete evidence of Nick's threat.

Pushing the shots back into the envelope, his attention snagged on her right arm. The photo had been cropped to cut off her right hand and wrist. Looking more closely, he could see a fragment of the charm bracelet dangling below where her hand should be.

Nick had claimed he'd recognised the bracelet. Anna didn't normally wear bracelets, said they interfered with her work. But she'd worn the charm bracelet the night of Marygai's party. Strange that it was almost deleted from the shot if Nick was relying on it for his evidence. The scar was more damaging. She hadn't disguised it. Anna had said she and a friend burst from the cake. Had they been holding hands? Could her friend be wearing the bracelet? He'd never get the chance to ask now.

"Doesn't matter," he muttered.

Except it did. He back-handed the papers off his desk, then crawled around the floor picking them up. Nick's note had spelled it out, he'd put his disgusting hands on Anna.

Hunter wanted to throw things, smash things, get drunk. Instead, tears stung his eyes.

Anna owned the bracelet, making the threat to her real. Digital images could be broadcast in an instant, and Anna's reputation would be trashed. Aside from the cops, getting the social media juggernauts to remove images was a near impossibility. Getting justice from them was even harder.

Locking the front door, he climbed to his apartment. The safest place for the photos was his safe. He wouldn't let Nick Richardson's latest attack slide, but it would take time to work out his defence. Time for Anna to move from devastation to rage to never wanting to see him again.

CHAPTER TWELVE

Anna found her way home on remote. One minute she was staring blindly where she knew a park should be, the next she was running until her breath sobbed in her lungs and she could run no further. Bent double, one hand on her knee, her other clasped around her bag so tightly her knuckles bled white, she pressed buttons on her phone. When the ride share arrived, she was upright, dark glasses jammed on her nose.

The journey passed in a blur.

Setting her bag down in the hall, she wandered into her kitchen. She filled the kettle, turned it on, opened the fridge door, then closed it.

Can I come over? she texted her sister.

Of course, came the immediate reply.

Can I stay tonight? Within seconds, her sister's ringtone bounced around the room.

"Do you want me to come and get you?"

"I'll call a ride share." Anna swallowed a sob.

"We'll be here."

I will not blubber in front of a ride share driver, even if he'll never see me again.

Anna knuckled tears from her eyes. Hunter wasn't

worth—hell, no man was worth her tears.

Who was she kidding? She and Hunter had something special, and he'd trashed it.

She knocked on her sister's door, and her tears started all by themselves.

The door opened, and Kate opened her arms. Anna dropped her overnight bag to step into her sister's embrace.

"I'm so glad I can properly hug you again. How the hell did you and Liam cuddle when you were the size of a baby whale?"

"We had our ways. Do you want chocolate?"

"Buckets of it."

Her sister led her down the hall and into their kitchen. "Sit down, Anna."

Parking her suitcase near the door, Anna propped her laptop bag on top. She sagged onto a chair, crossed her arms on the table, and rested her head on them. Her mind was a fog of confusion. Nothing made sense, and she didn't know how to make it make sense. Leaving Hunter had severed her connection to the world in some significant sense. She was floating untethered.

"Where's Lily?"

"She's asleep. And you don't have my permission to wake her up."

"I don't want her to see me crying."

"What happened?" Her sister set a mug of hot chocolate at her elbow.

Anna lifted her head. "You made me the deluxe."

"You look like you need pampering." Whereas, her sister stuck strictly to her mummy diet and sipped her herbal tea. Three ginger by the delicate aroma.

"He wouldn't talk to me."

"He being Hunter? What wouldn't he talk to you about?"

"Anything." And Anna had thought they were well beyond that.

"Shit. Is he crazy? Does he want you to end the

relationship?"

"You swore. I love you." Anna sniffed at her mug, inhaling the comfort of her sister's calm presence, then licked chocolate flakes off the frothy topping. "Hunter's not crazy. He keeps promises to other people's children. He works for his friends for free. He keeps his employees for years. He's a kind, decent man." Her chest was bursting with the need to defend him.

"But he wasn't kind and decent today," Kate said.

"It was terrifying in a way." Anna recalled the weirdness of seeing his usually bustling premises silent. "His office was empty. All the staff gone. At first, I thought something terrible had happened to the business."

"What's the worst thing that could happen to the business?"

"Financially, I would have said nothing. The risks he takes are calculated. You heard him at dinner. He's given Lucy the same advice."

"I've only met him a few times, but I wouldn't have put money at the top of his list of worries or priorities."

"His staff. He'd worry about them. The people he calls family." She blew her nose and blotted her eyes. She'd thought she'd joined that select group.

"Then ask yourself why, Anna." Kate's head turned at the sound of the front door opening.

"You told Liam," Anna accused.

"She told me I was needed at home." Liam walked through the door, stopping first to press a kiss to Kate's head, before coming around to Anna's side of the table, crouching beside her. "I want to help too."

"You can get drunk with me." Anna gestured to her sister's herbal tea. "Your lactating wife's off alcohol for the duration."

"Works for me. Beer or whiskey?" He stood. "From the pile of abandoned tissues, I reckon whiskey's the go. And a change of scene. Let's move this to the living room."

"It's my turn to cook." Kate offered the non sequitur

while rising to collect glasses and a jug of water. "I'll order Thai." Kate hated cooking more than Anna did.

"I heard that," he called.

Anna rummaged in her bag for more tissues and found the envelope.

"What's that?" Kate asked.

"Exhibit A," Anna replied, carrying it with her to the living room. "I got it at work earlier today. No sender identified. Hunter wouldn't discuss the contents."

"Did you get witnesses when you opened it earlier?"

Anna rolled her eyes. "You spend too much time with the lawyer."

Her sister knew Anna hated to lose control. Knew asking Liam to come home would comfort her, calm her, and allow her to keep some pride. She didn't care much about pride anymore. Taking the corner of the sofa, she kicked off her boots and curled her feet beneath her. She needed this. To be in a different place, to have to talk about different topics. Kate had helped her pick up the pieces after Helen's death.

In a different way, losing Hunter was worse.

She swallowed a sob.

"Kate just said come home." Liam poured a few fingers of fine Scottish whiskey into two heavy crystal tumblers and set one on a small table beside Anna. "Is there anything I need to know?"

"I dumped Hunter, or he dumped me."

"Why?"

"Jees, if I get any more rational questions, I'll smash something."

"Not our wedding present whiskey glasses, please. Your mother would notice."

Liam sipped his whiskey, and in gratitude for his solidarity, Anna sipped hers.

"Have a look." Anna nudged the envelope across the table with her finger.

"Is Hunter capable of doing that to a woman?" Her sister glanced briefly at the first photo, winced, then focused on Anna.

"No."

Anna would bet her life on it. He couldn't knowingly hurt another person like that. She'd had his hands on her body. Seen him with children and vulnerable work-experience teenagers. Seen him in unguarded moments and moments when he hadn't known she'd been watching. Doing that to a woman wasn't something you could hide.

"The note says he is." Liam used a pen to move the note to one side.

"I know."

"Did Hunter say anything?" Liam used the same pen to push the photos into some sort of order.

"He said he didn't have to explain himself to me."

"Any idea who might have sent them?" Liam was astute.

"I'd decided it was his father—Nick Richardson. I wanted to talk the theory over with Hunter, but he didn't give me a chance."

"Why Nick?" Kate prodded.

"Because he can't bear for Hunter to be more successful than he is. He's tried bribery and threats to get Hunter to join forces. Hunter refused. The only reason Hunter bought the building my childcare centre is in is because Nick—Hunter never calls him his father—was mounting a hostile takeover to cripple Raed Hariri financially."

"Again, I ask why?" Liam smiled.

"Raed was more father to Hunter than Nick Richardson. Hunter was brought up by the Hariris and his maternal uncle and aunt."

"Hunter didn't take a penny of his mother's money," Liam said.

Liam's unrelated announcement had Anna jerking upright, her mind whirling.

"How the hell do you know that?" Anna set down her drink, instantly protective of Hunter's privacy. "And why the hell do you know that? Have you been snooping on Hunter?"

"For the love of Mary and Joseph"—Liam held up a hand—"I'm the messenger here. Niall has contacts who have contacts, and after Hunter helped stage Niall's exhibition, someone told Niall the story. According to Niall, the bloke figured Niall was part of Hunter's secret magic circle. Apparently, he helps a lot of people."

"The inheritance funded his lucky break in property development, according to some pundits," Anna said, recalling Bizgos, who attacked Hunter with surprising regularity.

"No talent. Mummy's money enabled him to go head-to-head with his father."

"He got his break when his uncle took him along on jobs and cut him into some profits." Liam waited.

"He told me about his uncle. They split profits on small renovations." Anna punched her brother-in-law's upper arm. "Stop looking so bloody smug and all prosecutor-making-his-final-arguments-to-the-court. This is not a bloody play or a novel where you do the big reveal at the end."

"Hunter used his inheritance so his uncle and aunt could establish a charity for the families of construction workers killed on the job. Often there's not enough insurance, or it won't cover extras for the kids' education." Liam sat back and steepled his hands over his mouth—claiming silence now when he must have cross-examined Niall at length to get the information he had.

"You said 'secret magic circle.' Is there any public record of Hunter's involvement with the charity?"

Anna doubted it was common knowledge in the industry. Nick had informers there too. She remembered the old brickie at the hospital. Hunter had given him a card for a charity.

"Are you asking me to make inquiries?" Liam raised an eyebrow.

"To quote a lawyer friend of mine—*for the love of Mary*, no. Nick targeted Raed Hariri for being a father figure to

Hunter, and Nick's bankrupted Ben Thompson in the past. I don't like to think what he'd do to Ben if he discovered Hunter gave Ben his inheritance."

"Good enough reason to keep Hunter's connection to the charity quiet," Kate said.

"Maybe I should have been calling him Samwise." Anna had missed so many details.

"Samwise Gamgee—Lord of the Rings—loyalty-is-my-middle-name Samwise? Who are you talking about?" Liam swallowed a mouthful of his whiskey.

"H. S. Thompson. The S is for Samuel. I've been calling him Sam-I-Am."

"Probably more all-purpose than stud or hunk." Kate battered her eyelashes.

"Why are you telling me about the charity?" Anna was struggling to make the facts connect. Why wouldn't Hunter mention it?"

"Because I'm guessing he hasn't, and it's a reason for Nick to target Hunter."

"He keeps secrets." All the fight left Anna. "I understand privacy. I understand embarrassment and not wanting the mistakes you made as an adolescent or twenty-something to condemn you all the days of your life. He keeps good things quiet. That doesn't make sense. And he uses his secrets as weapons to keep people out. To keep me out." Self-preservation had taught him to keep people at a distance. She didn't like those rules applied to herself.

"You're closer than most," said Liam, a startling truth. "He came to dinner with us. He's helped Niall and Lucy." His voice softened. "He was with us when Lily was born. Did he drop you at home afterwards?"

"No." She frowned. Hunter had cosseted her.

"Is Nick Richardson the sort of man who carries out his threats?" Liam was relentless in this mood.

Anna flinched.

"I'll take that as a yes," Liam said. "Here's my take. These photos look like police or hospital shots."

"You're not comforting me." Anna took another smaller sip of her whiskey while she added that puzzle piece to the jigsaw in her head.

"Look at them the way I've arranged them. In my early days when I was an environmental defender, occasionally I found myself representing protestors. Unfortunately, I saw a few too many photos of assault injuries, and the occasional car accident. There's a strong possibility those bruises there"—he pointed—"are the result of a seat belt biting into her."

"Can we check?"

"I'll get on to it tomorrow. Now, tell me about the visit starting from the beginning."

"When I arrived at five, the place was weirdly quiet." Anna spoke slowly, summoning an image of Hunter's HQ. "No vehicles parked outside. No staff. He came out of his office, and we went back there. The blinds were shut. I thought something was wrong, and then he started acting oddly—"

"Did you ask about the missing staff?"

"No, although at the end I asked if delaying work on the centre was some sort of hit at me." Anna replayed that bit of the conversation in her head. "He seemed more concerned that I'd think he'd renege on the centre than about the photos. What's that about?"

"Not sure." Her brother-in-law added the detail to the huge calculator he carried in his head "So, you showed him the photos of his battered ex-girlfriend. Anything else?"

"He shuffled some papers, tucked the envelope that had been on top underneath." She frowned in remembrance. "The envelope was express delivery. Same size as mine."

"Could Nick have compromising photos of you?"

"Where would he get them?" Anna stared at her sister. "Neither of us has shared even a vaguely compromising photo in the last decade."

"Photos can be doctored," Liam reminded them. "Although there are more publicly available tools to check whether a photo's been tampered with these days, and you can pay for a proper analysis."

"OMG!" Anna sat upright. "The most embarrassing moment of my life was that party. Nick Richardson was there."

"You said there were no photos." Kate studied her.

"Yeah, and the agreement said no sex, but they honoured that rule. Like hell!" Anna scanned her memory, going over her movements at the party. "Nick, or someone with him, must have taken photos of me when I bounced out of his birthday cake." She curled her hand into a fist. "But that's ridiculous. I was wearing a pretty impenetrable disguise."

"You were naked," Kate said meaningfully. "Did you put makeup over your scar?"

"What scar, and why is it important?" Liam leaned forward in his chair.

"Upper thigh, a crescent moon. That night was the zenith of my teenage rebellion. Makeup, wig—Dad's new play was premiering in Sydney. One of the makeup crew was happy to give me pointers on how to distract. No one would recognise me except for the scar. Don't look at me like that, Maybelline."

"Like what?" Kate held up innocent hands.

"Like you were responsible for me being pissed off with Dad."

"Dad was unshockable." Kate repeated an old argument. "Thought your anarchy reflected well on him."

"You were eighteen. You're thirty-two this year." Liam was trying to make some sort of point.

"I'm younger than her." Anna jutted her chin in her sister's direction.

"Fourteen years, Anna." Liam waved his hand to attract her attention. "We're talking before any of the social media behemoths became big. Before wide-scale use of mobile phones for sharing videos and dick and tit pics. Before ready access to AI tools. These days people bent on revenge steal real photos and plaster them on naked bodies, even naked bodies having sex, to trash someone's reputation. It's a crime, but you've got to get the police to take notice and provide evidence the photo was taken and/or distributed without consent. Even if you prove that, it's almost impossible to get the stuff taken off the internet."

"Nick could use the photos to target me, to trash my reputation." The idea made terrible sense to Anna.

"It's plausible," Kate said.

"Hunter was lying to me to protect me." It was the sort of thing Hunter would do—send Anna out of harm's way. "The idiot."

"Again, plausible. Does Hunter know about the party?"

"I told him about it the first time I saw Nick Richardson. Told him what I did and gave him a chance to walk away early."

"Even though all men are superheroes, sometimes we have doubts. And sometimes we step away from the woman we love because of some half-arsed concept of chivalry."

"Chivalry and stubbornness don't leave much room to manoeuvre." Anna sighed, because she was sure that's why Hunter hadn't called.

"Bottom line. Would Hunter cut you off to protect you?" Liam asked.

"Yes, but for me, locking me out is also a kind of betrayal." Her eyes were starting to sting again. "We're better together. Like you and Kate. If he can't see that, we have nothing."

"Does Hunter know about Helen?" Kate sipped her tea like a woman who'd found the Holy Grail.

CHAPTER THIRTEEN

"This is a friendly visit." Niall's hands were raised in surrender.

"Phone dead?" Hunter leaned against the door jamb. He guessed Anna had provided the detail he lived above the office, with a hard-to-find entrance at the side of the building. She'd been gone seventy-two hours, but who was counting?

"How'd you guess?"

"Come in."

His guest surveyed the comfortable living arrangement. "Nice. You've got one of my bowls."

Niall Quinn made straight for the sideboard under the window. His bowl formed from the burl of a tree was centred, framed by the park's huge figs visible through the picture window. The bowl's multiple brown shades were accentuated by the pile of oranges and lemons sitting in it.

"Anna gave it to me for my birthday."

"She didn't mention it was for your birthday." Niall swung around.

So, Niall had known Hunter had one of his bowls, and like any artist, was pleased at its prominent position.

"It wasn't. It was her way of getting me to tell her when

my birthday was." The memory of her teasing the date from him held a sad sweetness.

"She's honestly devious or deviously honest. Not sure of the right description except honest and loyal are her defining character traits."

"Ouch." Hunter gestured toward a sofa. "You did say friendly?"

"Whisht lad, I'm still smiling." Niall exaggerated the Irish lilt he'd picked up while undertaking an apprenticeship of sorts with a well-respected cabinet-maker in Ireland.

"Beer."

"Please." Niall settled in a corner of the sofa.

Hunter snagged two bottles of Peroni from the fridge, topped them, then handed one to the quiet carpenter before taking the opposite sofa.

"Thanks again for providing the venue for my exhibition." Niall held the bottle loosely by the neck, seemingly relaxed.

"A friend had an empty warehouse, you needed a space. It was a commercial transaction." Hunter swallowed a mouthful of beer.

"I'd run out of options, professionally and personally, and you gave me a way out." In his understated, yet direct way, Niall was giving him an opening. "Lucy loves me."

"It's not that simple."

Niall leaned forward, setting his bottle on the coffee table. "If I can help, I will."

Hunter slid down on his sofa, his head falling back. The ceiling offered the same inspiration it had every night since Anna had left. Zero. He closed his eyes.

"If you repeat a word of what I'm saying, I'll call you a liar." Niall's voice dropped to a whisper, mesmerising with its capacity to reel Hunter in. "You know I didn't tell Lucy I was planning an exhibition of my work. She only found out when I cancelled. What you don't know is that we each kept secrets. I won't speak for her, but I was ashamed of things I'd done in my life, felt I didn't deserve her. I let the shame drive my choices, instead of hope." He slapped a hand on the table. "And feck, that has to be one of the soppiest things I've ever said. What's your problem?"

Hunter lowered his head and met Niall's gaze. "Perhaps I don't love her."

"If there was a vengeful god you'd be vaporised by now."

"Let's say it's in her best interests to steer clear of me."

"Why?"

"I carry baggage."

"There's not a soul born who doesn't collect baggage by the time they're thirty-four."

"Thirty-five." Hunter raised his bottle to him and downed a mouthful.

"What about that baloney you spouted at Kate and Liam's place? Only risking what you're prepared to lose? Knowing what you're prepared to lose? I thought you had all the odds figured."

"I gambled, and I lost." Hunter had misjudged the situation. Knowing Anna wouldn't give Nick the time of day, Hunter had underestimated Nick's ability to attack Hunter through Anna.

"Loving Anna isn't a game." Niall exploded. "You're not making sense."

"Some British lord once said 'Gambling is when you bet something you can't afford to lose.' I thought loving Anna was no one's business but mine and hers. I was wrong."

"You're wrong now," Niall insisted. "There's another reason I'm here."

"I'll fight you, if you're here to take your bowl back."

"You helped me. Anna says there's some problem at the centre. You're down to fit-out, some customised bits and pieces. I can help. I've got friends who can give you a few days to catch up."

Hunter stared at him. "You mean that."

"Help one member of the Quinn family and you get the lot of us. Anna didn't know if it was a supply chain issue, a labour shortage, or sabotage." The carpenter let his last word hang in the air.

"Yeah, it's like that when everything goes pear-shaped. Conspiracy is appealing." Hunter was still checking the details of the glitch in his order, a transposing of dates on the computer so the delivery was ten days late. A regular supplier, who was endlessly apologetic. "From what I can tell, it was cock-up, rather than conspiracy."

"Good to know." Niall drained his beer and stood. "People in the building game talk to me. I'm not competition, but might have ideas."

"Go on."

"Nick Richardson is late on payments to his contractors. He's putting them off with bullshit for the most part, but hinting he's about to get an influx of cash. Know anything about that?"

"He'd like me to become his junior partner."

"What would you like?"

"To see someone take him down."

"Not you?"

"I'm working on it." Hunter flashed his teeth. "I appreciate the offer of help and the information." He appreciated the generosity behind Niall's presence and knew Anna was part of it. "How's Anna?"

"You'll have to ask her. But I'll give you something for nothing. Anna doesn't give up on her friends just because they're being an arse." His guest's Irish lilt was stronger when he was moved by strong emotion. "You know where to find me."

Hunter's mind was spinning when he climbed the stairs to his living room after seeing Niall out. Anna was worried about him and had sent help. That made them even. He was worried about her too. And missing her.

He picked up his bottle, then set it down. Opening his safe, he extracted an envelope and upended it. The glossy photos weren't the issue, the fake digital images Nick wouldn't hesitate to create and use were. A minute's work for his father to broadcast the shots of a naked Anna to the world. By the time Hunter or the cops could prove the shots were illegally obtained, Nick could have superimposed a current picture of Anna onto the body, and the scar would give her away.

And Nick's merry-go-round would start again.

Why? Why the fuck now? Problems paying contractors? *Is money the trigger?*

Nick had reappeared in Hunter's life at his mother's funeral. At the will reading, Nick had been apoplectic with rage, his comments libellous. Hunter had sold him his mother's house at less than market price, but Nick had demanded it as a gift. Nick's harassment started after that. Maybe this was all about money, and the sleazy attacks on Anna were a sideshow?

The scar would identify her.

Anna had the right of it. Nick was a disgusting old lecher and a champion hater. Hunter couldn't ask Anna to wait out the old man. Not when Nick's weapons were so obscene.

Hell, he noticed her absence with every breath he breathed.

As a kid, he'd plotted to disappear. That would have been a declaration of surrender. Would Anna run with him now? Unfair to ask. Better for her to think he was an arsehole.

Hunter's life was empty without her and her occasionally outrageous clothes, her repertoire of smiles, her rapier sharp insights. Teasing him, loving him, trusting him with her secrets and her dreams. He loved her. With Anna, he'd understood contentment.

On the point of returning the photos to the envelope, his gaze returned to Anna's upraised arm. The moment she should have been yelling "Surprise," her body at full stretch, her arms flung upward, her mouth open on the word. Setting the photo down, he positioned his phone above it and used the magnifying feature to zero in. It was possible Anna hadn't been wearing the bracelet that night, even though she owned it now. Nick's note claimed he'd recognised the bracelet, not the scar.

Had Nick identified the wrong woman?

Hunter's attention had been on Anna. Only Anna, when he'd first received them. He'd noted the wig she'd told him she'd worn to burst naked out of a birthday cake. To his mind, her heavy makeup accentuated her innocence. She was more beautiful now, more comfortable in her skin, sure of who she was as a woman. Demanding he hear the truth so he knew who shared his kisses, shared his bed. He loved her brutal honesty.

But he'd doubted her. He had to own that.

Hunter had lived and breathed betrayal as a child. Nick belittled him as a kid, treated him as if he was stupid, pretended he cared while trying to get Hunter's playmates to swap their allegiance to Nick. Hunter had always been on guard.

Since the funeral, Nick had tracked the people Hunter loved, rather than face Hunter himself. If the end game was taking over Hunter's company, there were only two possible motives—humiliating Hunter and money. Time to follow the money.

Hunter glanced again at the photo. Who was the missing woman? Had Nick cut her out of the photo? Unlikely. Had the photographer focused on Anna, not her friend? Possible. Nick remembered the bracelet. Had he remembered the right woman?

What had Anna said?

"I was getting wilder, angrier."

"A bloke I knew said we'd get good money for an hour's work."

"Out of the cake, circulate a bit, smile."

"He promised no touching. No serious touching. Maybe a tit squeeze, a crotch against my butt, a kiss, but that was the limit. There were rules. He knew them. The punters knew them. The bloke organising it would be with us all the time."

"He was wrong. Later he told me he kept the bond. For damages. Offered to split it between us. I gave my share to a friend. Blood

money."

"She said *us*." Hunter leaned back against the sofa, his eyes closed.

The night Anna had told him her story, Hunter had been struggling to get past the idea of Nick seeing Anna naked, of Anna's disgust, and Hunter's fear she'd see him in the same light. He'd let her distract him, or she'd chosen to keep her friend's story to herself. By the time Hunter had got his head straight that night, she was asking him about why he'd changed his name.

"What happened to your friend, Anna?" And did it matter after all this time? Someone at the birthday party got a little too familiar, maybe a bit rough—part of Anna's litany of men who'd enraged her. Not something that would stop Nick's attack.

What am I missing?

Anna had listed a string of incidents to explain her rage and her uncompromising advocacy for women who'd run out of choices. Had there been a specific incident more important than the others?

What happened to your friend, Anna?

Hunter wasn't on the kind of terms with Anna for him to ask.

The relentless ringing of his bell forced Hunter to open his front door, and Casildo pushed through.

"What's going on, Hunt?" Casildo's face was creased in concern. "You don't answer calls for three days, Donna's been acting like there's a death in the family, you look like you haven't slept in days, and it's three in the morning."

"Is it?" Hunter glanced at his watch. "Sorry. Go home."

"Not without some answers." Casildo headed for the kitchen. "I'll make the coffee. Start talking."

"Remember Marygai." Weird place to start, but Hunter had to start somewhere.

"The woman who sexually assaulted you when we were

at school." Casildo placed one cup under the nozzle of the coffee machine, pressed the button, and turned to face Hunter. "I'm not likely to forget."

"Right." Hunter pushed both hands into his hair.

"Take this." Casildo passed him the black coffee and set the machine for a second. "Find a seat. We'll talk."

Hunter walked into the lounge, the sharp scent of coffee cutting through the fog in his brain, but he was too restless to sit.

Casildo followed with his own cup, dropping onto a lounge. "Why bring her up now?"

"Nick told me at Mum's funeral that he put her up to it." Hunter placed the cup carefully on a shelf so he wouldn't smash it against the far wall. "He was her pimp."

"Al'ama." Casildo jack-knifed to his feet and put his arms around Hunter. "I'm sorry, Hunt."

Resting his head on Casildo's shoulder, Hunter allowed himself to be held. Cas had never let him down, never turned his back, never treated him as less. Never demanded chapter and verse.

Hunter lifted his head and stared at his friend. "I love you, Cas."

"Back at you." Cas knuckled his head. "Drink your coffee before it gets cold."

Hunter picked up his coffee and sank into the opposite lounge. Nursing it in his hands, he struggled to find the words. "I thought I was good. Those consent classes at school helped me get my head around it. One of the case studies came close to what happened to me. Having a hard-on, even ejaculating didn't mean I consented, that I wanted it."

"You didn't want it," Casildo assured him.

"I wondered if guilt and shame was the killer in my relationships with women."

"Was it?" Not curiosity from Cas, just a nudge to keep him talking.

"I've worked it out. I keep expecting to be shafted. But

that's on Nick, and after the divorce, on Mum." Hunter leaned back on the lounge, taking his mug with him.

"That's probably cold."

"Right." Hunter set the cup down.

"Parents aren't supposed to betray you," Casildo said gently.

"Right again." Hunter winced. "Because he's fucked on so many levels, Nick's betrayal takes a particular form. He uses women to feed his ego. He even wanted the girls from school to declare he was better than me—or he'd say something nasty to them. Repeatedly."

"That's why you stopped having birthday parties," Casildo guessed.

"If they didn't say he was great, he'd mention one was fat, or stupid, or that I didn't really want her at the party. I was too young to know why it was so wrong, but it was"— Hunter searched for a word—"viciously cruel."

"Yeah."

The one word was enough. "What did he tell you, Cas?"

"Lies."

"I'm sorry."

"Not your sin. Childhood parties, then Marygai." Casildo's tone was careful. "Then Gina. What's Nick done to Anna, Hunt?"

"It's just a matter of joining the dots, isn't it?" Hunter looked at his friend. "Of course he'd target Anna."

"Anna would hate him on sight."

"She did." Hunter gave a half-smile. "But Anna made a mistake when she was eighteen, and Nick happened to be present."

"You think Anna betrayed you?" Cas leaned forward, disbelief in his tense focus, and Hunter loved him even more for his faith in Anna. Cursed himself for his failure.

"I thought he coerced her or tricked her or engineered some setup, like he did with me and Marygai. Maybe, like me, she was too ashamed to talk about it."

Hunter had betrayed Anna in that split second, he'd

believed Nick. His doubt was unforgivable. And he wasn't confessing to anyone until he tried to speak to Anna.

"You're wrong." Casildo's conviction shook Hunter. "What did Anna tell you?"

"Nick sent me photos of Anna as an eighteen-year-old. Naked photos. Nick threatened to post them on social media. Even if I call the cops, he could still post, get one of his lackeys to post. Her reputation's important to her. Her family, her new niece …" He was babbling, trying to justify himself.

"You didn't tell her? Show her the photos Nick sent you?"

"He's only targeting Anna to pull me into line." Hunter willed Casildo to understand. "Breaking it off with her keeps her safe."

"You're an idiot if you think Nick won't go after her anyway."

"I'm trying to buy time. Will you help me bring Nick down? Then I can go after Anna and see if we have anything worth salvaging."

"What's your plan?"

"The beginnings of a plan. Niall Quinn picked up gossip that Nick's got money trouble. Delays in paying contractors. I've made a few calls. Contractors aren't the only people waiting for money. That's the missing link. I thought it was ego or Mum's money or even disdain for me driving his obsession to take over my business. That's why I couldn't get a proper handle on how to get him off my back."

"You mean he couldn't have paid Dad if he'd matched your bid?" Casildo snorted his contempt. "You and your mum are still his goods and chattels."

"Let's pool our resources to shut this down. Nick can back off, or we encourage unhappy people to plant stories about his finances and wait for the dominoes to fall. The market will kill him with very little help from us."

"I like it, but how about one more? Get Anna's agreement to go to the cops."

"I'm responsible for Nick's sins as long as I live and breathe." Hunter exhaled on the words and discovered he no longer carried that weight.

"I hope you know that's not true." Casildo raised an eyebrow. "Your turn to make the coffee. And breakfast. When are you calling Anna?"

"When—*if*—we get this closed down."

"You're wrong, Hunt. Locking her out is the worst mistake of your life."

"I make my living weighing up whether something is a calculated risk or a gamble." Hunter grimaced. "If Nick's in financial death throes, he'll be even more volatile. I don't know enough yet to risk her well-being by including her." Hunter met his friend's gaze. "She's too important for me to gamble with her privacy much less her physical safety."

CHAPTER FOURTEEN

Anna watched the lights of the ride share disappear around the corner of the park. If Hunter wouldn't even talk to her, she'd call another time. Five nights tossing and turning alone.

I'm downstairs. I'd like ten minutes of your time. She pressed send.

Lights came on in the stairwell, and the door was pushed open. She strolled across the road, her casual sashay a lie. Her stomach did an old-fashioned jitterbug that threatened to bring up the one meal she'd managed to keep down today: dry toast and flat lemonade—Kate's staple through early pregnancy. Anna's nausea had a different source.

"What do you want, Anna?" he growled. Teddy bears did scary-gruff as well as grizzlies.

"Ten minutes of your time"—she glanced around—"without witnesses."

"Come in." Not a great welcome, but she'd get a hearing.

She passed him in the entrance, sought out his sage-smoky scent in the confined space, and regretted the legacies people carried that never let them breathe freely. Inside his living room, she stopped. He'd been reading a book or maybe watching TV or listening to music or all

199

three simultaneously—having as much trouble as her settling to a single activity. Choosing the dining room rather than the lounge, she moved toward the far side of the table and sat down. Upright chairs, some distance between them, a table to lay out the evidence. But first things first.

"You look like shit."

"Thanks." He pushed his hands in his pockets. "There's no point in rehashing what we said the other night."

"You destroyed something in me the other night." She placed her bag on the table to one side, aware he'd flinched. Your body keeps your secrets or betrays them. He was hurting too. "I hate lies—big, small, kind, cruel. There's always a trap. So, I tell the truth to the people I care about." She shook her head, still bewildered. "I thought if I always told the truth, people would believe me. You cured me of that."

"Anna—"

"My photos came from Mr. Anonymous, only I'd put money on Mr. Anonymous being your narcissistic arsehole of a father." Stacking the photos in a pile gave her something to do with her hands. "Although I shouldn't tease. I confirmed my source was"—she paused for the equivalent of a mental drumroll—"Nick Richardson."

"Men beating up women and children makes you sick to your stomach." He dropped onto the chair opposite. "You received photos of me beating up my ex-girlfriend. Nick knows how to target his attacks."

"That's not strictly accurate."

"So, I'm not in the pictures." He was watching her, wary, but his eyes looked bruised. "The note named me."

"That kind of crap evidence wouldn't get you far in a court of law. But you're right. Violence, physical, mental, or emotional makes me sick to my stomach. Identifying the perpetrator can be tricky, but it's a pretty essential part of the exercise.

"Nick's not as smart as he thinks. Liam's assessment was car crash injury, but a few photos appeared in a social media feed, then were withdrawn. Seems Gina—"

He jerked at the name.

"Gina published the photos on her Insta feed, then regretted her action, and took them down. Too late to stop the bullshit commentary." Anna shook her head. "I can't believe anyone finds Nick charming. I didn't find Nick charming a decade ago," she said. "He's like the portrait of Dorian Grey. His face shows every obscene act he's ever committed."

"What's your point?"

"Gina, your ex-girlfriend, was pushing for marriage. You explained you'd rather be stung by a box jellyfish than get married. She threw a tantrum. You were booking a taxi when Gina took off with your car keys and smashed your car. For good measure, you paid all the medical and rehab bills."

"Who told you that?" He pushed back from the table, and she waited for him to withdraw—again.

"I asked her." Anna shrugged.

"It was still my fault. I should have anticipated, handled everything better."

"Is that why you don't drive?"

"Part of the reason."

"Another secret or another secret shame? Next you'll be ashamed of living and breathing." Anna's search had produced a few other interesting details. "Her initial post didn't mention an accident, or that the shots were taken in hospital. The great unwashed commentariat pushed for a different story. 'C'mon,' they said. 'Tell us what really happened. You were bashed by your boyfriend.' Gina let that sit a little too long."

"Gina was angry."

"Who are you trying to convince?" Anna heard the roar of a distant siren, then silence. "Gina was the author of the ambiguous *Guess what happened to me* caption with the photos. There's no justification for letting a false accusation of assault gain traction on social media." Anna's heart ached at

Hunter's distrust in what they'd created. "Your turn to guess. Did I track Gina down to trash your privacy, or because I wanted to prove she lied?"

"You didn't believe I hit her." His turn to be bewildered.

"I believed something was terribly wrong." Anna jammed the photos into the envelope and pushed them across the table. "Because you wouldn't talk to me. That left me without a compass. Like now—you're offering no confession, no excuse, no denial. After a few months, where I've had to pry every confidence from you as if I'm excavating for rare earth minerals, I've had enough."

"Fair enough," he said, straightening his shoulders, preparing for a blow.

Couldn't he see? Nick Richardson was still dictating his actions.

"So, did you get naked photos of me from Mr. Anonymous? Photos at that birthday party were against the rules, but, hey, rules are meant to be broken, especially by entitled men."

His head snapped back.

"That's answer enough." Anna pointed a finger at him. "What's the probability of you receiving nude photos of me and me receiving photos of your battered ex-girlfriend on the same day?"

"Unlikely."

"Agreed. So that leaves your Mr. Anonymous as Nick Richardson."

"Cas agrees."

"A good man, Casildo. I suspect he tells the truth to the people he cares about."

"Okay—I got photos of you naked bursting from a cake."

"Show me." Anna froze, trapped by an old fear. Until this moment she hadn't been one hundred percent sure he had photos. "I'm not leaving until I see them."

He rose, crossed to the bedroom, and returned a few minutes later. Upending the envelope, he watched as they tumbled onto the table, then silently resumed his seat.

Anna forced herself to focus on the top photo. The zigzag scar from her fall on a serrated bit of rusted metal was as visible as when she wore a swimsuit or shorts.

"I told you I'd worked as a stripper, burst from a special birthday cake, and you've seen me naked, so you know I have a scar, where it is. Unlike most people, you know how I got it."

"Not sure how this is relevant." He sounded weary to his bones.

"A scar's not much to identify me. I could have weathered a scandal."

It had taken Anna a long time to find her anger after Helen's death. To look around and see Helen wasn't the only silent victim. Longer still to find the best way to apologise for her failure to help her friend. Anna studied Hunter closely when he didn't answer. She wanted to laugh and cry and beat the table with her fists. Telling the truth was her magic amulet, her way to identify friend and foe. If he didn't believe her, they truly were finished.

"I see. You got a note too. What did it say?"

He deflated. "Nick recognised you from the bracelet, not the scar."

Anna slapped a hand to her mouth, pushing away from the table, and racing for the bathroom. Grief slammed into her, making her knees buckle. The bastard, was all she could think. The bracelet alone wasn't proof Nick had assaulted Helen, but she'd always believed he'd been the one to convince Helen to withdraw charges. Anna had seen him in the carpark of the hospital. Helen had been terrified when Anna had reached her—the charges already cancelled.

Helen had lived half a life until the day she died. Blaming herself. Ultimately hating herself.

A few minutes later, Hunter knocked on the door. "Can I come in?"

"I'll be out in a minute."

Anna was kneeling on the floor in front of the toilet

bowl. Finally she pushed to her feet, rinsed her mouth, and washed her face. She rolled her shoulders, and it made not a damn bit of difference to the tension lodged in her neck and back muscles.

Her helplessness when she'd heard Helen had suicided swamped her now. Other images of that night scrolled through her head with unrelenting horror. Helen's bruises, her silent sobs of pain. Anna pressed a hand to her throat to stop herself from throwing up again.

Closing the door behind her, she made her way back to the table and sat down. "What else?"

* * *

"Verbatim"—Hunter had memorised the words, but Anna's reaction to Nick's identification of the bracelet cemented his doubts—"'Anna and I fucked at my party. She's an 'okay fuck.' Happy for the few extra bucks for the night's work. She came on to me.'"

Her skin turned the pale yellowy green of parchment, and she pressed a hand to her stomach. He expected her to turn tail again.

"He'll publish the photos and his accusations to as many sites as he can find."

"For a split second you believed him." She tilted her head to one side, and Hunter knew he'd failed her.

He held up both hands in surrender. Hunter hadn't believed she'd chased Nick, but he'd believed she'd been set up, taken advantage of, as he'd been, and like him, been unable to say aloud what had happened.

"I believed—thought—considered—I don't know what word fits the disorientation that felled me when I received the photos. Not that you'd been willing. Never that. But that he'd coerced you in some way, and you were ashamed and blamed yourself."

"You've got part of it right."

Hunter closed his eyes. How the hell could he give back

what Nick had stolen from her? How the hell could he protect her?

"Nick will destroy you."

"I wasn't wearing the bracelet that night."

"I wasn't sure," he said. *What a pathetic excuse.*

"But you didn't ask. You didn't talk to me." The finality in her words sliced through him. "The bracelet belonged to a friend, Helen. Her mother gave it to me when Helen died."

"How did Helen die?" He held his breath, afraid of the answer.

"Helen was ashamed. Helen blamed herself." She scrubbed at the tears running down her cheeks. "Two women jumped out of your father's birthday cake."

Hunter hissed, and she filled in the missing pieces.

"I didn't tell you everything before. It was Nick's birthday. His party wasn't a safe place to be. When I found Helen, she'd been sexually assaulted. She was incoherent with shock and pain. Injured enough to need a hospital. I made a full statement to the police to go with Helen's complaint. Helen withdrew the charges. I don't know who got to her, but I have my suspicions."

"What do you want, Anna?" *Jesus—Did Nick set Helen up the same way he had me and Marygai?*

"My dreams to come true," she sing-songed. "But that's a bit fanciful for a tough cookie like me. And trust is impossible for you."

"How did Helen die?" Hunter tasted ash.

"She killed herself three years ago. Still ashamed and blaming herself. I spent all night on the phone with her. She promised she was getting off the phone and calling Lifeline. I was wrong."

"I'm sorry." He blinked rapidly several times, tears stinging the backs of his eyes, recalling his constantly shifting emotions after Marygai, the fleeting thoughts of death as escape. "And sorry doesn't cut it. She must have been in endless pain."

"I guessed you had photos from the party, that

somehow Nick had worked out I'd been there. It never occurred to me Helen's bracelet was the key." She licked up a tear that had reached her upper lip. "I failed Helen."

"No, you didn't." Hunter wouldn't allow her to criticise herself.

"But you failed Gina? Because that's part of this story." She flung her hand in the air.

"I didn't make her happy, so that's on me. But I wasn't responsible for her injuries."

Hunter rose to his feet, energised by what she'd told him and anxious to work out his next steps. He'd need to let Anna go tonight, figure out if Helen's story helped in any way to neutralise Nick. Despite calling in every marker he had, Hunter still had a few missing pieces to bring Nick down financially. "We can talk more later."

"You're dismissing me?" She stared at Hunter as if he'd sprouted a second head. "You're handing Nick the victory?"

"No." How to convince her.

Pushing to her feet, she pulled a small envelope from her bag and set it on the table. "I refused to be a victim then. I won't be a victim now. I guessed Nick sent you photos of me. I'm more than happy to go to the cops. I also came here to tell you about Helen.

"That's a copy of Helen's hospital discharge report, her police complaint, and my supporting statement. I'll also give you her charm bracelet. There would have been DNA testing as part of the initial sexual assault complaint. I'm guessing either there were no matches on the database at the time, or the cops stopped the investigation before identifying the perpetrator. But the cops store things like that for future reference."

"Why are you giving me this?"

"Nick's a narcissist. He sees betraying others as self-defence, because he's the only person who counts. I didn't fully understand all the marks of the beast when I was eighteen, but over the years, I've built an identikit in my head. The fragments I've been assembling came from images of Nick I remembered from his birthday bash."

"Why didn't you tell me it was his birthday sooner?"

"A mistake. You didn't need me to confirm Nick preys on vulnerable people."

"Jesus. There are things I should have told you, warned you about."

"If you think dumping me will protect me, you're wrong. I'm a target all by myself. Not because you were dating me. Nick will open another battlefield, and another, until he wins. If you'd told me about Gina then, shared your photos, I'd have told you about Helen, given you what I had. Liam would have taken our case to the police."

"Did Helen name him?"

"Helen didn't see the man's face. I can't swear to where Nick Richardson was every minute I was in that hell hole. But recognising the bracelet is pretty telling. Either way, he was complicit. I saw him in the hospital carpark. She'd dropped the charges by the time I reached her room."

"Thank you."

"What for?" she spat her self-disgust. "I talked her into that night. She died."

"For coming here, for telling me Helen's story." Hunter sounded so bloody formal, even to himself. He was making a hash of it. "I thought Nick would destroy you." In that moment, he'd been prepared to do anything—to never see Anna again—if it removed her from Nick's orbit. "You've got a family, a new niece. Your reputation's important."

"Yes, it is. It brings in work. But in the end, it's who I am, what I do when no one's watching that's more important to me." She thumped her chest. "You should have asked. I'm not ashamed of my body. I'm not ashamed of being a woman, of making stupid mistakes by using my body to gain attention or affection.

"If Nick broadcasts those photos, I'll own them. I'll also make sure a helluva lot of people know that Nick shouldn't have them, that he exploited women, some of whom were underage, to titillate fifty-year-old men at his birthday party, and now he's using them to coerce and control my behaviour."

"Not everyone in your life will look for the explanation. Dirt sticks." That was the gamble Hunter hadn't been prepared to take.

"I don't care about everyone," she cried passionately. "I hate that I didn't help Helen enough, and that I wasn't fast enough to recognise that an obsessive, entitled arsehole was targeting my sister. I should have forgotten rules, niceties, and politeness, and shouted in every forum I could that women are not and never have been possessions. Sexual violence is about power. That's why you see it in wars. Show as many naked pictures of me as you please. I won't like it, but I refuse to be silenced." A tear spilled onto her cheek. "That would be a betrayal of every woman who's been crushed."

"I'm going after him. I had a plan before you came tonight. Your evidence gives me more." Hell, Hunter had totally cocked this up. His silence about Nick had encouraged Anna's. "I have another story, if you'll listen."

She nodded, scrubbing away her tears.

"I told you my parents divorced." He led her back to the chair. "That Mum found Nick screwing his secretary in their bed. I was with her. He wanted a divorce and wanted her to sell the house, figured he'd make it so the memories were too bad to stay there." Unable to sit, Hunter paced.

"He got his divorce, but Mum refused to sell. I didn't know what to think at the time. But I knew my family was stuffed. Mum started sleeping with Nick's associates, an attempt to make him jealous. I never knew who I'd find at home. Nick toyed with her—came by, he used to say, for a fuck for old times' sake or because he was at a loose end. She let him in." He rubbed his face, disgust with them, with himself, making his throat dry.

"What did he do next?"

While she was making spilling his guts easier than Hunter would have believed possible, listening wasn't forgiving.

"I was fifteen. I woke up to a woman sucking my cock. She was naked. Before I knew what was happening, Marygai was on top of me. I came."

"Was she your first?"

"Damn it, yes." He threw his hands in the air. Marygai had taken advantage, but he'd endlessly workshopped the what-ifs if he'd leapt out of the bed screaming assault. "A party at home. Marygai stayed over because she was *tired and emotional.*"

"Crap."

"I responded." When Anna looked disbelieving, Hunter backpedalled. "Or my body responded. And I know intellectually that doesn't mean I wanted or invited her attack."

"Did Nick ask Marygai to assault you?" She was icy in her rage.

"Yes."

"Was your mother also in on the scheme?"

"Jesus. I don't know. Don't go there." The possibility had added to Hunter's confusion.

"When did you find out?"

"At Mum's funeral." Hunter knew he'd have to fill in the gaps. "Maybe he chose that day because Gina was with me." He swallowed the bile rising in his throat. "At least he took me aside to boast about it. Reckoned I must have been thinking about seeing him fuck his secretary that day. Thought he'd give me a taste. Dripping poison at Mum's funeral was one way of attracting attention."

"He's evil."

"He was right. I was disgusted and enthralled at the same time. Ashamed of what I was thinking, about how my body was reacting. I was terrified after that night that Marygai would get drunk at another one of my mother's parties and say I came on to her."

"Is that what she threatened?"

"I was fifteen years old. Sex was my every second

thought. She pretended she'd had one too many drinks to know exactly what she was doing. Walked into the wrong bedroom, and I pounced." He recalled his helplessness.

"Hunter, they were the adults. It was premeditated child abuse." Her uncompromising verdict erased the humiliation, which had clouded that memory.

"Yeah. I was lucky I had Cas, and decent consent education at school. I finally accepted I'd been assaulted"

"Helen told me it doesn't completely remove the shame."

"She's right. Nick's boast that he arranged it brought it back," Hunter admitted.

"Did Nick assault Gina?"

"Not according to her." Hunter pushed a hand through his hair. "She said they'd been drinking, he'd been commiserating with her about my refusal to commit, and one thing led to another."

"But add it all together and you keep expecting to be ambushed by people who claim to love you. Any women between Gina and me?" She waved a hand in the air. "Stupid question."

"Not stupid. I've seen women. Occasional dates, sex when it suits us both."

"Never the same woman twice?"

"Not until I met you." Compliment or insult? From the look on her face, he had no idea what she thought.

"What happens now?"

"I'll let you know if I use what you've given me."

God, Hunter wanted her to stay, wanted to tell her every sordid detail of his past, but he wasn't sure he could protect her yet.

Pulling out her phone, she tapped in some numbers. "Don't bother." She sucked in a breath. "You talk about gambling and risks. You don't have to do this alone. Clearly, by your calculations, I'm expendable."

* * *

He hadn't contradicted Anna at the end. And damn him for that. If he loved her, surely he'd have asked Anna to stay, to plan Nick's downfall together. Well, damn him to hell and back again. A girl had her pride, and sitting around mooning over Hunter Samuel Thompson, when she'd given him second and third chances, was not going to happen.

Suck it up, Anna.

She sniffled—quietly—in the back of the ride share.

Anna hadn't guessed at the depth of Nick's betrayal of Hunter. Hunter had been arming himself for years in readiness for ambush. And Nick had form where Hunter's women were concerned.

Stupid, bloody, protective idiot. Hunter had been dealing with Nick before Anna's arrival on the scene. She was missing something. Hunter had bought The Hariri building to protect Casildo's family. He'd set up the foundation secretly to disguise where his mother's money had gone. She bet that was to protect his uncle. He'd circled the wagons. He had his loved ones safe when she'd met him.

He hadn't expected to have a relationship with Anna.

"Never the same woman twice?"

"Not until you."

Hunter was trying to put her inside the circle of wagons.

Did the stupid idiot know he loved her?

Anna opened the door to Casildo twenty-four hours later. "Are you escort, peace-maker, or bodyguard?"

"All three," he said. "Depending on the moment. Right now, I'm escort."

"Where are we going?"

Anna collected her bag and followed him down the stairs. Hunter had proposed, and she'd accepted, this meeting via text, ridiculous hope flaring at the invitation.

"The childcare centre. I've brought the armoured vehicle and have access to the underground carpark."

Placing a hand on his arm to stop their descent, Anna turned to him. "Not funny."

"Sorry. Dad's car. It's got heavily tinted windows, so it's not easy to identify who's in it. Gives us some privacy. No one will comment on Hunter being in the building."

"What's going on, Casildo?"

"Hunt's changing the game plan."

"His plan to stop Nick?"

"Yeah. I don't trust the snake even with all the evidence we've got."

"Did Hunter tell you about Helen?"

Casildo was Hunter's lifelong friend. Hunter didn't accept it, but he had integrity and loyalty, qualities Casildo was also known for in their industry. She'd bet Hariri senior set the example for both of them.

"No need to answer that," she said. "I'm glad he's got you in his life. Has Nick always hovered in the background?"

"Like that snake I was talking about, Nick has slithered in and out of Hunt's life at different times. We thought he was gone. Hunt's mum's death triggered this cycle of hell. Nick's got the kind of ego that can't accept no. He'll coax and cajole, but if you tell him to piss off, he has to punish."

"Hunter told him to piss off, and trying to bankrupt your father was part of Hunter's punishment."

Casildo nodded. "Hunt says Nick has turned his big guns on you."

"I'm a big girl. I can look after myself." Although Hunter's rejection was testing that resolve. She hadn't completely forgiven Hunter's high-handedness, even when his goal was to protect her. The jury was out until after this meeting.

"All I'll say is that Hunt blames himself for Nick turning his gunsights on you. If Hunt wasn't in your life, this wouldn't be happening." Casildo hit the remote to unlock the car.

"I'll grant him that. But teams often achieve more than

individuals"—Anna settled in the car and allowed some of her frustration to surface—"he's accepting help from you."

"Nick destroyed Hunt's mother, almost destroyed his uncle, and has tried his damnedest to beat the goodness out of Hunt. Hunter's my hero." Casildo was a staunch defender. "And he hates it when I say that. He's tired of having his loved ones attacked."

"What happens if Hunter's plan doesn't work?" She stole a sideways look at Hunter's closest friend. "Will he banish me permanently?"

"Yes."

"As the closest thing he has to family, you should be telling him he's crazy to let me go."

"I have."

The finality in Casildo's voice frightened her more than anything else had in the last few days, snuffing out the few shoots of hope she'd had. When she gazed at her lap, she was holding the handle of her bag in a death grip.

CHAPTER FIFTEEN

The tight knots in Hunter's shoulders eased when Anna walked through the door. Just seeing her made his day better. "I've got drinks." He handed Anna a keep cup of hot chocolate and Cas a coffee. "Want a tour of the site?"

"Not today." She peered into his cup. "Your favourite inky-evil brew."

Hunter couldn't read her. Knew he'd hurt her. Hopefully today was a start to changing that. "We can use the childcare director's office." He turned and led the way.

Casildo stopped at the doorway. "I'll be here if you need me." Then closed the door with him on the outside.

"Please sit." Hunter gestured to the new furniture still covered in plastic. "Not quite ready to go."

"Why am I here, Hunter?"

"Clearly, by your calculation, I'm expendable."

He hadn't been able to get those words out of his head.

"You're not expendable." He huffed out a breath. "I didn't want you to remember me as a man who beat up women, but I made the decision that if you tossed me aside for that reason, you'd keep your pride, and ultimately your heart, intact."

The word *expendable*, and all its dreary companions—of

little significance, disposable, non-essential, unnecessary—tormented him. She was as necessary as his next breath, as essential as water, the love of his life. His plan might not work; he wasn't sure how he'd let Anna go if he failed.

"I'd like your help to bring Nick down." And asking was easier than anything Hunter had done in his life. Her answer mattered, but being able to ask set him free.

"I have a few questions first."

"Ask."

"Cas said your mum's death brought Nick back into your life. Back when I read that stuff, Bizgos claimed you inherited everything."

"Yeah. The house, contents, plus some investments and cash."

"The house your father wanted. What happened to the house?"

"Nick bought it, bulldozed it and put up shonky apartments. Pissed off the entire neighbourhood." He rolled his shoulders and eased back in his seat, abandoning a burden. "The new owners are still fighting poor construction claims."

"Liam told me what you did with the money."

Hunter snorted. "How the hell did he find out?"

"Your good deed for Niall. Turns out it wasn't the first good deed you did. A third party just assumed you were a friend of Niall's, and that Niall would be interested in knowing how to return the favour."

"Niall did return the favour."

"Tell me."

"Ben's always been involved with a workers' union charity for the partners and kids of workers killed on construction sites," Hunter said without hesitation. "He's started a related charity. He and Ellie handle all the work. I'm on the fundraising committee."

"Donna's husband died on site."

"Yeah."

"The steady stream of work experience school children

I see, either in the office or on various jobs, they're all part of the program." She was following loose ends, and Hunter was happy for her to continue, although he wasn't sure where they were heading.

"Yeah. But there was so much happening, it took me a while to work out that Nick was after the money. It's been a series of jigsaw pieces where I was jamming things in the wrong places.

"Ostensibly Nick re-entered my life because I bought an old building he was interested in. He's moved on from houses to buying medium and high-rise office blocks for redevelopment. He offered me a 'role' in his business—always vague—junior, certainly, poorly paid, probably, gaining access to my network, definitely. When he realised my refusal was for real, it was payback time."

"He doesn't seem the type to take on a partner." She moved her chair close enough for him to sniff the air and find her, find some balance.

"Took me too long to work that out. After Niall's tip-off, I started looking harder at Nick Richardson Enterprises. In true narcissist style, the crap he fed Bizgos about me—cash flow problems, over-commitment of capital, dissatisfied customers—all applied to him. It was useful to join his name to mine, to tell his lenders a merger was in the offing. He'd pick up my assets, not my debts."

"Broadcasting his financial difficulties is a brilliant idea. Hit him where it hurts."

"Still too big a gamble. The odds are too high, he'll outmanoeuvre me, especially holding naked photos of you. I want to confront Nick with your evidence about Helen before witnesses." Hunter covered her hand with his own, and she waited through his silence. He had the sense she'd always give him time to find the words. Would she give him another chance? "I let his lies come between us. I'd like to explain why."

"You're not responsible for him or his actions," she insisted with the clarity of absolute conviction.

"No, but sometimes I feel more hunted than Hunter. Did Helen feel like that?" Hunter forced himself to ask.

"Helen felt that night defined her. She couldn't see past it, couldn't be convinced of all the good parts of herself. Shame consumed her."

"Pain has its own colour, shape and temperature," he murmured.

"Helen's was grey, tear-shaped, and despite the gap in time, red-hot."

"I felt betrayed. Didn't matter which way I turned in that house, I felt betrayed. But I was angry as well. Maybe that saved me. I'm sorry for what happened to Helen." Hunter sucked in a breath. "Sorry because I think there's a better than even chance Nick was the person who assaulted Helen. Essentially, Nick killed her and is trying to scare you now. Not that we could prove it after all this time."

"You *do* know you're not like him."

"I'm not like him. Thank you, Jesus. But he's tainted my life and dictated a lot of my choices. I was lucky I had Cas and my uncle."

"Leaving home was the right choice, the brave choice. Better to see-saw between your uncle's house and the Hariris' than stay where you were and wait for another attack." She was telling him she loved him—without words.

Hunter had to find his own, because if he didn't, they had no future.

"You chose father figures, Hunter. That's healthy."

"They didn't give up on me. Money and sex. Nick's two gods, or his way of defining himself." Hunter shook his head.

"He's the kind of man who comes through a door with his ego ten feet in front of him."

"Not all women read him so clearly." He shook his head.

"He spoke to me at that party. I've never forgotten his words. 'I don't need long with a woman before I know what I want to do with her, how I want to do it, and when I want to do it.'"

"He's amoral when it comes to women. I want you to know, there were a lot of reasons I split with Gina, but sleeping with Nick wasn't the main one, if that makes sense?"

"What was the main one?"

"Nick wasn't the only one. Not the first or the last. She didn't see her actions as disloyal in any way."

Anna set her cup down, a frown creasing her forehead. "Did we go to Marygai's party to exorcise her memory?"

"In a way. I wanted to show you off. Someone good and clean and honest was choosing to be with me. I was a stupid idiot, and it meant Nick saw you."

"He didn't see me." She brushed his attempt at an apology aside. "He saw a body and a bracelet."

"You showed me something that night. You're not ashamed of your body. By your own admission, you stuffed up as a teenager, made some wrong choices, and got taken advantage of by cock-happy idiots who lacked brains and charm. You defeated them all. You exorcised Marygai simply by being."

"But you didn't remember that when you got the photos."

"Knowing what Nick's capable of, I thought he could have coerced you, then blackmailed you. He threatened to destroy you now. I don't know what sick fantasy he was brewing. I just wanted to get you away from him."

She was wearing her speculative expression, her cut-and-dice facts and fake-news expression. She drew her own conclusion. "Did you think he might have assaulted me?"

"It crossed my mind," he whispered. "I knew you'd never have had sex with him willingly that night."

"Good answer, Sam-I-am. It hasn't been easy thinking you didn't trust me." She pressed a fist to her chest.

Pain ricocheted off her, and he cursed his part in contributing to that.

"My reaction to the photos was because I don't trust Nick."

She nodded. "Have we covered everything?"

"I might have left out a few small details, but that's the gist. To be clear. I'm glad he didn't touch you that night, but it wouldn't make a blind bit of difference to how I feel about you."

"How do you feel about me? I can guess, but guessing isn't good enough." A few heartbeats later, and she continued, her voice softer. "No answer?"

"I'll answer when this is over." *Because if I say I love you, you'll never walk away.*

She exhaled loudly, as if summoning her courage. "Last question."

"I wish." But Hunter smiled, because she was still in the room with him.

"Do you think I'll betray you—"

"No."

"Not finished the question." She rested her hand at the top of his thighs. "In your body?"—then moved her hand to rest against his chest—"in your heart?"—before touching a finger to his temple—"in your head? Because for you it has to be body, heart and mind."

"You told me about Nick's birthday party. You sent Niall to offer help when you thought my business was in trouble. You gave me Helen's story. You turned up tonight. If you wanted to tell me something, you'd do it to my face."

"I love you," she said.

"I know you do." Hearing the words strengthened Hunter's resolve to permanently banish Nick from his life. "I also know you're strong enough to walk away. I don't deserve you."

"It's not a matter of deserving, it's a matter of accepting. That's always been the hurdle with you."

"I'm doing this to give us another chance."

"And if it doesn't work? Will you cut me off again?"

"I've considered all the angles. I'm not gambling with your safety, but I *am* asking you to take a calculated risk."

"Tell me the plan."

* * *

Anna pictured Hunter standing alone in the main office, the lights muted. Everyone had their assigned place, although Anna had made a last-minute adjustment to Hunter's plan. Casildo, charged with getting her here, hadn't been able to change her mind. The plan had been for Kate and Liam, Niall and Lucy, and Helen's mum to be with Anna, but she'd shooed them away, choosing to wait alone in the dark in Hunter's office.

She'd caught a quick glimpse of Hunter before she'd locked herself in. He'd dressed for the part—Tom Ford suit, Oxford shoes, Hugo Boss fragrance—all part of his disguise as a successful businessman. She loved the man behind the mask and had to believe he loved her. He'd let her in, and that was huge for him.

Forty-eight hours since they'd developed this plan.

Casildo's family, Donna because she was family, Antonio because he was family to Anna, were also in the larger room.

The sound of the front-door bell echoing through the building steadied her. They'd choreographed the main moves like any theatrical presentation.

"Showtime," she muttered, the light under the door telling her Hunter had hit the light switch to the main room and was opening the front door.

"Nick, come in."

Hunter had lured him with a suggestion a deal was on the table. Hunter sent the next signal to his guests, slamming the heavy door shut.

"Don't mind if I do." Nick was on the premises, probably cocky with the conviction Hunter would be begging for mercy.

Anna slammed the office door open and stepped out. She held her hands above her head. "Well, if it isn't the birthday boy."

Nick slipped the button on his jacket, one hand running down his front. Preening like a cock on a dung heap, convinced of his power.

Doors burst open on the other side of the room. Hunter and her friends and family tumbled through shouting "Surprise."

CHAPTER SIXTEEN

Hunter was proud of her. Wearing the dress she'd worn to Niall's exhibition opening, she showcased what she was—professional, capable, confident, and to him, the most beautiful woman on earth. Her dress said she was comfortable in her own skin and trusted the men around her. A woman who stirred the air as she passed and invited admiring or envious looks. She was dignified and delicious. Seeing her walk toward him boosted Hunter's confidence. Loyalty for her was an absolute. He'd missed her every second they'd been apart.

"What the hell is going on?" Nick roared. "I'm leaving."

"Not so fast." Casildo stepped behind him, blocking the exit.

"A little conversation." Hunter shrugged. "Before a few interested parties." He'd opted for the nuclear option. He wanted Nick to pay for every moment of distress he'd caused Anna in the last few weeks.

The elegant dress said it all, and Hunter hadn't got the full message until she'd spelled it out for him in his apartment days ago. She owned every mistake she'd ever made, while he'd refused to talk about most of his.

"You got me here under false pretences," Nick snapped.

"A friendly chat." Casildo smiled.

"Hariri, isn't it?" Nick dismissed Casildo with a glance. "You're a friend of my son, aren't you?"

"I'm a friend of Hunt's."

"He is my son. His mother hadn't prostituted herself at that stage." Nick surveyed the crowd in the room, his eyes narrowing in recognition of some of those present. "Seems the gang's all here." Nick's insolent gaze rested on Anna. "You've aged well, Anna. That little shimmy you did when you burst out of my fiftieth birthday cake was delightfully provocative. You followed it up with some moves my fellow guests reminisce about to this day. Such smooth, silky skin—"

"That was a professional performance. Wasted on you and your 'friends.'"

"You're wrong." Nick puffed out his chest. "We enjoyed it very much."

"Enough to take photos?" Anna was baiting Nick.

"You're very photogenic. A few mementoes of a special occasion seemed fitting." Nick seemed indifferent to the watching crowd, intent on his own revenge.

"Recording and distributing images without permission is a crime in this state," she said sweetly.

Nick laughed. "Watch your mouth, missy. I'll sue."

"Crime, Anna?" Hunter tut-tutted. "Photos of his own birthday party? Everyone knowing what they were there for? I'd say he has plausible deniability on consent. No one in this room would pick you as the birthday girl. I'm more interested in how Nick identified you. Did you hand out business cards?"

"My professional name was Brandy Alexander." Anna pouted. "My favourite drink at the time."

"You want to talk charges. Kidnapping is a crime." Nick waved his hand in Hunter's face.

"Interesting charge, when we're just having a friendly chat."

"I'm finished," Nick said.

"Are we finished, Anna?" Hunter's voice held enough menace to fluster Nick.

"No."

"I'm finished." Nick made to turn away.

"I sure as hell hope so." Casildo grabbed a chair and set it down. "Have a seat."

"No." The sheen of sweat on Nick's forehead was another good sign. "What do you want?"

"An answer." Hunter leaned back against Donna's desk.

"The organiser must have given me your name." Nick glanced around the room, possibly checking for other exits.

"Why would he do that?" Hunter pretended to give it some thought. "Unless you made it worth his while? And you've remembered Anna's name all this time. Except, it's not her name you remembered, but her bracelet."

"Gina is pretty pissed at you, Nick."

At the left-field attack, Nick's gaze snapped to Anna, his Adam's apple working. "Who's Gina?"

Anna was close enough for Nick to lash out, so Hunter moved to put himself between them.

"My ex-girlfriend," Hunter said. "She stole my car when we broke up, then crashed it. Fortunately, her injuries weren't serious. Lots of bruises though. She looked battered. Battered enough that when she posted photos to her Insta feed, a few people started up a chat about domestic violence."

"It happens." Nick shrugged.

"She pulled the photos, when the posts got creepy, and called me."

"Is there a point to this?" Nick glanced at the ceiling, seemingly bored, but sweat was now trickling down the side of his face.

"Cas got his tech friend onto it." The tension in Hunter's gut eased when Nick's gaze met his, then slid away. "He traced your interactions with Gina, your escalation of the situation. I think the legal term is leading the witness."

"Which is how I come in." Anna's scent swirled around

Hunter, a new one. God, he'd missed the game of parsing out her scents to work out why he could smell Anna through them all. "Someone sent me photos of a badly beaten Gina the same day Hunter got naked photos of me. A bit obvious, don't you think?"

"You're a trollop; he hands out the occasional back-hander." Nick must be rattled to issue what amounted to a confession. "Why wouldn't someone want to let you know?"

"Hints in Gina's feed that I'd attacked her in a fit of jealousy had your fingerprints all over them. Only you, Gina, and I knew you'd screwed Gina. I use the word screw deliberately. You set her up and bought her off. You knew I'd never mention it." Hunter was baring his history to his closest friends and Anna's, and to hell with it.

"That Gina. She wanted a bit more man than you could offer."

"That's enough." Anna sounded in complete control. "You're pathetic. You told Hunter you remembered the bracelet, the bracelet worn by a woman attacked and viciously sexually assaulted at your party that night."

"There were no charges laid," Nick snapped.

"Because you threatened Helen and demanded she insist on my silence."

"You can't prove that." Nick's gaze darted from him to Anna and back, alerted by the new name.

"I saw you at the hospital shortly after she withdrew the complaint. How did you find her?" Anna studied him. "You had someone follow us from the party, didn't you?"

"You really are a fantasist." Nick scoffed, but his gaze slid to Casildo and the door.

"You must have still been worried about that party. The photos were to silence me. Sure, you wanted to make Hunter hate me, but really, the photos were to keep me quiet. Mistake number one—you expected Hunter to show me the photos. He didn't. Mistake two—you expected me to dump him without checking the authenticity of the photos of Gina. Mistake three—I'm not Helen. I inherited her bracelet."

Nick's face turned a bilious green.

"I'm perfectly happy to go public, tell the police you're targeting me, and remind them they took a DNA sample, which could identify Helen's attacker. I'm sure they wouldn't have discarded that."

"You're bluffing."

"Try me." She leaned toward him. "Funny thing is, I couldn't have linked you directly to Helen without the photos. The assault at your birthday party led Helen to suicide. I've got nothing to lose."

"Nothing to do with me." Nick held up his hands, backing away.

"She left a note. She was ashamed. She blamed herself. You denied her justice." Anna's voice wobbled.

Hunter caught the flash of fear on Nick's face, and the pieces fell into place.

"You assaulted her," Hunter said. He and Anna hadn't discussed this, but from long experience, Hunter smelled the guilt seeping through Nick's pores. "You recognised the bracelet at Marygai's party because Helen was wearing it when you molested her. Anna's right. You believed Anna was the woman you attacked.

"The purpose of the photos was twofold, to silence Anna and bring me to heel. You picked the wrong victim this time. Anna will shred you. And I'm happy to watch. Anna would have kneed you in the balls, birthday boy or not. I don't know, or care, about the years you've lied to me, but I won't be silent about this."

"I've had enough of this bullshit," Nick roared.

"There's more." Hunter drew himself up, sensing Anna's trembling rather than seeing it, his entire attention on Nick. "You're as near as bankrupt as bedamned."

Anna, his brave, battle-hardened warrior, stepped up to his shoulder.

"You've been trading off the possibility of a merger with

me for weeks now. Never going to happen."

"I've got the backing of this town." Nick blustered, but the stale scent of his sweat muddied his sickly sweet cologne.

"Look around." Hunter gestured to Raed Hariri and Ben Thompson standing silently behind him. "If we spread the word, you're done in this town."

"You've been happily threatening all of us with trial by social media for events years old." Anna raked Nick from head to toe with a disdainful gaze. "Branding is my bread and butter. Releasing a new brand for you would give me enormous pleasure."

"Stay out of my life," Hunter said. "If you come near me or mine again, I'll present the evidence we've collected to the police. We might not win, but you'll lose."

Hunter felt hollowed out. Nick Richardson was his father, and he'd trafficked his son and assaulted and all but killed Anna's best friend.

Dear god, will she ever forgive me?

"Your turn to sweat for a bit."

"I expect you might hear from the police soon." Liam stepped forward. "I'm obliged to hand evidence of wrongdoing to the police. Done that."

"Time for you to go." Anna turned her back on Nick.

Hunter loved her for her presence and support, even as he expected her to walk out of his life. His own fault. He'd wanted to be a stupid knight in shining armour for her, when she'd been the one on the white horse rescuing him.

Casildo shuffled Nick out the door, returning a few moments later. "Do you think you've stopped him?"

"What's your take, Anna?" Hunter gave a nod in Donna's direction.

"Slowed him down, but he'll be calling his lawyer." Exhaustion, rather than elation echoed in her voice.

"He'll need more than a lawyer. Remember I said I knew a man who knew a man …" Cas grinned. "Turns out he knows Bizgos. The story of Nick Richardson's parlous financial state goes live overnight."

"Then I'd say Nick's finished." Hunter let the certainty roll through him. "I appreciate the support, everyone. Now, let's lighten this party up."

Donna opened the door to Hunter's apartment and a steady stream of waiters came down the stairs, carrying nibbles and drinks on trays.

"You're still my hero." Casildo enfolded Hunter in a tight hug.

"Cas—"

"Don't say another word. I'll speak to you later. I didn't know Maha knew Antonio."

"I introduced them."

"Looks like they might have taken that further." Cas loosened his tie, snagged a beer and headed across the room.

Hunter waited twenty minutes, until the mood was mellower. Anna had spent most of that time with Helen's mother. Lots of hugs and kisses. Anna was magic. His magic, and she deserved to hear the words. He signalled to Cas, who gave a piercing wolf whistle, silencing the room.

"He was always better at that than me." Hunter laughed. "Thanks for coming tonight. I appreciate your support. Anna can speak for herself."

She studied him from across the room.

"I love you, Anna Turner." Her loyalty to her friends was legendary—Casildo had warned Hunter not to confuse loyalty with love—she'd have supported Hunter against Nick even if she planned to cut him out of her life. Risk or gamble? He no longer cared. Winning any time with her was worth it. "I don't want to imagine a future without you. Marry me?"

"Yes."

Anna being Anna didn't make him wait, strolling across the room to plant a lush kiss on him. Hunter vaguely heard the cheers in the background.

* * *

229

Anna sagged against him. Fear, which had swamped her when Nick had as good as admitted attacking Helen, slowly leached out of her bones, leaving her dizzy with relief.

"I thought you'd blame yourself for Nick's attack on Helen," she whispered.

"For a split second, I did," he confessed. "But I'm not strong enough to send you away again."

"It takes strength to stick."

"I love you, Anna. I can't believe how lucky I am you chose me." He wrapped her in his arms and gently rocked her.

"Then we might start to move these lovely people along, so you can show me." Anna traced his upper lip with her tongue, while walking her fingers down his chest.

"Are you going all X-rated with a room full of people?" He caught her hand before she went lower.

"Just providing extra incentive." She kissed his chin.

"Fifteen minutes. You start near the door, I'll work from the back."

Anna hugged Kate, who, with Liam, was among the stragglers. "Thanks for coming. I didn't think you'd want to leave Lily so soon."

"Mary couldn't wait to have her granddaughter all to herself for a bit. And I wouldn't have missed this for worlds. Hunter's a good man, Anna. He's the one." Kate hugged Anna.

"I think so." Anna smiled through her tears.

"Talk later," Kate said, then left, Liam's fingers linked with hers.

Turning, Anna found Hunter at her side.

"We've done it." Hunter closed, locked the door, then leaned back against it, pulling her into his arms. "We brought him down." He nuzzled her throat. "I love the way you smell." He brushed his lips across her temple. "And taste. Hot chocolate as a nightcap?"

"Maybe later." She took his hand. "Are we going home

now?"

"You make everything so easy." He tucked her under his arm and turned toward to staircase.

"I understand you pushed me away because you wanted to keep me safe." Anna watched for a Hunter-withdrawal special.

"Then you're more understanding than a lot of people. Cas told me if I ever did anything like that again, he'd renounce me as his blood brother."

"He's a smart man. You should listen to him more."

"I love you. I love who you are, what you've made of yourself, and the future you dream of." He picked her up and swung her in a circle before dropping onto the sofa with her in his lap. "Most of all, I love that you're here, now."

She wriggled around until she straddled him. "I've worked out the marriage vows—with this ring, I promise thee I'll always talk to you—and a few other details." She brushed her lips across his.

"Loving you is not a detail." He closed his eyes. "It's everything."

"Another good answer." She lowered herself to his chest, her ear pressed to his heart. Steady, maybe racing a little when she gave another wriggle.

"You smell like home. Blame it on my upbringing, but I need you to be safe."

"I was safe when you kissed me on the beach, when you bought a sick old man a coffee, when you cared for me after Lily was born. When you locked me out, I became unsure of my ground. You told me you loved me with everything except words, and without you I was adrift."

A ripple undulated through his body.

"I love you, Anna Turner, and I want to make love to you."

"That can be arranged."

AUTHOR'S NOTE

The female lead in *Betrayal*, Anna Turner is introduced in *Masquerade* and makes another appearance in *Quinn, by design*. A lot of readers have been asking me when I'd tell Anna's story.

No pressure then.

My first challenge was: who would be Anna's perfect match? Then I met Hunter S. Thompson. The S stands for Samuel, not Stockton, the famous US journalist's name. My Hunter was a builder's labourer, trained as an architect, and is now a property developer—a man who's used his body and his brain to build a life. A very private man.

Trust is a theme that runs through romance, physical, mental and emotional trust in yourself, in other people, and in a lover. Trust and betrayal aren't opposites, but mistrust often grows from betrayal. Imagine the impact of repeated betrayals, including childhood betrayals.

When I decided to call this book Betrayal, I found myself exploring how others see and feel betrayal. A quote that resonated with me was one by the famous Russian spy, Kim Philby. In 1967, in an interview with the UK's *Sunday Times*, he said *"To betray, you must first belong."*

Essentially you need to be close to someone to truly betray them. Parents are close, family is close, friends and lovers are close. What are your choices if you confront betrayal at every turn?

Choosing love would be the hardest choice. Anna and Hunter choose love.

I'd like to again thank Yezanira Venecia for her thoughtful and patient editing and Emily from Emily's World of Design for her cover art. It goes without saying that this book would not be published without the continuing support of Melissa Keir, Inkspell Publishing. Thank you Melissa.

Don't Miss a Sneak Peek at the Next Book in the Choosing Family Series

A Just Man

Chapter One
17 years later

Kelly stood, waiting for her two friends to finish weaving their way through packed tables to the one she'd reserved. A celebration called for their favourite bistro.

"I've ordered champagne. Bella's sprung for it." Bella was Arabella Steele, foster parent and fairy godmother to Kelly Steele, previously Kelly Manners. Although Kelly was also prepared to award sainthood to Lahn Nguyen, the case worker who hadn't turned her back when Kelly had slunk back into Sydney after her nightmare in Hay over a decade and a half before.

"You got the job." Lucy McTavish tightened her hold before stepping back. "Congratulations."

"I've been 'acting' in the job a few months." Kelly smiled. "But, yeah, it's been confirmed."

"Move aside, Lucy." Clem—Clementine—Delgado nudged Lucy out of the way with her hip and took her place, dancing a little on the spot. "Go, girl. I knew you'd get it."

"You're both way more confident than I was." Kelly sank into her seat.

"But you're pleased?" Lucy dropped beside her.

"Over the moon." She grinned. "I love the idea of combining school and community libraries. They make sense in small country towns. Plus, they're a better use of public resources."

"But the job's based in Sydney. You're the NSW Education Department's state-wide co-ordinator for school community libraries. You advise, you suggest, you research models to improve school library services across NSW, right? You just visit sites occasionally?" An edge of concern entered Clem's voice.

"Mostly."

A waiter appeared at Kelly's elbow, champagne bottle in hand. The cork popped, and he filled three glass flutes. Kelly saw Lucy signal Clem to zip it while the waiter hovered and prepared herself for the cross-examination. They loved her, so they were entitled.

"Don't you just love champagne?" Kelly searched for the right words in her glass. "The pop of the cork, the bubbles tumbling into the crystal flute, the scent of the effervescence."

"You can smell the effervescence?" Clem drawled.

"Can't you?" Kelly offered a question for a question, a time-honoured way of avoiding difficult subjects. "Thank you." She smiled, and the waiter retreated.

"What does 'mostly' mean?" Lucy barely waited until he was out of earshot.

"Here's to new opportunities." Kelly raised her glass. Her friends did the same.

"New opportunities." Lucy clinked her glass against Kelly's.

"Add 'new' to 'mostly' and I want to know what this opportunity is." Clem wouldn't be distracted.

"The Department supervises a few school community libraries, but it's a growing trend. One of our most ambitious ventures is in Tullamore."

"Tullamore. Brand new building. Ayesha Patel. Your equivalent of a guru." Lucy rolled her eyes. "You were present for the handover of the completed, but empty building to the school just before Christmas. Ayesha is deputy principal and has carriage of the project."

"You're a broken record on the subject." Clem agreed.

"Am not."

"Are too." Lucy shot back.

"Ayesha has taken emergency leave, and I've been asked

to go to Tullamore to make sure the library opens as planned in late January, after the summer school holidays. Get hands-on experience of doing this from scratch," Kelly blurted it out in one go, and hoped they didn't ask for details on Ayesha's emergency. Kelly didn't know, but had a gut feeling something at the school, not something in Ayesha's private life, had precipitated the deputy principal's sudden departure.

"Are you sure, Kel?" Lucy exchanged a worried glance with Clem.

Coming Soon…

Be Sure To Catch The Books In The Choosing Family Series....

MASQUERADE

Fool me once...

Money won't bring LIAM QUINN'S father back, but it'll save his mother's home. A high-paying law partnership is in his sights. To win it, he needs to successfully land a project. Problem is the project requires absolute confidentiality, and he's just discovered his estranged identical twin is appearing life size on a billboard across the city. The second catch is a return to environmental law. His earlier career imploded after his lover was revealed as a mining company spy.

Researcher and soon-to-be-published romance author KATE TURNER needs a disguise. Maybe more than one. Her famous playwright father despises 'trashy' novels. Her ex-boyfriend mocked her 'dirty little secret', then stalked her when she left him. Her identical twin coaxes her into appearing on a billboard to prove she can be notorious and anonymous at the same time. No one connects the billboard model to the dowdy researcher Kate has become, and no one knows about her author pseudonym and second disguise as Ms. Sexy Romance.

Kate and Liam's lives collide when she's hired as Liam's research assistant. Liam's boss laughs off the billboard. Having doubles is the perfect cover for confidential field work.

A masquerade, a road trip, a steamy attraction, the sudden appearance of Liam's old lover, and Ms. Sexy Romance's unexpected arrival in the wrong place at the wrong time, and Liam and Kate discover the steps they took to protect their hearts might break them.

--"A Jennifer Raines romance will make you sigh in the best possible way!"-- Best Selling Author, Grace Burrowes

EXCERPT

Liam gestured to her report, open in front of him. "Simple summaries of assorted environmental disputes across Australia. That's not a lot to work with."

"Have you read my report, Mr. Quinn?" Kate emphasised his surname, annoyance at the snub for her research trumping her anxiety at exposure. She'd back her research skills against anyone in this room.

"I've scanned it." His shoulder lifted in an offhand shrug.

Arrogant moron. Another man living in an echo chamber, so sure his worldview was right not even a drone buzzing overhead would alert him to imminent attack. Was he hostile because his identical twin Niall had kept the billboard campaign secret from him? Or generally hostile to new ideas? "Then you're being deliberately offensive."

"Not yet," he answered, leaning forward—a panther preparing to spring.

Dismayed to be so attuned to his slightest movement, she stiffened her spine.

Liam had her second-guessing her defence strategy.

Until Liam, Kate had trusted that Ms. Dowdy Researcher couldn't be linked to the billboard—the final stress test to confirm no one, especially not her besuited, controlling ex-boyfriend, would recognise Ms. Dowdy as Anna Turner's twin.

Quinn, by design

She's antiques royalty, he's relentlessly modern

Master carpenter NIALL QUINN's passion is creating bespoke furniture. Everything else comes second until his ex-fiancé ditches him when he gifts another creation to a friend, and he discovers his brother has been carrying his dead father debts. Niall's self-respect demands he pay his share. He's landed a prestigious exhibition of his work with a top gallery, possible in part because of the support of an antiques dealer who's been mentor, patron, and generous landlord. Niall's hoping the exhibition will establish his reputation and boost his bank balance.

LUCY McTAVISH's grandfather, antiques supremo Cameron (Cam) McTavish raised her. His death leaves her totally alone. Lucy drained their personal accounts to provide twenty-four-seven in-home palliative care for Cam. The thought of poverty paralyses her, a crippling reminder of life before Cam found her. Laden with debt, she plans to sell Cam's workshop to ensure his antiques emporium survives.

When the will is read, Niall Quinn holds the keys to Cam's workshop. Lucy's convinced he conned her grandpa in his last days and demands he restore antiques for her. Niall is blindsided by the bequest, but worries about yet another debt and agrees to the work.

Lucy and Niall circle each other. In sharing stories and drawing closer, Lucy figures out debt is her childhood bogeyman resurrected by Cam's death. Niall has real debts and, unaware of his exhibition, she looks for clients who'll pay him for the work she'd been demanding for free.

With the exhibition drawing closer, it's crunch time. Will Niall choose his exhibition or Lucy? Does Lucy want a man who won't share his dreams with her?

Award winning author Jennifer Raines' stories combine a love of romance with contemporary conflicts. Her writing is both relevant and heart-warming. Each story is a journey across the world. Jennifer likes to think her readers get occasional hints of the deep passion of a Nora Roberts or the unshakeable loyalty of a Grace Burrowes where love conquers loneliness, distrust and fear.

EXCERPT:

"I didn't ask for that." She made a face at the oversized sandwich he'd set in front of her.

"It's lunchtime." Niall took the chair opposite her.

Her guilty glance at her smartwatch told him she'd lost track of time, while her unfashionably baggy clothes told him eating was a faint memory. Loss of appetite was another by-product of heartache.

He'd been there too. "I hate to eat alone."

"I thought you lived alone." She cut one half of her sandwich in half and added pickles. Eating his food was another nod to politeness. Referring to his living arrangements was her opening salvo in hostilities.

"What else did your granda tell you?" Niall waited for her to swallow her first mouthful, then took a bite of his own, setting himself the task of keeping her in his kitchen long enough to finish her sandwich. Food was his currency for sympathy, although Lucy McTavish's unannounced arrival declared she wasn't here for comfort.

"Months ago, Grandpa talked about meeting a furniture restorer at an antiques auction."

"I've done the odd bit of restoration." Niall was pretty positive Cam had offered those pieces as a sop to Niall's dignity. While the profit from their sale had covered the rent, over time, Niall worked out Cam had become his patron rather than his landlord.

And wasn't that a feckin' indictment. At thirty-four, he needed an old man's patronage because his passion for making bespoke furniture had yet to deliver a decent living.

"Three pieces." She placed her left hand on his table as if drawing strength from the age and beauty of the timber. "Three pieces of furniture were delivered to McTavish's Antiques five months ago."

"Cam said they earned a good profit." Niall wrapped both hands around his Blue Italian Spode cup, watching as she raised the Flora Danica, Royal Copenhagen to her mouth; a distraction while she framed her answer. Like most of his cups, the matching saucers were lost in the mists of time.

"They did." Her chin jut signalled a full stop on McTavish profits.

"Cam said he told you about our arrangement." Niall's doubts were growing. Furniture restorer was a half-arsed description of him.

"He told me he offered you accommodation in return for restoring furniture. Three pieces of furniture over eight months gives you a higher hourly rate than a top-class hooker." The insult rolled off her tongue, the barb sinking deeper than she could have known. Unaware, she popped the last morsel of the second quarter of sandwich into her luscious, bow-shaped mouth.

Available now in Ebook and Print- At all Major Book Retailers

ABOUT THE AUTHOR

Australian Jennifer Raines writes contemporary romances set mainly, but not exclusively, in Australia – think Malta, Finland, New Zealand or ? A dreamer and an optimist, her stories are a delicious cocktail of passion, mutual respect and loyalty because she still believes in happily-ever-afters.

Jennifer fell in love with romance as a teenager. Starting with historical romance. Everything in the school library and then a personal treasured collection of Georgette Heyer, hard copies, paperbacks and ebooks. Comfort food, she calls them, like Vegemite toast, for those times when she feels low. Her library of comfort food has grown over the years but Georgette Heyer was an early star, under the blankets after lights out using a torch.

Jennifer is a member of Romance Writers of Australia. Three times a finalist in the Emerald competition, including in 2017 (*Common Cause*, renamed *Lela's Choice*), 2018 (*Taylor's*

Law) and 2022 (*Quinn, by design* – Choosing Family Book 2). She's a member of Romance Writers of New Zealand, winning the Pacific Hearts competition twice, including in 2019 with *Grace Under Fire*, the sequel to *Taylor's Law*. She's also a member of Romance Writers of America and has been a finalist in chapter competitions in 2019, 2020 and 2021 (*Taylor's Law*). Jennifer won the contemporary romance section in the 2020 Orange Rose Contest for *Planting Hope* and was second overall. Jennifer values competitions for the constructive, honest, not always comfortable feedback they provide.

In 2023 *Taylor's Law* placed second in the Romance Writers of New Zealand Koru Best First Book

Jennifer loves those days when words flow and the joy of writing makes the hard slog worthwhile. She's always made up stories about strangers in the street, in a café or strolling through an airport terminal; finding inspiration in snippets of conversations, news items and the sheer puzzle of human interactions.

Jennifer lives in inner-city Sydney, Australia, with the requisite number of partners (1) and animals (2). Her desk overlooks a park which nourishes her soul when she raises her head from her keyboard. She gets some of her best ideas during long yin yoga poses or walking – anywhere. While Jennifer adores historical romance, she chose to write contemporary because she thought (wrongly) it needed less research while she was holding down a full-time job.

You can find out more about Jennifer and her writing at https://jenniferrainesauthor.com   or   via https://www.facebook.com/jenniferrainesauthor

Or https://www.instagram.com/romanceauthorjen/

Her book(s) are available through major providers.